Beyond the Break

Beyond the Break

HEATHER BUCHTA

Penguin Workshop

PENGUIN WORKSHOP
An Imprint of Penguin Random House LLC, New York

Text copyright © 2020 by Heather Buchta. All rights reserved. Published by
Penguin Workshop, an imprint of Penguin Random House LLC, New York.
PENGUIN and PENGUIN WORKSHOP are trademarks of Penguin Books Ltd,
and the W colophon is a registered trademark of Penguin Random House LLC.
Printed in the USA.

Visit us online at www.penguinrandomhouse.com.

Library of Congress Cataloging-in-Publication Data is available upon request.

ISBN 9780593097014 (pbk)   10 9 8 7 6 5 4 3 2
ISBN 9780593096994 (hc)   10 9 8 7 6 5 4 3 2 1

For my nieces, Macy and Cassidy.

May you always know Whose you are.

—Aunt Heather

a

Chapter One

The first time a guy felt me up was in the big church prayer room.

All the parents of youth-group kids thought church lock-ins were a fantastic "outreach." So many sign-ups from non-church kids for a night of innocent fun playing sardines and capture the flag, with the gospel message given! Even if "Jesus died for you" was thrown into the five minutes between Oreo-eating contests and discussions about which church Justin Bieber attends, seeds were planted!

It must be from the Lord.

Well, it wasn't, unless the Lord was the one fanning the flame of rumors about the endless possibilities at lock-ins. Dark rooms. Dark hallways. Lots of games requiring dark rooms and hallways.

I was in ninth grade, and this was my first lock-in with our high-school youth group. I had just graduated from junior-high youth group and was nervous, but I had my two best friends Kelly and Lydia, so it was okay. We were playing sardines, where one person hides in the church building with the lights off, and then the masses are released to find that person. After finding the "hider," you hide with him or her until there's one dogpile of quiet, giggly teenagers waiting for that last scared-poopless soul wandering in the dark after watching everyone disappear.

Please don't let me be the last one, I prayed to Jesus. *Oh, and thank you for the cross.* I always felt guilty asking God for something without at least thanking him, too. Lydia, who was Catholic and didn't go to my church except for lock-ins, had sashayed off with some tenth-grade guy named Max, so I was hand in hand with Kelly. "My goodness, don't leave me, Lovette," Kelly begged, but then released my hand and turned a corner into the main sanctuary. When I turned the corner, she was nowhere.

"Oh God—I mean, gosh." I squinted at the shadowed pews. "Kelly!" I whisper-yelled. Nothing. I felt my way, back pressed against the wall, searching for a glimmer of movement. A few outlines crept across the balcony, everyone searching for Tim.

Tim Rainsforth was a junior and a leader on our worship team, SQUAD, so he'd nominated himself to hide first. I'd never find him. He spent, like, six days a week here and for sure knew every inch of this place.

My hand bumped against the doorknob to the prayer room. I'd been here once before, when I asked God for help with my pimples and making the volleyball team, and thanked Him for dogs and the weather. Inside, I couldn't make out much, but I knew the space was tiny: just a rug, a couch, some pillows to kneel on, and a card table draped with a cloth. On one wall were curtains and a cross. On the opposite wall was a Bible verse: *"And we know that all things work together for good to those who love God. Romans 8:28."*

Something brushed my leg, and I jumped. My foot landed on a pillow, and I toppled to the ground. An arm wrapped around my stomach and pulled me in.

"Shh . . . ," he said, and I sighed with relief. Tim. I'd found him. And first!

We were under the card table, and the cloth draped to the ground, so until our group became bigger than four, this hiding place was killer.

"Wow!" I whispered. "Nice spot!"

"Shh," he repeated, but I could tell he was grinning, proud. Someone opened the door, and I held my breath. The person was feeling the walls like a blind person reading braille. He or she tapped the top of our card table. I could feel Tim wrapped around me, a leg on each side, and I suddenly forgot about the game. Was this allowed? *Sorry, Jesus, sorry, Jesus, sorry, Jesus.* My heart thumped loud enough to give us away. Sweating this much had to mean sin. I started to move, but Tim held me firmly. I swear he was more still than a statue. He was so good at this! Tim was always somehow on the winning Ultimate Frisbee or capture the flag team. He also picked the teams. The shadow-person moved the pillows and left the room.

"Fooled!" Tim whispered.

Okay, it's just legs wrapped around you. It's just a body. He's just trying to win. I repeated these lines like a memorized Bible verse. As guilty as I felt, I liked his legs around me. I scrunched my eyes shut. God heard that. *Were legs around me considered going too far? How far was too far?*

We heard another noise outside the door—someone tripped on a hymnal, probably—followed by a thump and laughter. Tim responded by clutching me tighter, but his hand accidentally cupped my bra, and I sucked in my breath like someone had walked into the room again. *Oh God, oh God, oh God* and not *gosh* because I really meant God. My eyes started to adjust, and I could see his purity ring pressed against my bra. I know I should've felt giddy or whatever people feel when hot guys do this, but it was so shocking, I could only gape.

Oh God, does this mean I don't like guys? I mean, gosh.

Tim was really good-looking and popular, but this was really weird. He had never held my hand, but now he was holding my boob. I was no relationship expert, but I thought we were skipping some steps in this whole "courting" thing. Didn't he just give a talk on this? Through the crack in the tablecloth, I knew the cross was peeking back. Jesus was glaring at me for sure. There's no way He'd let me make the volleyball team now.

"Um . . . ," was all I could say.

He looked down at what he was holding, and his eyes went wide. "Sorry," he whispered. "I didn't—I swear I didn't realize—you kept moving and—shit." He let go like my breast was on fire. "What's your name?" he stuttered.

Something near the small of my back pressed against me. His hand? Oh no, wait. Ew. I leaped forward, knocking my head on the table. Two people entered the room.

"I heard that," one whispered. I was too busy rubbing my head to tuck myself back under the table.

They scrambled over and kicked into me.

"Way to kill my hiding place," Tim grumbled. I could

see the outline of his mini Bible sticking out of his pocket. My face flooded with embarrassment. *How inexperienced did someone have to be to get a Bible confused with an erection?*

Anyway, that was two years ago. Tim wasn't a jerk afterward, either, or weird. Or anything, really. He was always nice to me, and sometimes I wonder if he even knew it was me. We couldn't fully see each other in the dark, and if I'm honest, back then, my boob could have doubled for a flat stomach. Anyway, that's the most I've ever done with a guy by a long shot, and I'm proud of it. After all, I'm in eleventh grade and live in Los Angeles! I'm like a walking miracle.

Tim goes to community college now, and sometimes I see him in big church, but mostly on holidays with his parents. I hear he still plays guitar but more for gigs, and he wears a puka-shell necklace like a lot of the surfers do, except he doesn't surf. Or maybe he does, and that's where he lost his purity ring. It's not on his finger anymore.

Chapter Two

Waves. I'm thinking of waves the first time I meet him. Maybe it would've been different if I was thinking about God. But I'm not. I'm imagining the waves lapping at the beach, one swell cresting higher like it's winding up but then delivering smooth and even, perfect for riding the line. I don't notice that someone's asked me a question until the second time he asks.

"Have we met?"

It's 8:55 p.m. on Monday, toward the end of my shift at Billy's Buns, and I'm staring at a six-inch hoagie layered with roast beef and cheese. No onion, lettuce, pickle. A plain guy. But when I look up at him, he's anything but plain. I notice his eyes first—big, dark brown eyes that make me feel like I'm someone he knows—and then his shoulders, the kind guys get only after high school. His light brown hair's longer than it should be but just barely, which makes it adorable when he blows it out of his face. I suddenly feel ridiculous in my mousy flop of brown hair smushed to my scalp by a hairnet. Holding up the yellow and white bottles like maracas, I'm double-fisting the mustard and mayo, one in each hand, asking him which, but through the plexiglass, he grins and shakes his head.

Neither.

This isn't your future husband, I remind myself. God would never have me meet my future husband like this. Ordering a sandwich from me? No way. Besides, God's not introducing us to each other in high school. I know. We've got a plan, and it's not happening my junior year.

I look down at his sandwich. Did I mess up his order? No, he said plain. I look up at him, my throat dry. "Did I . . . ?"

"I'm Jake," he says. "Jake Evans?"

He says it like a question, like his last name should ring a bell. Kim, my coworker, takes the next lady in line.

"Lovette," I manage.

"I know," he says, and I freeze. How does he know me?

Then Jake points to my name tag, and I laugh. "Right." At the cash register, the plexiglass no longer separates us. There's something vaguely familiar, but I can't place it, like the feeling of seeing an old friend.

"Lovette," he repeats. "That's different. I like it."

"Thank you," I say, busying myself with the bill. "Six fifty."

"Can you add a coffee?"

I look at the clock.

He notices. "Two-hour drive ahead of me."

"Of course. Cream and sugar?"

"Nah. Just black." Definitely out of high school.

He hands me a ten, and I make change for him. Why is my hand shaking? Not because I'm interested. Definitely not interested. I don't date. I wonder if this is what God means when He says, "The flesh is weak." My hand is weak, but my heart knows better. There's no way college-shoulders Jake is for real. I feel my whole body exhale when he turns to leave, but then he stops. U-turns. I suck in my breath.

"Lovette, what time's your shift over?"

I shake my head, unable to speak, trying to convey "never."

"Right now," Kim pipes in and hands me my time card.

"I, uh, have to race home."

"Well, then," he says, smiling warmly. "You better hurry." He holds up his sandwich bag. "Thank you."

I nod way too vigorously, and he turns and leaves. Everything in me collapses, and I rest against the counter for support. Kim nudges me so the lady can pay for her sandwich. I clock out, turn the OPEN sign to CLOSED, and remove my hairnet and apron.

"Are you out of your mind?" Kim whirls to face me as soon as the lady exits. I grab my backpack from the back room, ignoring her. "Hello?"

I fiddle with my phone. "Too old for me."

"No, he wasn't!"

"Yes, he was. Did you see his shoulders?"

"That means he works out, not that he's forty!"

I fumble with my backpack zipper, my hand still not cooperating. As I pull my swimsuit out of my pack, I mumble, "I don't date, remember?"

"So?"

"So," I say and head to the bathroom to change.

Once I'm outside, the beach breeze blows cool against my sweaty neck. I unlock my bike by the light of the moon, coast down the three blocks to the ocean, and then ride ten short blocks south, parking at Old Man Mike's place. He's my old surf coach from when I was a kid, a retired guy who lets me stash my bike in his side yard.

And my wetsuit.

I wriggle into the neoprene, and it's a bit of a struggle since it's still damp from yesterday. With my legs and arms suctioned in the suit, I reach over my shoulder and pull the zipper up my back. I get goose bumps from the cold, and my teeth start chattering, but it's worth it. It's always worth it.

I hurdle over the pile of towels, his skateboards, and his two surfboards, then back out the gate. I jog through the alley to the boardwalk, empty except for one lone cyclist with a flashing light. The cold sand squeezing between my toes, I walk onto the beach, look out at the majestic expanse of dark water, and charge at it in full sprint. The moon, whose reflection makes a walkway from me to her, shimmers as white water explodes and crashes at my feet. I don't hesitate before I leap into the ocean and dive under the cool, churning waters. A smile starts deep inside of me and finishes on my face. *The heavens declare the glory of God.*

This is where I'm home.

I don't know why I feel more alive in the water than on the land, but it's like I can float and fly and dive, and nothing's impossible, and the world's okay. It's where I feel closest to God, like He's holding me on all sides and reminding me, "I've got you." And I feel His embrace most in the waves. I don't care if they crash over me, if they tumble me, if I get tossed around, because even when I'm submerged, I still feel safe. When it all settles, I know the ground's right there.

○))) ◐ ● ◖ ◖ ◖ ○

An hour later, I walk into my house, my hair still tangled and wet from hosing it off at Old Man Mike's. I wrap it in a T-shirt as I walk down the hall. Dad pokes his head out of my parents' bedroom.

"Hi," he whispers. "Mom's already asleep. How was the Y?"

Usually he says, "How was it?" so I don't feel like I'm lying when I say, "Great," but today, he asks how the YMCA was— which is where he's assumed I go every day since it's right next to my work, and I come home from Billy's Buns with wet hair. I've never corrected him.

"Hmm?" I say because I hate lying. Like *hate* hate it. There are certain sins you do without thinking about them, and that's bad enough, knowing sin put Jesus on the cross. But lying's one of those sins that you know you're doing, and that's just mean to Jesus. It's like saying you're His friend while hammering another nail on that cross.

"How was it?"

I exhale, because the YMCA's no longer part of his question. How was *it? It* could mean anything. "Good! Really good," I say.

He comes into the hallway, closing his door. Darts a look back toward their room. "Matty's coming home next month to surprise your mom for her birthday."

My brother's in his third year at UC Santa Cruz, and he's way closer to my parents than I am, but I'm fine with that because when he was younger, he almost died. If I had a kid who was basically brought back from the dead, every day with him would feel like my birthday.

"Hey." Dad puckers his lips, brings his face close to my scalp, and inhales. "They cleaning that pool at the Y?"

I don't answer because, again, the lying thing.

"You don't smell like chlorine."

"Oh," I say to his second statement. "I rinsed off before I came home." Which is true, and once again, I've avoided lying. But I feel a little twisty in my stomach.

Dad salutes me. "Well done, soldier," he says, which is kind of dorky, but I like it, because he musses my hair and it makes me feel like he's proud and I've changed the world a little.

I enter my room, close the door, and apologize to God for my non-lie lies. My mind drifts back to Jake Evans. Why did he want to know when my shift was over? Was he really interested? I've never been interested in dating. I mean, why bother entertaining those thoughts if I'm not going to marry the guy? And I'm definitely not getting married until I finish college, which is, like, in six years. So he's off-limits, which means thinking about him now would only be bad. Remember King David? He thought about Bathsheba when she was off-limits and ended up having sex with her and getting her pregnant, then sending her husband to the front lines of war to cover his butt. No, thank you.

But what if I think about *future* Jake Evans—like the Jake Evans that I meet again six years from now. I can dream about *that* Jake . . . right? He would love animals, build houses for the homeless, and lead worship, and we'd go on night hikes, live on the ocean, and swim twice a day. His shoulders would be the same, I think as I sink into my pillow. They're already perfect.

Chapter Three

At youth group two days later, I'm still in the parking lot looking for Kelly when I see her wave and hop off the brick wall she's sitting on. That should've been my first clue. Kelly doesn't hop. She moseys. Her feet don't leave the ground when she walks. Her hair's always in a messy bun, with that single inch-wide streak of purple bright against her blond.

One of the leaders blows the conch, which means we're starting the group game downstairs in five minutes.

Church has been a second home to me since sixth grade, and there's a rhythm to it that I've come to love. Big-group game, followed by same-sex small groups, and then back together for worship and prayer. I love the pattern of it, the routine. Every week, I know what I get. Lydia tried to explain to me once that's why she loves her Catholic church. Something about tradition, and how we're creatures of habit, and something else that I'm sure's all good, but there's no way I'd ever leave my church for hers, not when this place is the reason I love God so much. Or at all.

"Did you see him?" Kelly says and squeezes my hand. She loves touching people while she talks.

"Who?"

"Who!" she squeals back, which doesn't help me. She twirls my hair into ringlets. "You're going to say 'hit' with an *S* in front, you'll see, but I call dibs."

Is someone back from college? Sometimes old youth-group kids come back to visit for a night. Whenever it's a guy, the girls swoon, like being out of high school makes him perfect boyfriend material.

Of my two best friends, Lydia's the crazy one, but Kelly's usually mellow, so seeing her like this means she must like this guy, whoever he is. I'm guessing Tim Rainsforth. It's like a movie premiere when he comes back on his semester breaks.

The music blares from the speakers downstairs, something about eternity, and the way the drums and the bass pound, it makes me feel like heaven's gotta be way better than roller coasters or bungee jumping. Kelly loops her arm through mine as we walk down the steps to the youth room, side-hugging anyone we pass.

Brett, our youth pastor, is on the microphone as we enter. "Hey, hey! There are three large squares on the carpet I made with painter's tape. Find your way into one of those squares."

The carpet's so thin that you could sweep up a spilled can of Coke with a broom. Or drape it with long pieces of painter's tape.

Our youth room is how I imagine college apartments. Mismatched, comfy couches. A Ping-Pong and foosball table in one corner. Three Nerf basketball hoops. The walls covered in posters of extreme sports—a skier midair with a snow cliff above, a rock climber hanging from a precipice by his fingertips, a base jumper sailing through a bottomless sky—

and on each poster, a quote about living for Christ.

Some kids start yelling, "Poop deck!" and divide themselves up between the three carpet "squares." Brett laughs. "Yes! We're playing poop deck! It's about to get 'lit' in here, you know what I'm sayin', brahs?" He doesn't notice the groans and eye rolls. Brett is the best youth pastor. He doesn't talk to us like we're five, or yell at us to stop chatting when we're playing games.

The only problem is that he tries to talk like a teenager, but he uses the words in all the wrong places. No one cares, because for the most part, Brett puts up with way more than our parents would. And his talks make you get so fired up for God. "Okay, okay." He holds the microphone close. "Miggity-miggity-mic check! For the one person who grew up in a cave and hasn't played this game, here are the rules. There are three large squares in the room: poop deck on the left, half deck in the middle, and quarter deck to the right. If I yell 'Half deck!' everyone run to that square. If you're already in that square, you're safe. Our leaders will be the refs. Last two people to each square are out. Oh, if I call 'Hit the deck!' you've all gotta jump down to your bellies. Last two people to the ground are 'Bye, Felicia.' If you're one of the last five remaining, you win—wait for it, wait for it—a five-dollar gift card to Two Guns Espresso."

Everyone keeps talking and giggling over him, but Brett doesn't care. "And one, two, three . . . poop deck!" Instantly fifty teenagers scramble. Kelly and I are already in the poop-deck square, so she embraces me in a bear hug like we've already won. The square's not big enough for fifty teenagers, and it's a giant mosh pit of laughter and squished bodies. "There he is!" she says in my ear. I try to turn my body around, but I can only stretch my neck. In the corner of the square, his eyes, barely above the other heads, look back at me. Deep brown eyes peeking out of his slightly too long hair. It can't be.

The refs must've pulled the last two people out from that round because I hear Brett holler, "Hit the deck!" and the masses drop to the ground. I don't. I can't. Everything in me's stiff as a surfboard. Not sure I even blink.

"Ooh, Lovette, no replay needed," Brett says through the microphone. Candy, one of the youth leaders, touches me on the shoulder to move me to the wall with the others who are out, now four of us.

What's he doing here? How did he find me? Did he ask my coworker Kim, and did she rat me out? It's too much. I step outside for some air.

"You okay?" someone says in my ear, and I practically jump out of my clothes. It's Candy. She's in her thirties, and holy Bibles, she's intense about the Lord.

"Oh. Yeah, just needed a bathroom break."

"Praise God."

"I suppose." Should I praise Him for that too?

"I just mean you looked like something was wrong. I thought you might need prayer."

"Don't we all?" I smile.

"Amen." She extends her arm for a high five. I slap her hand. Should I tell her about Jake? I imagine her praying in tongues over me for protection.

"Thanks, Candy. I'm good."

"No one's good but God."

"Right. Okay, well, I'm just gonna go pee."

"Be blessed!" she calls.

On my way back to the youth room, someone taps me on the shoulder, and I jump again. What's with Candy sneaking up on me? Then I remember she's probably on "pot patrol." Every week, one of the adult leaders is designated to do the rounds of the church property, making sure that none of the teens are slinking away to engage in activities that would make Baby Jesus cry. We call them the "pot patrol."

I turn and say, "I swear I only peed," but I'm face-to-face with Jake Evans.

He grins and scratches his head right above his ear. "I'm not keeping score."

Chapter Four

"Ohmygoshyou'renotCandy." I'm more breathing than talking.

"No," Jake says. "Candy would've probably told you not to swear."

I smile and stop. "Wait, how do you know that?"

He starts to say something and then doesn't. He cocks his head, and his hair falls to the side. "You really don't remember me."

"Of course I do," I say, as professional as I can. "You bought a sandwich from me."

He smiles, looks up at the ceiling, and then down again. "Yes. Yes, I sure did. I, uh"—he rakes his hand through his hair—"I was in youth group here in sixth grade. It was called Fire, right? The first year you started coming to church. Mine too."

"How do you—"

"We were new the same night. I remember because I was so glad they didn't make me stand in front of the group by myself."

I'm drawing a blank. That following year was rough for me, but I don't remem—and then I look. Really look. Dark brown eyes. It's a faint memory, like the wisps of a dream as you wake up. "Jacoby," I murmur. We weren't close; I mean, not that I remember. Not sure we even talked.

"Just Jake now."

"You were so little," I blurt. He really was. Like a doll. Scrawny with a buzz cut. "I'm sorry, I just—"

"No, no. I get it." He laughs. "Yeah, I was a drop in the bucket. Anyway"—he motions toward the youth room, and we start walking back—"I just moved back. Well, for the weekdays. Long story. Military brat."

I feel my shoulders relax. "Me too. Military kid, that is. Well, Dad's retired."

"Yeah? Look, we weren't that good of friends back then. But I remember you. Maybe your name stuck out. When I saw you at the sandwich shop, I thought, she has to be the same Lovette. Anyway, I was going to tell you all that when you got off work, but you rushed off, so . . ."

Oh man, I feel like such a tool. He wasn't trying to flirt with me at all.

"I'm sorry," I say, and I don't feel the giddiness of that first night. I just feel kind of self-absorbed.

He shoos my words away with his hand. "Please. I shouldn't have bugged you at work. Probably looked like a creeper. Anyway, I'm a senior, and it really sucks being the new kid. Just was trying to—"

"No, I get it! And I'm so sorry. It was one of those days." Was it? Am I non-lie lying again?

He repeats, "One of those days," as if he had one, too, and now I wish I did have one.

We enter the youth room as kids are filing out to their small groups. "Oh, by the way," I say. "You're in room fifteen. Senior guys."

"Right. Thanks." He smiles again. He has a dimple in his left cheek. "I'll, uh, see you back in here for worship?" I nod, and he turns to go, but then he turns back. "Hey, do you still surf?"

Something catches in my throat, stopping my words. I lick my lips, and I can taste my Dr Pepper ChapStick. I shake my head. At least it's not a lie—it's true, I don't surf—but it feels as crummy as a lie.

"Aw, that's too bad. You were amazing."

The compliment warms me, and I find my voice. "Eh. Maybe for a sixth-grader."

"Nah. For anyone. You could've competed against high-schoolers back then."

Wait. That means he *does* remember more about me than just my name.

The rest of youth group's a blur. In our junior girls' small group, Kelly draws designs on my jeans with her finger as we all talk about effective ways to evangelize at school. The girls are having side conversations about "the new guy," who really isn't the new guy but the old guy who's just been out of town for five years. Only Kelly knows this. "Jacoby Evans," she whispers in my ear as Nicole suggests leaving encouragement notes from Jesus in student lockers.

"Just Jake now," I whisper, and Kelly stops drawing on my jeans. "I ran into him at the bathrooms."

Charlotte suggests making cookies and giving out plates of them for free with a Post-it that says friendship with Christ is free too.

"I can't believe how different he looks," I say. He's nothing like I remember.

Kelly shifts like the floor got uncomfortable. "Oh, but you still don't date, right? Besides, I totally said—"

"You guys would make a cute couple," I say, and I squeeze her arm to emphasize it. "I just mean he used to be so little, I didn't even recognize him."

"Right?" She resumes squiggling on my pant leg.

Back in the youth room, I sit in the front row. I need time to think about God. To sing and remind myself how much I love Him. To remember His faithfulness to me back in seventh grade. The ways He totally took care of me when no one else did. And my single simple promise I made back, not because I had to, but because I *wanted* to.

By the end of worship, it's a no-brainer. God has given Jake to be my friend and maybe Kelly's boyfriend. As soon as I hear the final "Amen," I stand to exit, but Kelly's hand finds mine.

"Kel, I gotta jet," I say.

"You can hang for two seconds. Let's just make sure he feels welcome."

I look over at Jake, and there are at least two guys and four girls already talking with him.

"He looks like he's doing fine."

But she's already pulling me, weaving in and out of teens and chairs and trash cans full of empty chip bags and Capri Suns. I recognize Dave among them, leaning on a table, strumming his guitar. He's not on the worship team or anything. He just likes to bring his guitar everywhere.

"—so bummed you're not at Mira Costa High," one of the girls (Carrie, I think) says.

"My aunt lives closer to the 405," Jake says. "So it was either Hawthorne or the charter."

"Ooh, Hawthorne High," Dave says, and there's a collective wince from the group. "Yeah, definitely the charter."

The charter? As in *Maritime Academy?*

"Hey, Lovette goes there," Dave says as he sees me. "She could show you around."

Wait, no.

"Jake, this is Kelly," I say quickly, then add, "She—"

"I remember you from Fire," Kelly jumps in, releasing my hand to shake his.

"Oh, right!" He gives her a friendly handshake, but he glances at me, and I wonder if he remembers her. "Hey, how are you?"

"Same. I mean, not same since then, but, you know, nothing much. You?"

Oh boy, she's nervous. I should help. "Kelly goes to Maritime too. She also attends this poetry thing on Tuesday nights at this coffee shop." He looks from me to her. "It's a great way to meet people," I add.

"Yeah," Dave says, plucking his guitar. "It's cool. I've played some of my songs there."

"Kelly can tell you the details," I say, nudging her forward. "I've gotta go."

"Stay," Kelly pleads.

"I'm on my bike, and—"

"But you always stay for at least fifteen."

I back out and wave. "I know, but I've gotta hurry."

Jake says, "One of those days again?"

I see him grinning at me with that dimple, and I laugh, and he laughs, and then I realize we have our first inside joke. "Yeah, something like that."

I take the stairs two at a time to my bike and pedal down the long driveway before anyone's made it back to the parking lot. Maybe I should've given him my number or a place to meet at school where I can show him around. But that all feels wrong as I picture the look in Kelly's eyes when she saw him. My feelings feel like sin and not sin at the same time. Dark blurs of trees and houses whiz by, and I look up at the night sky. Clouds cover the moon tonight, and I try to pray but everything feels jumbled, so I settle on one word. *Help?*

Chapter Five

I sleep okay, but I wake up a lot. I thought I'd get through all four years of high school without ever liking a guy. I mean, I prayed for that. And a guy my best friend called dibs on? Luckily, it's only been a couple of days of these weird new feelings. It can't be from God.

God says to look at the heart, and I've looked at Jake's face. I know nothing about him, which means my attraction's physical. Or is it? What was that something I felt—that something that went beyond his dimple and easy smile? The way he felt so comfortable in his skin, how that made me want to be around him. What's that called? Or the way he paid attention to people when they talked, even Dave when he mentioned his guitar songs. Like you could share stuff with him and he'd instantly be in your corner. Or how he wasn't just polite but engaging to Kelly, though I'm almost positive he didn't remember her. What are those things?

Today at school, I keep expecting to see him during passing period. Our school isn't big. But so far, he hasn't been in the halls or in any of my classes.

"Nice shirt," Cecilia Grayson says to me as she walks by my desk to borrow the teacher's stapler. She says it like she means the opposite, like I've ruined her day, her hair, and her life by wearing it.

I look down at my favorite vintage tee. It's a red shirt with the word LIFEGUARD on the front, a cross underneath, and below that, the words MINE WALKS ON WATER. Most of us growing up on the beach were Junior Guards, so I think it's perfect to wear a Jesus shirt that's relevant. Especially after last night's small group about school evangelizing. God wants people to know Him, and it's not like I'm banging a Bible on people's heads or screaming *"Turn or burn!"* with a megaphone at our pep rallies. I'm just wearing clothes, which everyone does. And, besides, I never comment on Cecilia's soccer sweats and how much they *swish-swish* when she walks, even in noisy hallways.

She's probably mad because her boyfriend and I were Junior Guards growing up, and maybe my shirt reminded her. Trevor Walker and I surfed at pretty much the same level then. He's the top surfer at Mira Costa now, and once in tenth grade I ran into them at the Manhattan Beach Creamery. I hadn't seen him in years, and when he recognized me, he gave me a high five like I had just gotten tubed by a wave. Then he fixed his hair in case our hand slap had moved it. I remember Cecilia's eyes and the way they narrowed to slits and she gripped her waffle cone when I told Trevor that I went to the same school as she did. That was over a year ago, and she's been a brat to me ever since. I know God reminds me, "It's Me they hate, not you," but her words still sting. *Sorry, God.*

I'm probably oversensitive right now because of this in-class assignment that people like Cecilia are already finished with. And stapling! Which means she wrote *multiple* pages.

I look down at my blank paper and then back at the whiteboard, where today's assignment smirks at me: *Write about your passion. Must give examples! One page minimum, due at the bell. HW: textbook 1–30, complete sentences.*

Passion? I know what my passion is. It pulses through my veins and wakes me up before dawn and keeps me up at night. But I can't write about it because no one knows. Well, I mean, God knows, but that doesn't count, and I can't chance my parents ever finding out. I'd never see daylight again. So it stays off the paper, except for a little wave I draw in the margin, but I scribble that out too. No evidence.

The only thing that I seem to be passionate about right now is sweating. I can feel my body perspiring as the time ticks by. Great. Now I'm going to smell AND fail this assignment.

With seven minutes left, I write about my other passion, which is God, even though I'm missing the point of this assignment because I'm sure Ms. Jensen wanted us to think about our futures. She doesn't even read these; she gives everyone five points and a sloppy star on top of our scribbly paragraphs, so I fill my paper with whatever comes to mind:

Jesus is my passion. I love Him with everything, like more than ice cream or the smell of the sidewalk after it rains. Or dolphins, and if you know me, I really love dolphins, even though I still eat them. I mean tuna, but the safe kind. Anyway, Jesus. I love youth group. It's where I get filled up for the week. Also, I've made big commitments there, and when you stand for things no matter what, that's kind of like passion. For example, I decided back when I was twelve that I was going to wait until I was married. And not just for sex. My first kiss is going to be at the altar when the pastor says, "You may kiss the bride." It's the most romantic thing I can imagine. Well, used to imagine. In seventh grade, it sounded cool. I even signed a purity contract. Now it feels like forever. Saying you've never kissed a guy sounds really dumb and embarrassing, and maybe that's what Paul meant in the Bible when he said to consider it pure joy when you face trials. But it's not like people walk around asking that, so it's fine. Anyway, if you read this, Ms. Jensen, which I know you won't, no kissing and telling. Lol. Get it?

The bell rings as I'm filling the bottom line of page one. My hand's cramped, and I can see dark red under the armpits of my light-red Jesus tee. *How'd that happen?* I've been nervous all day, I guess. I say a quick prayer that I have an extra shirt in my locker and then hurry there because if I go fast enough, people won't read my shirt and think, *Do all Christians stink like this?* Plus, it would be just my luck to run into Jake. I spin the numbers on my lock, for a moment forgetting my combo. "Hey," I hear over my shoulder.

Chapter Six

I exhale loudly. Lydia's voice, not Jake's. She continues, "Are we going out tomorrow night?" Oh, man. There's a full moon this Friday. Which means a fully lit ocean. Perfect conditions for night swimming, which I only get once every twenty-nine days.

"I can't, Lyds."

"But it's Friday!"

"Nope." I click open my locker.

"Friyay!"

"I work."

"*A*, You don't work Fridays. *B*, It's Friday! And three, what if your true love is out there?"

I know Lydia's waggling her eyebrows, even though I haven't turned to look. "I have to study."

"Girl, love takes residence over education."

"It's precedence," I correct, grabbing my physics book. Dang it. No extra shirt.

"Obviously, Lovette. That's what I said." She gives me an all-hips hip check like we're out on a dance floor, and I go sailing and slam into my locker. A few students stop and look, so I straighten up. Not because I'm embarrassed, I try to convince my hot face, but so they can read my shirt. Instead, they look at one another and move on.

My best friend Lydia's not perfect at grammar, but it doesn't matter. She's perfect at being perfect, which would make sense if you knew her. No matter what you're doing, you're having a good time if Lydia's around. She's fun in a way that makes you feel like you're always seeing Disneyland for the first time. Sure she's a little wild, but who doesn't want a friend who makes you believe you can scale buildings? And if you're ever feeling knocked down, she's the best to be with because she struts around as if she holds the entire world in checkmate. And if her personality weren't already perfect enough, she's also known at our school as "the pretty one," which sounds like our students are shallow, until you see her. Like you wonder what she's doing at school when she should be on a modeling shoot somewhere. She has the most gorgeous ebony skin, but she's not African American. Her family's from Colombia, but I'd sound like I had a stuttering problem if I called her South American American. I told her that once, and she said, "You stutter?"

Oh, she's also not the best listener.

Lydia slaps the row of lockers. "You're zoning out again. Did you hear me? We're going out tomorrow night."

"Going out" involves going to an eighteen-and-over dance club, the Venue, and no, this sixteen-year-old doesn't have a fake ID. Also, my mom knows I go there, so I'm not being sneaky. Lydia's uncle works in the dish room, and he lets us in through the back entrance. We do dishes for an hour and practice our Spanish with him, so I get smarter and work on my domestic skills, and when I tell my parents what I learned, my mom says things like "muy bien" and my dad salutes. He was in the Navy for thirty-four years, and I think he misses it. He gives me salutes for everything: homework, feeding the fish, walking through the front door. I'd tell him to stop, but I kinda like how important he makes me feel for brushing my teeth.

I'm honest with my parents, but I might skip the part in the retelling where Lydia drags me out of the kitchen and onto the dance floor while she dances and I stand there doing my award-winning impersonation of a pole. Her Latin blood just needs to "let loose" as she says, and so I go with her because she always counters my "No, thanks" with "What else are you gonna do? Go out on a date?" Which is a joke because she knows I don't date. So I say, "Of course not." And after Family Dinner Friday, I ride my bike to the Venue, where I meet Lydia and her uncle. Every week.

Lydia grabs my hand at the locker and spins me so I'm facing her, and I suck in my breath. Jake's standing a few feet behind her with an amused expression as he watches. How long has he been there? Did he see me fly into the lockers? My pit stains? I keep my arms by my sides and wave with just my fingers. Great, I'm a penguin.

Lydia says, "Come on. Come with me. What else are you gonna do? Go out on a date?"

I lift my eyebrows to communicate that there's a cute guy behind her who I'd like her to play it cool around. Instead, she screams and then blesses herself with the sign of the cross. She's Catholic in the big moments, and I'd explain, but I really can't.

"You do! You have a date! Holy Virgin Mary!" and then she lifts up a hand to heaven because she says it's not taking her name in vain if you acknowledge her, like, *What, I'm only proclaiming she exists.* "Who? Who are you going out with?"

"Yeah, who's the lucky guy?" Jake says, walking up. The friendly way he says it—curious, with zero jealousy—makes me a little sad.

"Hey, Jake," I say, "this is Lydia. Lydia, meet Jake. He just started at Maritime this week."

She looks from me to him to me again. I shake my head, but she slaps her hand to her mouth, and I'm so embarrassed, I could die. I'm hoping the khaki lockers camouflage my khaki pants. "Holaaaa," she says to him like we're in some telenovela, and for whatever reason it makes me burst out laughing.

"Oh my gosh, Lydia, Jake's new, so I'm showing him around. And no, you know I don't have a date."

"Right." Lydia rolls her eyes in Jake's direction. "Everyone knows she's, like, 'dating Jesus' or whatever." Part of me's grateful that Lydia's getting this out on the table for me. This is what I want, right? "What's our tour guide Lovette shown you so far?"

He looks from the left to the right of the hallway and says, "You're looking at it."

"Figures," Lydia says. *Wait.* My chin pulls back into my neck, and I look at her like, *What's that supposed to mean?* She ignores me and focuses on Jake. "How would you like to come to the Venue this Friday night?"

"Lydia, we wash dishes!"

"Not the whole night," she counters.

"I really don't think he wants to spend his Friday—"

"I'd love to." My jaw drops. First, because he sounds so charming. How does he do that? And second, because it works! Lydia's instantly charmed.

"Perfecto," she says. "We're usually there at seven thirty, near the back entrance."

"The Venue," he repeats. "Got it."

"Seriously?" I say. "We really do dishes."

"Real, actual dishes?"

It takes me a second before I realize he's making fun of me. "Okay. Ha. Ha." I want to punch him playfully, but I don't. I start to throw my hands up in surrender, but then remember my sweat issue and squeeze my arms against my sides. Now I'm a clothespin. "Just remember I gave you fair warning."

The bell rings. "Great. It's a date." Then he grins at Lydia and says, "I mean, not a date. Lovette's taken." He points up, and that cracks Lydia up, and he laughs a little. Then he waves, turns the corner, and disappears.

Lydia squeals and kisses me on both cheeks, slaps me on the butt, and pulls out her cross necklace, the kind with Jesus on the cross. She holds it to my lips and squeals, "Kiss it! For luck," and before I can say "No, gracias," I find my lips smushed up against a half-naked dead man's chest, which, if I were Catholic, might feel inappropriate. "Yes! Yes! Yes! YASSSS!" she yells and prances away, leaving me stunned.

Chapter Seven

In the cafeteria at lunch, I arrive at our table and for the first time in three years, I don't know what to do.

Every day it's Lydia, Lydia's boyfriend Kaj, and Kaj's best friend Niles on one bench. On the opposite bench are me and Kelly. But today, Jake's sitting in my spot next to Kelly. I would squish in with them, but Niles is also on their side. It's a Jake sandwich, which makes me a side dish, but Lydia scoots Kaj over to make room for me.

Everyone acts like this is the most normal thing in the world, like we haven't broken a three-year tradition. I'm sitting across from my usual seat, seeing a side of the cafeteria I've never even looked at. This feels wrong. We might as well be sipping from plastic straws in front of a sea turtle.

I'm sure it's Lydia who dragged Jake over to join us, and of course my friends make it look like no big deal. Lydia and Kelly are the only other Christians in the group, but honestly, my friends are better followers of Jesus than me sometimes. Here I am flipping out about different seating arrangements. Meanwhile, Kaj and Niles are laughing at something Jake said, treating him like the three guys have been besties for years.

"Lovette," Kelly says, "did you know Jake lived in Oahu?"

"Hawaii," Niles adds, in case I forgot my brain.

"The cockroaches there are the size of my middle finger!" Kaj says, holding up his middle finger in my face and cracking up. Lydia swats him. "Hey, I was just showing her the size of the cockroaches."

Niles says, "Three inches? Just unzip, bro," and the whole table erupts in laughter, and Kaj throws a tater tot at him but laughs, too.

"Where in Hawaii?" I ask. "Barbers Point?" I feel Kelly's eyes on me. Am I allowed to talk to him?

"Well," Jake says. "Someone knows her naval bases." I only know because Dad would talk about moving the family there when we were young, when he still had dreams of my brother becoming a pro surfer.

Jake shakes his head. "Nah, MCBH. East side."

Ah. His dad's a marine. "Semper Fi," I say.

"Ooh-rah," he answers but half-heartedly. He mumbles, "First on foot and—"

"Right of the line," I say at the same time he does. He looks at me funny. "What?"

"Did you ever feel like you were gonna die while surfing?" Kelly pipes in. "Six- to ten-foot waves? I'd die!" She's never surfed, so she probably would.

"Yeah, sometimes," Jake answers. He turns to me. "You ever ride that high?"

Lydia sucks in her breath. Everyone's eyeing one another, no points for subtlety. I shake my head.

I swear he can see all the way to my sadness because he says, "Yeah, me neither."

Kelly starts, "I thought you said—"

"Hell, no! I only *watched* at the marine base. I surfed Oahu but the smaller breaks. You seen the coral there? I don't have a death wish."

He means it jokingly, but the table goes awkwardly quiet. He sweeps his eyes across our group, curious. I feel bad for him. "My brother was in a bad surfing accident," I say. Everyone freezes. Kelly's eyes are saucers. They know I never talk about this, and I don't know why, but it feels okay right now. "When I was in seventh grade. Board knocked him out. Hit him real weird. He was in a coma. Not forever, he's fine," I say when I see Jake's alarmed face. "Like, totally fine now. But he had to repeat eleventh grade. You know, to relearn everything. Walking, talking, catching a ball." I open my sack lunch and pull out my peanut-butter-and-jelly sandwich. "Anyone want my Hot Cheetos?" Kaj throws an arm up, and I toss them over Lydia's head, but Niles intercepts them.

"Punk!"

"What'd you call me?" Niles says. "I didn't hear because I fell asleep." He fake yawns and opens the Cheetos bag. "I'm SO tired. It's hard being awesome." He stuffs a handful of Cheetos into his mouth.

And just like that, the guys are back to being guys, throwing food at one another and trying to catch it in their mouths. Lydia's in the line of fire of their Cheetos-and-tater-tots war, so she forgets that I breached a three-year taboo subject. Only Jake's looking at me, and Kelly sees Jake looking at me. I can see them out of the corner of my eye, so I focus on my peanut-butter-and-jelly sandwich like it's manna from heaven.

○)))) ● ((((○

Luckily, essays, homework, and my shift at Billy's Buns keep my head occupied for the next day and a half. As usual, I swim Thursday after work, and I bask in the almost-full moon as I bodysurf by God's night-light. I skip lunch with my friends on Friday and spend it in the library studying for a physics test, which is my MO most test days. Today's no different, except for Cecilia Grayson bumping my desk on her way to check out a book. She mumbles, "Watch it," and my mean side wants to ask if she's talking to the desk. I don't.

By Friday evening, I barely remember it. In fact, every thought of the week wisps away with the ocean breeze as I pedal up to the Venue and see Jake. I arrive just as he's locking up his bike, and my heart does that hummingbird thing again. "Hey, there," I say. "So I didn't tell you. We're washing dishes, but we do it so we can practice our Spanish. How much do you know?"

"Hola, hola, Coca-Cola," he responds.

I laugh. "Very convincing. You sound like you were born there."

"I was."

"Really?"

"No, not even close." He laughs. "You always this trusting?" He bumps me in the shoulder. This is his thing, and I love it. "Come on," he says. "Show me these dishes that we have to speak Spanish to."

We enter through the back door into the restaurant kitchen, and I'm immediately engulfed in a hug from Lydia's

Uncle Joe. He's hairy except for his head, and he gives the best hugs—big and bearlike—the kind I wish my dad would give me. Sometimes, I close my eyes and pretend he's Dad, but it's weird because he's like twice the size of Dad, and he speaks Spanish. "¿Qué pasa, hija?" he says in my ear, then releases me and hands us gloves and hairnets.

"Nada," I say.

"¡Híjole! ¿Quién es el muchacho guapo?" He says this while offering Jake a handshake, so I'm guessing he's talking about Jake, but his words are fast. "Who's the . . ." and that's as far as I got.

I reach for my phone to look up Google Translate, but Jake answers, "Mucho gusto. Jake Evans."

Lydia rattles off a paragraph in super-speed Spanish, which she knows I can't follow. She and Uncle Joe look back and forth between me and Jake, and Uncle Joe grins and makes noises like a schoolgirl.

The corners of Jake's mouth turn up. He's understanding every word of it! They're talking about us!

Uncle Joe pats Jake on the back. "Eres un muchacho con mucha suerte."

"Sí. ¡Es verdad! Pero no."

"Ahhh. ¿Tienes una novia?"

"Es complicado."

"Ay. Todas las mujeres."

Wait. *Novia?* I know what novia means!

"I'm not his girlfriend," I say. "Solamente soy un amigo."

"*Una* amig*a*," Uncle Joe corrects.

"No," Jake says. "Of course I wouldn't say that. You don't

date, remember?" He bumps my shoulder. "I was telling them about my girlfriend."

Girlfriend? It's like he says it in Spanish. It hangs there like a word that my brain can't process. Then the past few days come crashing down. I think back to my single word prayer, "Help," on Wednesday night. Jesus answered me. So many posters and memes talk about the power of prayer. I can't think of one that talks about the pain of prayer. There needs to be a picture of a bumblebee on a swollen arm: PRAYER STINGS.

"Ay, Lovette," Uncle Joe says. "¿Qué estás pensando? Regresa al mundo."

Something about thinking and returning to earth. "Lo siento," I say, which is my go-to when he says most things to me.

We head to the stacks of dishes. The Venue's a restaurant, a bar, and after 9:00 p.m., a nightclub, and thus, it has an endless stream of plates, glasses, and silverware. We lose ourselves in suds, warm water, and basic phrases. Uncle Joe asks me how the weather is, what my favorite music is, simple things in the present tense.

I'm hoping I can still get my full-moon swim in. My curfew's eleven, and I figure I can sneak out when we're done washing dishes. Lydia won't even notice once she's on the dance floor. Hopefully Jake won't ask too many questions, and he'll just assume I need to get home.

At 8:50 p.m., we hear the music cue up. Lydia tells Jake about the dance club at nine (Latin Music Fridays) and how Uncle Joe lets me and Lyds go out there as long as we don't drink, and how we both love to dance.

"Correction," I say, pointing a butter knife at her. "Lydia's the dancer. I'm the mannequin, hoping not to get knocked over."

He laughs. "It's okay. My dancing looks like I'm on a trampoline." As we wash, rinse, and stack, a tension releases in me. He has a girlfriend. We can only be friends. There doesn't have to be weirdness between us because *nothing's* going to happen.

"So where's Kaj?" Jake asks.

"Español," I remind him, flicking suds at his arms. "No inglés."

"¿Dondé está Kaj?"

"No sé," Lydia responds, shrugging. "Not his thing. Pero, he might show up luego." Uh-oh. The way she says it means he won't show up later. She only mixes English and Spanish when she's bothered.

Jake picks up on it too, I think, because he switches subjects. "So it's almost nine." He gestures in the direction of the music.

We're just about done, which was supposed to be my exit time, but Uncle Joe nods the go-ahead. Lydia gives a hip shake as a response.

"See?" Jake says, pulling off his gloves. "I mean, look at that. And you haven't seen how high I can jump to salsa music. And, Lovette—"

"I told you," I say, hoping this gets me out of it. "I'm useless out there. Mannequin."

"Well, Lovette clearly needs to practice her poses for the window display at Old Navy."

Lydia bolts through the double swinging kitchen doors, and Jake motions for me to lead the way. I glance at my watch. I guess I can go for five minutes.

Chapter Eight

The second we leave the kitchen into the Venue, it's a million decibels louder and twenty degrees warmer. A few minutes after nine, and already these sweaty dancers have heated up the place. The tables have been pushed to the sides, creating a square floor where couples dance, holding hands and swinging their hips in rhythm to the Latin music. Their feet step back and forward in sync like they've practiced nonstop together, but they haven't. They're just that good. Some dancers move to the music by themselves, legs lunging left and right, and maybe it's the ocean air mixed with their sweat and gorgeous moves, but it reminds me of what I think Brazil would be like. Lydia undulates, shifting her weight from hip to hip, her upper body so controlled. She looks like a professional dancer, fluid and natural—and apparently also sexy, judging by the number of guys watching her.

I think Jake will stare too, but true to his word, he starts bouncing like a pogo stick. I stand perfectly still as always, watching the dancers. After one song, Jake's a sweaty mess.

"You're good!" he shouts over the music, pointing at my statue posture.

I giggle and shake my head.

"No, really! The fall collection will look fab on you!" he jokes.

"Thanks! You too! Did you grow up dancing?"

He's still hopping. "You noticed?" And then he gets that big grin again, the one where his dimple shows, and I can't help but grin with him.

Over his shoulder, Kaj shows up and stomps over to Lydia on the far side of the dance floor.

"Here we go," I say.

Jake leans close. "What'd you say?"

I point behind him, where Lydia and Kaj are yelling at each other. The music drowns them out. People dance around them, ignoring their argument.

"Come on," I say, leading Jake to the bar. "Let's get a Coke."

"They okay?" Jake says. "What happened?"

"Nothing. Everything. The usual," I say. "Who knows. They fight about everything."

"Then why are they dating?" The bartender hands Jake two Cokes, and he gives me one. I take a sip and peer through the crowds of milling people.

"Because *that*." I point to the dance floor. On the far end, Lydia and Kaj are kissing and groping each other like it's their last night on earth. "They really like to make up."

"Odd," is all he says.

"Not when you've seen it for three years." I sip my soda. "I think they'd break up if they started getting along."

"Speaking of getting along, what's with that Cecilia Grayson chick?"

I bite hard on an ice cube. "What about her?"

He twirls his Coke with his mini straw. "Guess she saw us hanging out at school. Almost dragged me into the women's restroom to tell me to watch out for you. Says you're after her man."

I spit the cube back into my cup, laughing. "Trevor Walker?"

"He a bad guy?"

"No. It's just. I dunno, you have to know him. He's so over the top, like he studies Disney movies and picks the cheesiest cartoon prince to mimic." I'm imagining us back in Junior Guards and how he'd flip his wet hair back like a shampoo commercial. It makes me giggle, and Jake lifts an eyebrow. "The one who uses selfie mode on his phone to check his hair? That's Trevor."

Jake adjusts the barstool under him, his leg brushing mine, and I jump. He's amused, I can tell, but I'm not sure if it's because of me or Trevor. "Sounds like a little much."

I finish my Coke. "I wish I were exaggerating. I've grown up with him, so I don't mind—he's an incredible surfer—but as for dating, yeah, no."

"You don't date him because he's a Disney prince."

"Pretty much."

"Not because of Jesus."

I can't believe in all this I didn't mention God. "No. I mean of course because of Jesus. That was an example. I wouldn't date him. Anyone. I mean, I wouldn't date anyone." My words feel like swirling sea foam, a garbled mess.

He's enjoying this, I can tell. "You got somewhere to be?"

"Right now?"

"I dunno." He stands and sets his Coke on a barstool.

"You've been looking at your watch nonstop since we left the kitchen."

My face reddens. Have I been that obvious? I can't tell him about sneaking away to get a swim in. Nobody knows, and that's the way it works. I can't risk my parents finding out. Well, Old Man Mike knows, but he hasn't talked to my parents in years, so it's not like he's gonna snitch.

"Uh, I dunno. It's a full moon. I wanted to enjoy it before I had to be home."

He finishes his Coke in three gulps. "Well, then, let's go."

Let's go? As in both of us?

"Okay," I say. I mean, I can't say no. I said I wanted to see the full moon.

We head through the kitchen to grab our jackets. Outside, the cool breeze makes me catch my breath as we unlock our bikes. "You have any place in mind?"

It's a lie to say no, because I do have a place in mind. But I can't say that. I settle for, "Anywhere's good. I mean, the ocean's nice because you get two moons. The one in the sky and the one on the water."

He's quiet. Have I said something wrong?

"I mean, not really," I correct. "It's just a strip of light on the water. But it's so bright it looks like you can walk out on it." He's staring at me now, maybe waiting for me to say more, so I do. "Or we can just cruise the neighborhoods. I mean, we don't have to head to the beach."

He blinks, and his familiar smile is back. "The neighborhoods? Why would you settle for one moon when you can have two?" He throws a leg over his bike and starts pedaling, calling behind him, "Let's move, mannequin. You have a curfew!"

I pause, wondering if this is okay, this going alone somewhere with a guy. I've never done that. But we're bike riding for goodness' sake, and besides, he's turning a corner and almost out of sight, so I hop onto my seat and pedal after him.

Chapter Nine

Jake and I fly on our bikes to the beach, the wind whipping our jackets, making them flap like wings. My cheeks hurt from smiling and my gums are dry. I may not swim tonight, but this is worth waiting another twenty-nine days.

We lock our bikes next to a beach trash can and stuff our cell phones into our shoes. Jake jogs toward the shoreline, and I follow. When we get close, I hold out an arm, stopping him.

And I point.

The churning crash of the white water fills the silence while we gaze at the moons: the bulbous one in the sky, and the other one, clear and bright, reflecting off the dark water a pathway directly to us.

He finally murmurs, "Two moons."

"Mightier than the thunder of the great waters, mightier than the breakers of the sea—the LORD on high is mighty."

The Bible verse pops into my head, and although this is my space—where I go to be alone with God—it feels okay that Jake's here sharing it. No, it feels more than okay. It feels *right*.

That has to be wrong.

"So you have a girlfriend," I blurt out.

"Well, that's random." His voice is tight. He draws circles

in the sand with his big toe and digs his hands into his jeans pockets. Something about the moment's lost. "Had. We broke up the day before I left."

Why did I ask that?

"Distance is hard," he continues. "You know, we literally have an ocean between us."

"You still talk?"

He looks out like he can see her across the Pacific. "Every day."

"Good," I say, overly cheerful. "That's good."

He rolls his eyes. "What about you?"

"What about me?"

"You have a bad breakup or something?"

"No, why?"

"Your 'no dating' rule. Strict parents?"

Heat floods my face. "Oh. No, nothing like that." I stuff my hands into my jacket pockets. How do I explain this to someone who wasn't there? "Back when all the stuff went down with my brother, God picked up the slack in a lot of ways." Understatement of the year. Jake eyes me curiously, but it's too personal to elaborate. "So I made this promise to Him as a thank you."

"You couldn't just pray with five people? Or, like, read the Book of Leviticus?"

"I wanted it to be bigger."

"So you became a nun."

I laugh, and it bounces against the crashing tide in the quiet night. "No, gosh no. I just wanted to wait and push the dating thing for later. When I'm ready to get married, you know, since, like, marriage is His thing."

"You know there's other ways to thank God. Probably better ways."

I feel him pushing back a little, and it makes me feel defensive. "Maybe. But when I was twelve, that was the biggest thing I could think of. Everyone was getting boyfriends that year."

"Is that why you got rid of your other boyfriend?"

My eyebrows crease.

"Surfing," he clarifies. "I mean, closest thing to a boyfriend you've had, right? You surfed every day in sixth grade. So what, you broke up because of God?"

"No." There's so much emotion still attached to that memory. I feel the sadness, the frustration, the loneliness— even the anger—but I know it's not for Jake. I swallow it down and mutter, "My brother almost died doing it."

"So now you're afraid of surfing?"

"No." Why's he digging so much? "How would you know I surfed every day? We never talked."

"I listened."

"I didn't surf at youth group." It comes out snappier than I mean.

"No, but people talked about you."

I put my hand on my hip. "Really."

"Fearless," he adds. "That's what I remember." Something stirs in me, and it makes me want to cry, but I don't. "And I remember you always showed up with your hair wet, and people would whisper about how you could out-surf the guys, and you always won the group games, and you'd volunteer to pray, which nobody did in sixth grade. Every kid wanted to be on your team or sit next to you in worship. Of course I remembered you. Anyone would've. But now. I dunno. You don't dance. You don't date. You don't surf. You don't talk much at school."

"So?"

"So it's just a lot of don'ts." I haven't been angry in so long, but he's kindled a fire in me by bringing up so much at once. How would he know, anyway? He's been here a week!

"I'm not allowed to, okay?"

"Surf?"

"Anything!" I kick the sand. "And why's it your business suddenly? I'm not allowed to go into the water. My parents told me no ocean. Period. No way they're going through hell again."

I'm immediately embarrassed that I said so much. The waves crash and pound and make up for the silence. His shoulders and head drop a notch, but he reaches out and rubs my arm. "Hey, I'm sorry. That was out of line. I don't know what that was like for your family. I think I was just pissed you brought up Hannah."

I blink.

"My ex. Her name's Hannah. I didn't choose to move, ya know. And"—he sits on the sand, facing the waves—"my mom didn't come with us."

The last part hangs in the air. Oh, man.

"Sorry," I mumble.

He pats the sand next to him. When I hesitate, he adds, "Promise I'll get you home in time."

I sit down and feel the cold sand through my jeans. "You don't have a curfew?"

"Sort of. My aunt—who I live with on the weekdays— she's a flight attendant and gone most weekends. That's when I see my dad. I actually should be back at the base tonight, but I couldn't pass up the offer—washing dishes." He bumps my shoulder and I smile. "I'll drive down tomorrow morning. Dad'll get over it." He says the last bit all grumpy, like he's already in a fight with his dad about it, even though it's the night before.

"Sorry I was snappy."

He shrugs. "Wanna make up like Lydia and Kaj?"

He gives me a sly grin, and we both erupt in laughter. It gets quiet again. I don't think he tells many people about his home life, and that makes me feel close to him, even though we only re-met three days ago. I dig my hands through the cold sand, burying them to my wrists. "I do swim," I whisper, and I feel his gaze turn toward me. "Every night, if I can." I lift my chin at the waves. "Out there. They have no idea, my parents. They'd kill me . . . twice. No one knows, actually." I glance up at him, then back down to my buried hands. "Well, Old Man Mike knows."

I wait for him to ask who that is, but he doesn't. A comfortable silence settles between us.

I peer up at the bright path of moonlight, the shimmering walkway from the shore to the horizon. I inhale the majesty, the wet salty air, the crashing sound of the surf, the soft lapping sound of the water as it ebbs. "It's weird. Even though I'm disobeying them—my parents—it's where I feel closest to God."

We watch the waves in silence. I wonder what he's thinking, if he feels I shared too much, if he thinks I'm so boring compared to my sixth-grade self. Abruptly he stands, extends his hand, and I take it. Guess it's time to go home. He lifts me to my feet but then takes my hand the way we do with our friends during closing prayer, not interlinking fingers, but still. This is the first time a guy has held my hand outside of prayer circles, and I start to resist, but instead of going to our bikes, he pulls me toward the shoreline.

"What're we doing?"

"*This* is what you wanted to do tonight, wasn't it?" At the water's edge, all I can think is, *A guy is holding my hand. Not for real in the romantic fireworks way, but still.* It's only September, but the ocean's chilly as he walks me ankle deep. "Before I hijacked your night. You were trying to get away so you could swim with God."

"Yes, but—"

"Then I'm not keeping you from it." We wade deeper, the water lapping up to our waists.

"I usually wear a wetsuit!" I laugh, pulling back toward the shore.

"Where's your wetsuit?"

"Old Man Mike's. Corner of Ocean and Twenty-sixth, you know, by Bruce's Beach? I leave it in his side yard."

"Not enough time if we're gonna make curfew. Come on."

He leads me farther in. This is crazy. And cold. Jeans, jackets, and T-shirts—soaked straight through. But I don't resist. I don't want to let go of Jake's hand for anything.

Well, maybe one thing. I pull away and dive headfirst

under the white water. The ocean surges over my head and surrounds my body with its current. I'm where I belong. I pop up, the salty taste dripping through my huge smile.

He has that look again, the one he gave me when I told him about the two moons, where he's staring intently, like if he looks away, I might disappear.

"There you are," he says.

"What," I say.

"You're not all don'ts." He grins and grabs hold of me, lifting and dunking me under the surf again, but this time going with me.

We swim and body surf until we're prunes. After five years of being solo out here, I've forgotten how much fun it is to do this with another human. *Thank you,* I tell God. *This is our place still, I promise. But thanks for sharing it tonight.*

By the time we wring ourselves out and he bikes me home, I'm a Popsicle, my jacket heavy with seawater, hands numb on my handlebars as the wind whips past. It's 10:58 p.m. when we pull up to my curb.

"See?" he says, as I look at my watch for the millionth time tonight.

"Do you want me to get you a towel?" I ask between shivers.

"Nah. Get yourself inside. I'll see you Monday."

"Okay." I don't move. "I'm, uh, gonna take my bike in through the side yard."

He nods. "Good night."

"Okay." *Why do I keep saying okay?* "I mean, good night." I walk through the gate, resisting the urge to look behind me.

Inside, I press my lips together so my teeth won't chatter

and hurry through the house to the shower. I lock the bathroom door and turn on the water. Fully clothed, I stand under the steaming shower until I've rinsed off any evidence of the ocean. As I peel off my jeans and jacket and everything else, I hear knocking.

"Hey, Love," Dad says through the door.

"Hey, Dad."

"You have fun with Lydia?"

"Yeah."

"Full moon tonight."

"Oh yeah?"

"You biked. Didn't you see it?"

Actually, I saw two. I'm remembering Jake's awe. *"Two moons,"* I hear him say.

"Lovette?"

"Yeah, sorry. No, I saw it. Beautiful."

"Your mom wants to talk to you tomorrow. Something about the YMCA not having you listed as a member."

Oh no. I close my eyes and pray, but I know I'm busted. How will I get out of this without lying? "Okay, sounds good."

He waits at the door, I can feel it, wondering if I'll explain.

"Night, Dad." I turn the water off, ball up my clothes, and wrap myself in a towel. Tonight's the first night I've spent alone with a guy. Does that count as a date? I hope not. I apologize to God just in case. I made a promise, and I intend to stick to it. But why didn't it feel wrong? He even held my hand, and it felt normal. Natural, even. I drop my head to my hands and sit on the toilet seat until the hall light goes dark under the crack of the bathroom door.

Chapter Ten

The following morning, Mom clomps into my room like she's auditioning for clog dancing. Her AirPods are sticking out of her ears in weird directions, and her Saturday-morning hair looks messier than usual. "Where've you been going after work?"

I'm doing homework in bed, so I can't pretend I'm sleeping. "Mom—"

Her hands drop to her hips. "Don't 'Mom' me. The YMCA says you don't have a membership. Where've you been at night?"

I look to the wall at my collage of pictures from Hume Lake Christian Camp. Next to it is a framed poster of Kelly Slater riding a wave in the 2015 Billabong Pro Tahiti World Surf League tour. "I—"

"Who walked you home last night? That wasn't Lydia."

I forget how to breathe. "How did you—"

She crosses her arms smugly. "Windows."

"You were spying?"

"Just trying to figure out why our daughter, whom we *thought* we knew, hasn't been where we *thought* she was for the past eighteen months."

"Actually, longer," I admit.

"LONGER!" she repeats, just in case Dad can't hear from his men's Rotary meeting across town.

I want to tell the truth. My parents aren't religious, and the whole lying thing isn't gonna win any points for how they view the Big Guy. I'm just so afraid that if I tell them I've been out in the waves, the one thing I love will be taken from me. They think the Pacific Ocean's the devil. I suppose if I saw my son attached to that many tubes after almost drowning, I might, too.

I start with the obvious. "The guy you saw was Jake Evans. He goes to my school. Lydia invited him to wash dishes. His dad's in the military too." I'm hoping this last part will make him sound better. *See? Our dads are men of honor.*

Mom's face changes. Her smile says, *I know what you're going through.* Uh-oh. I'm not sure she does.

"I dated a guy for two months once before I got the nerve to tell my parents," she confesses.

Wait, what?

I start to protest, but she waves me off and sits down on the corner of my bed. Oh dang. This feels like the last five minutes of a family TV show, when the slow music starts and it always ends in a hug.

"Gary Ratchford," she continues.

"Oh yeah?" I say, because what else do I say? My nose crinkles, and my lips scrunch as if I've smelled a beached-whale carcass. I don't want to think of Mom with anyone but Dad.

She doesn't notice. "These are confusing times, you know,

being a teenager, hormones, and I'm sure you have questions."

"I don't, really."

"And ever since you've been doing that whole church thing, I . . ."

That's what Mom calls my love for Jesus. *"That whole church thing."*

Kelly brought me with her to a church camp called Hume Lake the summer before sixth grade. It was a blast, and it was the first time I had heard about Jesus in a way that made sense: how it wasn't about us working our way up to Him but about Him coming down to us. That clicked for me. Also, there was this friendship-with-God thing, like I could talk to Him about anything, *seriously anything,* and I loved it. When I came back from Hume Lake, I started going to her youth group. It was like a dose of summer camp once a week. Turns out it was perfect timing. One year and three months later, my brother Matt was hit by his own surfboard in a freak accident. For the next year, my parents would be MIA as they spent every day in the hospital and then the rehab facility with him. They'd check in with texts, and I'd visit him sometimes, but a lot of nights when I'd get home, there'd be a note on the fridge about what food to heat up for dinner and a reminder to turn the lights off before bed.

I spent a lot of time at Kelly's house or with other church families, and I'd go on every weekend youth-group trip. I joined a midweek Bible study. Even though I was going to junior-high group, Pastor Brett heard what happened and said I could also come to high-school youth group. In the loneliest year of my life, when I should've felt like an orphan,

God filled my life with more family than I could imagine. People wonder why I'm so in love with Jesus, but if they saw the way He filled every void and answered every question, they'd totally get it.

I sit up in my bed. "Mom, it's not a 'church thing.' I love Jesus."

"Of course you do. But I don't know the pressures they might put on you there at that church thing, and I want you to know, that if you're thinking about sex, then we can talk."

Whoa. "What?"

"And the lengths you went to cover it up! Coming home every night with your hair wet? I just know that if you've been keeping a boyfriend a secret—there may be other things." She pauses, tilts her head, and shifts to look at me. The bed bounces, and I wish it would bounce me out the window, because she adds, "So he picks you up after work—and then you shower at his house to make it look like you've been swimming?"

"No, I use the beach showers. Mom—"

"Oh, that makes sense. It's right by your work. And here, your father was afraid you'd gone back in the ocean."

"Really?" I swallow.

"He said you smelled like seawater the other night. I told him don't worry—we're all on the same page." She gets a twinkle in her eye. "I shoulda known it was a boy." She smiles like she's in on a big secret. "Mum's the word. I'll tell your father you've been practicing swim at a friend's house." She winks at me, and I feel knots in my belly. She's covering for me. And for something that isn't even true!

There are so many things I want to say. *"Mom, I've been swimming in the ocean." "Mom, I feel closest to Jesus when I'm out on the water." "Mom, I miss surfing." "Mom, I know you almost lost Matt, but you won't lose me."*

But I don't. Right now, I can keep swimming every night because Mom thinks I've been out with a boy and she's actually *okay* with it.

I reach out and squeeze her hand. "Mom, I haven't had sexual intercourse, but when I plan on it, I'll be sure to talk to you, okay?" This won't be until the night before my wedding, but she doesn't need details.

"Do kids still call it that? Intercourse? Huh. I thought it was, like, banging or hitting it or—"

"Mom!"

"What! Okay, fine. Intercourse it is. You sure you haven't?" She tries to look inside of me with her searchlight eyes. I sit in awkward silence until she embraces me like we're reuniting after years apart. I feel her tears as our cheeks press together. "I can't believe how old you're getting," she sniffles. "Where has time gone?" Now I'm twelve and in a maxi pad commercial, but I endure it because the ocean's worth it. It's always worth it. A single thought comes to me, and I don't know if it's God or my guilt, but either way, I hear Him asking:

"Do you love the ocean more than Me?"

Chapter Eleven

Every Monday morning, I leave ninety minutes early and my parents never notice, but when I wake up this morning, I'm afraid everything will be different and they'll have a guard posted at my door. I peek into the hallway, but everything's the same. Mom's out to her office already, and Dad's happy that I'm getting a head start on my education. Well, as long as I make my bed first.

Like every Monday, I bike five miles past my school to El Porto Beach to watch the other high-school surf teams. By 7:00 a.m., I'm tucked into my hoodie on the wet sand and doing my Bible study while the girls practice their rail-to-rail turns. A worship song plays in my earbuds as I watch the girls popping up, carving, and soaring against a backdrop of pink morning sky:

I see Your face in every sunrise.
The colors of the morning are inside Your eyes.
The world awakens in the light of the day.
I look up to the sky and say, "You're beautiful."

I watch a girl catch a left, angling down the wave as it chases her from behind. She traverses the face as she rides down the line. So clean. I could be this good by now, but who knows if I can still get to my feet? At the bottom, almost where the water's flat, she turns her shoulders and buries her rail, setting up for a graceful arcing turn. Her speed shoots her back up the face, and she whips her board back 180 degrees, catching a little air. I actually clap in response and shout, "Yes!" She offers a friendly wave when she hears me, rides in on her stomach, and trots over.

"Hey," she says, "I've seen you out here a few times. You go to Redondo?"

"Nah, Maritime Academy. We don't have a team."

She clucks her tongue. "Bummer. I'm Alix. With an *I*. Not an *E*."

"Hi, Alix with an *I*," I say. "Lovette. You cut back at seriously the perfect time."

"Thanks. Got lucky on that one. Sounds like you know a good wave. You doing any of the opens?"

I shake my head. "No way I'd be ready."

"What about the All Wave Junior Open? It's a five-series local competition hosted by different local shops and bars. The third one was a few weeks ago, but the next one's not till February. Watermans is hosting. You should sign up."

"Yeah, maybe." That's a definite no.

"Cool, maybe we'll compete!"

And like that, she jogs off.

Disappointment slouches my shoulders forward. I feel heartbroken, and then those words come up again: *"Do you love the ocean more than Me?"*

Do I love the created thing more than the creator? "No, of course not," I say out loud, kinda angry that the thought keeps popping up. I open my Bible-study journal to an empty page, one verse across the top: "You shall have no other gods before me."

"Really?" I say to the sky. He knows I love Him more than anything. He *knows.* To prove it, I leave the ocean right then, thirty minutes earlier than usual.

○))) ● ● ● (((○

School's back to normal—uneventful like most weeks. Well, except for Jake. Is it okay to be attracted to someone even though I know we won't date? My heart boxes my ribcage every time I see him in the hallway, so I U-turn whenever I see him coming my way. I don't think he notices, and luckily, he's no different than before our Friday-night swim. Still friendly, still hanging out with me and my friends. This week it feels like he's been part of our group forever—a party of six from the beginning— and we've always had these seat assignments at lunch.

○))) ● ● ● (((○

The following week, the steady "uneventfulness" has a mini hiccup. I go to bed like normal on Tuesday, but I'm woken by a bird chirping. I sit up in a panic. How am I gonna get a bird out of my room? Then I remember that's the sound of Kelly's texts.

You awake

I write back, *I am now*

I lie back down and try to calm my breathing.

Her next text chirps: *JAKE HAS A GF!!!*

Had, I start to write, but before I hit send, she interrupts with another chirp.

I can't believe he led me on

This worries me.

I turn the volume down and write, *He led you on?*

A softer chirp: *HE WENT TO POETRY NIGHT*

Oh right. That was tonight.

How was it

Horrible. My future husband has a gf

Future husband? I stare at her text.

She writes, *Hello?*

I finally type, *What did you say?*

Stuff. I can't believe he would dump me like that.

Dump? Whoa. Brakes, Kelly. *You know you weren't dating, right?*

The text bubbles are repeating. She's writing a lot about them not dating. Oh dear. Finally it comes through.

We could've been! Eventually! And then when was he planning on telling me he had a gf?

Oh, Kelly. So many texts. *So many birds,* I think sleepily.

I decide not to fight her on Jake's girlfriend/ex-girlfriend status and instead send her a hug emoji before silencing my phone. Maybe I'm the one who's wrong.

If Jake didn't tell Kelly he was broken up, does this mean he got back with Hannah? He told me they talked "every day." Maybe they were in the process of working things out. I know I shouldn't care, but I flop away from my phone like I'm turning my back on the possibility.

I see Kelly's final text in the morning when I wake up. *Maybe pastor brett should talk w him*

The rest of the week, Kelly's quiet at our lunch table. Her eyes, usually ogling at Jake, are glancing around at everything and everyone else. Every time he opens his mouth, no matter what he's saying, I can sense her looking at me, wanting me to return the look so she can lift her eyebrows to communicate, *Can you believe he would say that?*

At youth group, she pulls me into the front row to avoid Jake, and I do my best to be a good friend. Pastor Brett's sermon is fifteen minutes long, but I only remember one part, like he saw a highlight reel of my life last weekend while planning his talk. He says, "I know that when people hear things like God saying He's jealous, they think He's some drunk guy at a bar talkin' 'bout His woman, being like, 'Don't touch my property, yo.' But it's not like that. God's jealous because God knows He's the best thing for you, and He loves you too much to let you chase after things that are nothing but counterfeits in comparison. The world's makin' it rain with counterfeit hundred-dollar bills. Who wants a crisp hundy if it's fake? The world's hundies are yesterday's undies." Everyone groans at his bad pun. "Yeah, that's how God feels, too. So it's a good jealousy. Not a human jealousy. What's God jealous for in your life? Who's stealing His number one spot?"

I think of the ocean. I think of Jake. *I'm not letting either take your number one spot,* I silently say to Jesus, *double-pinkie swear,* and to prove it, I don't look back once at Jake to say hi or "sorry my best friend's being weird." But I also volunteer to close the group in prayer, and I secretly hope Jake notices. *"See? I'm not 'just a lot of don'ts,'"* I want to say as I finish praying. But instead, I settle for "Amen."

○))) ● ● (((○

I still go to work as usual, but I've stayed out of the ocean for two weeks, and I'm miserable. I don't want to chance Mom seeing my wet hair and assuming I'm having sex with some guy she thinks I've been dating for a year and a half. I can't bear the guilt of that lie. And plus, ew, so embarrassing.

By Thursday night, even my coworker Kim notices. "What's up with you?" she asks while slicing tomatoes.

"Not much." I pretend I don't know what she means and immediately feel guilty. "No, that's a lie. Just, you know, stuff."

"Glad we cleared that up," she says, but lets me be.

○))) ● ● (((○

On Friday, Jake's waiting at the curb in front of my house when I pedal up after school. I look around nervously. No cars in the driveway. Thank goodness. The bird chirping in my room on Tuesday night has found a way into my heart and is flapping to break out.

"How'd you get here so fast?" I ask.

He points to the Honda at the curb.

I nod.

He tilts his head. "You okay?"

"Yeah, why?"

"You've been—did I do something?"

"No." I fiddle with my handlebar.

"One of those . . . weeks?"

Everything warms inside of me, and I smile. "Yeah."

"Yeah."

Now what? He's here because he knows I've been avoiding him. I want to ask about Hannah. There's the small possibility that they're back together, but my bet is on Kelly misinterpreting things. Instead I blurt, "Sorry. My parents busted me with wet hair—I played it off, but—I haven't been in the ocean since, and it's made me—I've been really off lately."

His tension releases. "That explains it."

"Yeah." We stand quietly for a minute, the bike between us.

He inhales again. Uh-oh. "Your curfew's eleven, right?"

"Yeah . . ."

"Can I take you somewhere tonight?"

"No," I say quickly. Of course I want to go out with him. But I can't fight against my feelings if I keep encouraging him. He steps back, which makes me soften. "I mean, I can't because it's Friday. Lydia." There's no way she'd let me get out of the Venue.

"I mean afterward."

I want to say Kelly wouldn't approve. I want to say we have to stop hanging out one-on-one because it's not going anywhere, but I still have a crush that needs to go away. And that before he came into my life two weeks ago, I was loving God just fine, and now he's an idol, and the ocean's an idol, and I'm a bunch of don'ts, and Mom thinks I'm having sex. Just say no. Easy peasy. *N. O.* Two letters. I open my mouth. "Maybe."

He grins. "Pick you up at nine? Back kitchen entrance?" He walks backward toward his car.

I nod feebly.

"Good." He unlocks his car door. "I mean, unless you'll be inside working on your fashion-model dance moves."

He lifts a hand, juts a hip out, and freezes, striking a pose.

It takes every facial muscle I have to resist smiling. "No, I'll be there. I mean, maybe."

"Good. See you then." He gets into his car and starts the engine, rolling down the window. The corners of his mouth lift slightly, and he adds, "Maybe." I rest against my bike as he speeds away. What just happened?

Chapter Twelve

During Family Dinner Friday, I usually talk more, but my nerves are abuzz about tonight. My parents ask me about my week as I pick at my food.

"Good," I say.

Mom squints. "Dad asked if you had homework."

"Oh. Yeah."

Then, it's like something registers on Mom's face. She winks at me and asks how "swim" is. Seriously.

At the Venue, Lydia's in another fight with Kaj, so she takes up two hours of dishwashing time telling me and Uncle Joe about who said what and when and can you believe that? It's in rapid Spanish, and Uncle Joe says, "¡Híjole!" a lot. I only get every fourth word or so, but I'm relieved. Thanks to Kaj and how many different ways Lydia's gonna kick his A, I'm able to avoid any questions about my status with Jake. She knows I only side-hug guys, and she's already asked ten times this week if we've gone "breast to breast" yet. (We haven't. Hugged face-to-face, that is.) She'll mention him soon; I'm just glad it's not tonight because I don't know how to answer.

At 9:00 p.m., as soon as Lydia shimmies onto the dance floor, I slink out the back entrance. Jake's there waiting, his

Honda humming in the deliveries driveway. He's wearing boardshorts and a short-sleeve button-down. Without thinking, I sprint over—all plans to play it cool, gone.

It makes him smile, and I melt at his dimple.

I look down at my jeans and long-sleeve T-shirt. Red drops of splattered spaghetti sauce decorate my top. "I'm underdressed," I say, rubbing the stains.

"It's fine. You'll be out of that in no time."

"What?"

He laughs at my panicked face. "You're too easy, mannequin. Relax. I'm not taking off your clothes."

I'm not used to being around someone this easygoing. Kelly's uptight and worried, and Lydia's impulsive and emotional. He slaps the roof of his car twice and gestures to me with his chin to get in.

I slide into the front seat and buckle my seatbelt. "So."

"So."

"So where are you taking me?"

His eyes twinkle, and he presses his lips together. He's not gonna tell, but he looks like he's going to explode with excitement. It's contagious, and my heart flips.

○))) ● ● (((○

The windows are down, the ocean air tangling my hair, music blasting, and I'm sitting next to Jake Evans, who keeps smiling at me with that dimple that makes the world better. I'm in a movie.

We coast north on Hermosa Avenue until we come to

North End, a locals' bar where the LA Kings hang out, then turn right and drive up to Manhattan Avenue. As we approach all the restaurants of South Manhattan Beach, he turns the music down low so I can hear him. "I thought maybe you weren't talking to me because of Kelly."

I don't want to answer him, so instead I ask, "How was poetry night?"

We come to the stoplight at Manhattan Beach Boulevard and Manhattan Avenue. The iconic ice cream and candy shop on the corner, the Manhattan Beach Creamery, has a line out the door. A group of club-ready ladies in high heels and short skirts weave their way toward the bars by the pier, shouting and cackling.

"I mentioned Hannah," he says finally, and the light turns green.

"Did you say you broke up?"

"I didn't get the chance! Probably better she doesn't know. She got all weird after that. Said I shouldn't lead girls on and that I should protect their hearts and treat them like 'King's daughters.'"

Oh no. I was hoping she didn't go there, but she did. "What'd you say?"

"I told her, 'I thought you just asked me to poetry night. Were you asking me to prom?'"

I slap my forehead. "You didn't!"

"I was kidding! Trying to lighten her up. And technically"— he looks at me when he says this—"*you're* the one who asked me to check it out. But yeah. She was intense."

"Yeah, she's really . . . uh, Christian."

"Aren't you?"

"Of course! Sometimes—sometimes—" I'm struggling to explain how Kelly and I love Jesus the same but it's different. "Like, if she wants me to go somewhere with her, she won't say, 'Hey, I want you to go.' She'll be like, 'I've been praying about this, and the Lord's placed it on my heart that you go with me.'"

"Can't really argue with that one."

"No, you sure can't."

He pulls into a metered parking spot on Highland and Twenty-seventh, just past Bruce's Beach, the two-block stretch of grassy hills sloping down to the boardwalk.

"This is close to Old Man Mike's," I say as we walk the pathway toward the ocean. "My friend who lets me store my suit in his side yard."

"I know." When he sees my brow furrow, he adds, "You told me—Twenty-sixth and Ocean—remember? Good thing, too, or I'd have to be knocking on a lot of doors."

Before I can ask more, he's loping down the grass of Bruce's Beach, and I'm following. We stop at Mike's property, and Jake veers down the alley where the entrance to Mike's side yard is. He unlatches the waist-high gate, which means he's been here before. As if he can read my mind, he says, "I might've peeped in a couple of people's side yards before I found a wetsuit your size."

I follow him into Mike's tiny side yard patio with its skateboards, surfboards, towels, and lounge chairs all crammed into the narrow space. There, on the side rail, my wetsuit hangs as usual, and next to it, a larger wetsuit. Jake's.

"Are we swimmi—" But I stop when I notice that Mike's surfboards, his shortboard and his Fish, aren't alone. Stacked next to them are two longboards, leashes attached, waxed and ready to go.

Jake walks behind one and reaches down near the fins, presses something, and the inside of the board lights up a blue as bright as a neon sign.

"What the—"

"My friend's dad from Hawaii makes these. He has a shop up in Ventura. It's for night surfing. Cool, yeah?"

"But how?"

"RGB LEDs. They're lined into the surfboard before the glassing. Then a computer connection, some stoppers, and O-rings to avoid the water. It's safe."

I gawk at the beautiful light coming from *inside* the board, three lines in the center and one around the perimeter, outlining its perfect shape.

"So." He leans back on the waist-high gate and crosses his arms casually. "He loaned me two, but I haven't met anyone else to test them out with me." He waits a beat. "I mean, except for you."

My heart sinks. Every part of me wants to. I trace the longboard with my finger, touching its bumpy wax across the middle and the sides. I can still remember how the board felt on my stomach when I was a kid, how it bobbed so mellow over the rolling tide, the way it glided through the crests of waves as I paddled out, splashing water over my head and waking up my insides.

"I can't." I close my eyes but don't cry.

"I *thought* you might say that. Your parents, right?"

I force myself to swallow the painful lump in the back of my throat. "I can't . . ." I start again. "It's bad enough I swim. I can't do that to them."

"Which is why we're not going to."

Huh? He throws my wetsuit at me, the thick neoprene slapping my stomach as I catch it. I shake my head and step back, like standing near the boards is sinful, but he stops me with a hand in the air.

"No one said anything about surfing." He takes his wetsuit off the rail. "Surfing involves standing up." He unbuttons his shirt and slips it off. "Think of it as bodysurfing, which you do every night. Only there's going to be a board under you."

"That sounds like justifying."

My eyes are fixed on his shoulders, but he doesn't notice or doesn't mind. I've seen guys with their shirts off before—I live at the beach—but there's something about his chiseled chest that tells a story. Military kid to the core. The kind who's up before dawn to get in a set of push-ups, weighted pull-ups, and a run even before he surfs. Is it guilt that pushes him? *I'm concerned,* I tell myself. That's why I'm staring. I hear God saying back to me, *"That sounds like justifying."* I turn away.

"If you see someone riding a surfboard on their belly, do you ever call that surfing?"

That gets a little laugh out of me.

"Look, your dream's in direct contrast to your parents' wishes," he says. "I can't tell you how to fix that. But I *can* get you as close to your dream as possible, especially since I can't get remotely close to mine."

"What's yours?"

He presses his lips together and shakes his head. I'm deflated that he doesn't want to share, so I offer my best guess.

"Hannah?"

"Huh?" It looks like I just slammed a frying pan to his face. "No, actually." He starts shoving his legs into his wetsuit, tucking his boardshorts in.

"Hey, don't get mad. You said you talk to her every day."

His tense shoulders, almost touching his ears, relax. "That's fair." He pulls up the back zipper and turns his back on me. When I realize it's so I can change into my wetsuit, I'm mortified. Usually I have my bikini underneath.

No big deal, no big deal. I wrap myself in an oversize towel and shrug my wetsuit on in record time. "Okay!" I practically shout when I'm done. He turns around and gestures at the two boards. I pick up the longboard, and it instantly feels like an extension of me, like I've never stopped picking it up.

"You ready?"

I lift the board and wedge it under my armpit. "Not even close."

"Good." He kicks my jeans and tee underneath one of Mike's lounge chairs, grabs the other board, then pads barefoot toward the dark ocean without looking back to see if I follow.

Chapter Thirteen

I'm jittery, and not from the cold. At the shoreline, I'm strapping the leash to my ankle, readjusting it just so I can hear the Velcro rip. The ocean, true to its nature, has used its magical ability to make everything okay again. It sounds so beautiful and soothing that—

"A family that's not fucked up."

I freeze, mid–Velcro rip.

"That's my dream. There." His words hang thick in the air, making everything else seem unimportant. I drop my leash, turn my full attention to him.

"Sorry," he says, his words soft. "Didn't mean to be a buzzkill."

I adjust the neck of my wetsuit. "Well, I wouldn't know. I mean, I don't drink."

He chuckles at my bad joke, and I think there isn't a better feeling in the world than making him laugh. But his dream for his family feels like a lead anchor, sobering my smile. "Anyway," he mumbles, "of course you'd think Hannah. How were you supposed to know?"

"True, but maybe you could tell me more about her so I'm not always guessing." He looks away from me and at the horizon. "Or your family?" I plead with my eyes, but he doesn't look at me. He opens his mouth, like he's considering, but then his eyes start glistening, and he snaps his mouth closed and clears his throat. As an answer, he presses the button on his board, lighting it neon blue.

"They had other colors," he says, "red, green—even purple—but blue reminded me of what you said before about two moons."

I crinkle my forehead. The moment is lost, but it's okay. He tried.

"Blue moon," he continues. "You know, when you have two full moons in the—"

"Same month," I finish for him. "Which is, like, hardly ever."

"So yeah. Two moons."

He reaches down and pushes the button behind the fins of mine, and my board lights up an electric blue that matches his. Different designs, same exact color. It sends a current through me too. With nervous hands, I lift the board and wedge it under my armpit. "You know, I haven't surfed in four years."

He attaches his leash and says, "Well, good thing you're not surfing."

I grin and charge at the water. I toss my board over the first set of white water and flop onto the waxy fiberglass. I hear Jake splashing behind me. We glide through the water, floating over the rolling swells, letting the ocean do the talking. We paddle in sync, left arm then right, and my shoulders already ache, but I don't care. I feel the water, how it flirts, lapping over my board, and then dips, causing my board to drop and then slap it.

The blue lights from our boards make the water shimmer, reflecting an eerie glow in the half-moon darkness. The surf's small tonight, only one- to two-foot breakers, but our boards feel like unsheathed lances as they spar with the waves. We duck close to our boards, letting the waves spray over us. Side by side, we continue with long arm strokes until we paddle out past the farthest set. The waves and shore are behind us, and we maneuver to straddle our boards, facing the endless expanse of dark water.

I rotate my legs under my board like an eggbeater and twirl my surfboard in a full circle one direction, then a full circle the opposite way. My eyes sting and there's salt in my nose, and I couldn't be happier. I tip my head back to the sky and laugh, splash the water with my fingers and slide off my board, diving under the cold Pacific. When I come up, I giggle again, and I snort some salt water and cough. I climb back onto the board and lie flat, my chest against her. *Breast to breast*, I think, and that makes me laugh again.

Jake lies down, cheek to his board, and watches it all with his dimply smile. Finally, he speaks. "You hated it. I can tell."

I wipe the blurry salt from my face so I can see him clearly. "Yeah. It was horrible." I rest my cheek against my arm and face him. I keep thinking about what he said about his family. Or rather, didn't say. He told me his mom stayed behind when they moved, but I feel like there's more to it than that. There's a heaviness in the air—it sags his whole body—when we start to talk about it. Even though he's the one who cussed, I feel like it's me who owes him an apology. "Sorry your family's"—I wonder if God's okay with cursing if you're quoting someone, so I whisper—"*fucked* up."

He laughs. "I'm sorry, I couldn't hear that last part. What'd you say?"

I splash him. "And sorry I brought up Hannah."

We bob quietly.

With his hand, he makes swirls and whirlpools in the water. Finally, he says, "Nah, I mean, how would you know? I wish I could explain it, but you don't know Hannah. I can't just cut things off."

"Do you want to?"

"That's a loaded question."

"Why?"

He threads his hands together and tucks them under his chin. He rests his head on the board, not looking at me. "My dad did a tour of duty a few years back. Seventh to eighth grade he was deployed. Afghanistan."

"Okay." I have no idea what this has to do with Hannah, but I don't care. He's actually opening up. I want to think of the right thing to say, but I don't know what that is. Dad always says to thank every military person, especially those who serve away from their families for the greater good. "Will you thank him for me?"

He scoffs. "Yeah, sure." He unthreads his hands and flicks the water with his thumb and middle finger. "He came back *different.* And there's stuff that only she knows. About my family. My dad. So I can call her, like whenever, like when shit goes down, and, well, she gets it. Her dad's deployed right now, so, you know, sometimes she needs me, too. And I get it."

There's not much I can say to that. I want to say, "*I get it, too.*" But I don't. My dad was never deployed. He's been stationed here for years. But it's not like he hasn't done great things. He was in the Navy, not the Cub Scouts. Still, it feels inferior right now compared to two marines fighting a war, and one coming back with what sounds like PTSD. And why should it matter? Jake's finally being honest, which I know is hard for him, and all I can think about is how Hannah shares something with him that I won't ever be able to match.

What can I say, God? Give me something wise. I open my mouth. "Oh."

Oh? Way to make him feel better. I'm a regular spiritual giant.

"So, uh, does Hannah surf?"

He chuckles under his breath. "Maybe the Internet." He slicks his wet hair back with one hand. "Nah, she's more of a mall rat than a gym rat."

It seems like it should be a cutting remark, but he says it fondly, like he's remembering some fun memory they had at Macy's. I feel a pang of jealousy, and then he continues. "She's not really into this stuff . . . but we've been through a lot together."

Well, Jake and I have matching boards, boards he matched on *purpose* because a blue moon is two full moons in the same month, and he wanted two moons. He wanted us to have a *thing*, which has to be better than any possible *thing* they could've had at the mall. It has to.

And there's surfing. We have surfing. Well, I mean, we'd

have that if I actually surfed. But I'd be disobeying my parents, which would mean disobeying God. But what if my parents are actually wrong for keeping me from surfing? Then is it okay?

Sorry, Jesus.

I spin my board so I'm facing the shore and gather armfuls of ocean as I paddle hard. I hear him shouting my name, but I ignore it, instead focusing on the blue lights making my wetsuit glow.

I'm greedily pulling at the water, gaining speed and gulping chestfuls of air. I glance behind me at the mound of water forming and then to the left and right to measure how it's breaking. The swell pushes me and lifts me high. I'm looking down the sloping hill of water, belly to belly, my shoulders tense. With a snapping push-up, I stand.

I'm surfing.

Take that, Hannah. I ride hard, attempting a simple cutback, but my feet are bigger than four years ago. I tip over and forget to jump back, so I land in the wave, tumbling like I'm in a washing machine. The board tugs me by the leash, and I try to suck in a mouthful of air, but I'm underwater. Panic seizes me as water fills my lungs.

Chapter Fourteen

Jake's strong hand grips me by the bicep and drags me up until I grab my board and rest my head on it. He's by my side and we're in the whitewash, and I'm coughing, panicking, and thinking of the psalm about crying out to God: *"Then they cried out to the LORD in their trouble, and he brought them out of their distress. He stilled the storm to a whisper; the waves of the sea were hushed."*

I've memorized every Bible verse that mentions waves, and I don't know why this one comes to mind. I couldn't cry out because I was too busy swallowing water. Did He answer anyway? Does He answer even when we're going against Him? My adrenaline's surging. So many thoughts of my brother's accident race through my head. This is so stupid. If I got injured tonight, my parents would never recover.

"You're okay." It's like Jake can read my mind.

I wipe my face, but it's hard to breathe.

"You're okay," he repeats.

"I shouldn't be doing this," I sputter. I've been wanting to surf since the moment I stopped five years ago. But not like this. Not because I was jealous of some girl. The guilt washes over me like high tide. It's only a few feet deep here, and

Jake's standing next to me, steadying his board and keeping it facing the shoreline. I weakly stand, then reach down to remove my leash. He stops me with a hand.

"You're not walking out of the ocean after that."

"This was a mistake."

"Then try again."

I'm shaking—he can tell—and I'm angry that I look weak. "I can't! I don't even remember how!"

"Yes, you do." His voice is steady, calm. Unmoved by my volume. "Get back on your board."

"No! Seriously, Jake, my parents said no! And look what happened the first time I tried!"

He holds my board down when I try to lift it out of the water. I glare at him, but he's looking at me without blinking.

"You know your brother's accident was a freak occurrence, right?"

"You don't even know what happened," I choke out.

"I do. I looked it up."

I turn away to face the crashing and churning tide. He cared enough to look up my past. To try to understand why I no longer do the thing I loved most in life. I feel my anger slip, but not my fear.

I hear him in my ear, almost whispering. "Get back on your board."

I shakily climb back onto my stomach. He turns the board so it faces the oncoming waves. I reach forward and begin my slow paddle out.

A small wave forms, and before I can spend too much time thinking about it, I turn and grab fistfuls of water so I can match its pace as it swells under me and catches my fins, pitching me forward with speed.

Every muscle in me is taut, and I'm terrified. With a grunt, I pop up onto my feet and curl my toes, gripping the wax and staying low.

I hear a loud whoop before I realize it's me. I did it. I'm balanced perfectly, and it makes me feel more alive than I've been in five years. I don't turn, just ride it clean and sure, reveling in the moment and wanting it to last for eternity, until I'm face-to-face with my maker.

I look behind me. Jake's caught the next wave and jumped off, climbing back onto his board to paddle over to me. When he glides up, he has this gleam in his eye. "There's the girl I remember." He reaches out his fist.

I bring my knuckles up to his. I'm panting from holding my breath through the entire ride. "You realize you're cheering for me to disobey my parents."

"I'm not. I want you to talk to them. Tell them what you want."

I paddle away from him, back out to beyond the break. Over my shoulder, I yell, "You say that like it's so easy."

"You ever try?" He paddles up to me.

I don't answer.

"Figured."

"What's that supposed to mean?" He has no clue what he's asking. "You don't talk to Hannah about us, I bet."

He looks like I slapped him across the face. "What. About. Us." He says it calmly.

"Nothing." I'm saying too much. Time to stop. "But we hang

out. More than Kaj and Niles, and they're my guy friends."
Stop, Lovette. No more. "And you talk to me. Like, a lot."

"You haven't even given me your phone number."

Ugh, he's missing the point! "Can you honestly say you feel nothing?"

The question catches him off guard. Me too, a little. I can't believe I said it out loud.

"I feel"—he hesitates, rakes his hand through his hair—"things."

"Same," I admit. "But I don't date."

"So then why does it matter?"

"Because it does! You're not gonna stop talking to Hannah, and I'm not about to start dating you. How's it helpful to either of us to hang out alone with each other?"

"Would you date me if I stopped talking to Hannah?"

This time, it's me who's caught off guard. I never thought he'd ask something like that. I busy myself by turning my board to face the oncoming waves. "You're not doing that."

"You're not answering my question."

As an answer, I mount another wave and ride it to shore. I step off when it's only two feet deep. I hear Jake easing off his board behind me.

Once we remove our leashes, we walk to the dry sand, set down our boards, and sit side by side, facing the ocean. Our neoprene-armored shoulders lean against each other.

I wish my life was as simple as nature. The moon tells the waves how high they should be. The tide goes in and out at precise times, and you can even buy calendars that tell you the exact times in the future. Everything makes sense in God's creation. Everything but us. Humans and their unpredictability. The way they march into your life and make you question everything. Your promise to your parents. Your promises to God.

"Look," he starts. He pulls his knees in, grabs fistfuls of sand. "Yes, I still talk to Hannah, but we're broken up. Either way, it's okay because you don't date. And I don't want you to." I sideways glance at him, but he's staring at the horizon. "You made a commitment to God, and I don't want to come between that. I'm not about to pull you away from something you feel strongly about." He looks at me then. "But I like being with you. And I think you like it too. So if we just hang out, and don't *do* anything, what's that make you?"

"I dunno." I like him around. I *want* him around. "Not a girlfriend, I suppose."

"I was going to say 'friend,' but okay. Then be my 'not a girlfriend.'"

I stifle a giggle, then sober up. "I just don't want to end up sinning against God."

"Look around at this." He gestures to the waves, to the sand, to our brightly lit blue boards. "This doesn't feel like sin. Are we sinning right now?"

"No." I lean my elbows on my knees. "Well, I mean, not with each other. But sin doesn't always look like sin, you know?"

"No, I get it. But I like this. I kinda like us." He bumps me with his shoulder, and this time, I bump him back. "See? We make pretty good friends. And if I won't date and you *don't* date, well then, we can't really lead each other wrong, right?"

He stands and gets down on one knee. "Lovette, would you like to be my 'not a girlfriend'?"

I'm trying not to laugh, but he's making it difficult. This is a dangerous road, and I feel it. "I don't know—"

"Listen. God's placed it on my heart for you to be my non-girlfriend. I've been praying about this, and—"

I erupt in laughter, and it bounces off the water. "You have not."

"Is that a yes? I need to take more lessons from Kelly."

I can't stop giggling. "Fine. I'll be your non-girlfriend."

"Good. Way to agree with God."

He's right about one thing: I have to talk to my parents. After tonight, I need to surf again, more than I need to breathe. But I feel sick to my stomach when I think about that conversation.

Jake puts his arm around me, and I tip my head and lean on his shoulder. The butterflies are flapping into one another in my stomach. *"Is this okay?"* I want to ask God. But I don't. Tonight I need it to be okay.

Chapter Fifteen

As soon as I get home Friday night, still electrified like the LED lights of the surfboards, I'm ready to march into my parents' room and demand they let me surf again. But when I walk into the house, it's dark. I lock the front door and turn to see my dad like two feet from my face, and I yelp. He puts a finger to his lips and motions toward their bedroom. "Migraine," he mouths. I still feel my body moving on the waves, and I step off balance and catch myself. Dad eyes me funny but doesn't say anything.

Saturday, I wake up even more amped. I'm ready to say that surfing's an extension of my body, and I need my limbs back. It sounds so poetic, and I practice it in my head. When I find them in the kitchen, I start with, "Can I talk to you guys?"

And Mom says to Dad, "See, honey? I told you she'd talk to us about it." She smiles with concerned eyes. "Your dad says you were a little unsteady last night. Were you drinking?"

What? "No."

"Good," Dad says, "because you were on your bicycle, and you can still get a CUI—cycling under the influence—just as dangerous as what your brother did."

"Matty got a CUI?"

"No! Of course not," he snaps, and I stand at attention. "It was an analogy. Your head to that concrete or his head to the surfboard. Same. You remember you gotta think of others and not just you. If there's one thing the military has taught me, it's—"

"Dad, I wasn't drinking."

"Well, good."

Mom isn't so convinced. "You know you can talk to us. We've had our share of alcohol in our days. And if you're switching Zima for 7UP, don't think we haven't been there."

"What's Zima?"

"Very funny. Just know we're here for you."

Dad nods sharply, like a genie granting a wish. "But no CUIs."

"Yessir."

Mom puts her earbuds in and fiddles with her iPad. They never ask what I wanted to talk to them about, and I'm glad because no way I can tell them now. My head to concrete is how they envision surfing. It's hopeless.

The following Monday, I see my friends in the quad before school. Somewhere between Niles and Kaj making each other flinch and Lydia asking about ACT dates, I blurt, "I started surfing again." The world stops for one second. Niles pauses mid-swing. Lydia slaps her hand to her mouth and holds it there. Kelly whips her head in my direction and doesn't blink. Then Kaj coughs once, and everything goes back into motion.

"Oh yeah?" Niles says.

"That's nice," Lydia adds, which she says with such a monotone that I smile. They know it's a big deal and they're totally trying to downplay it for me. However, I catch Kaj handing Niles a one-dollar bill.

"You bet on me?" I say, laughing.

Kaj holds his hands up. "Not whether you'd surf again," he says. "Just when."

Jake jogs up as I'm heading to first period, and he gives me a look like, "Well?" My parents. I shake my head. "I tried." Jake shrugs an *Oh well*, but I feel like one of those sandy puddles underneath the beach showers.

After fourth period, he finds me in the hall and swings an arm around my shoulder. "I know you'll tell your parents when the time is right." My heart fills to overflowing. How can someone *do* that to me so easily? "So in the meantime," he adds, "why don't we start training?" I swing my arm around his waist, and his eyes grow wide. "Is Lovette showing some PDA?"

"Side hug!" I correct, laughing. "Okay, let's train. I'm so sore from Friday, and we barely paddled."

We spend the next day at lunch making a workout schedule, and all my friends chime in. Lydia says that dancing works out the hips and core. Kaj and Niles argue about whether I should work triceps or biceps first during a workout, and Jake says I'm going to do a minimum of one hundred pop-ups a day. Kelly's silent, but she does ask Jake, "What's a pop-up?" and we explain it's when you lie on your stomach and pretend you're on a wave, popping up to your surfboard. Basically a burpee with a squat.

"Hmph," is all she says.

Tuesday, I'm walking down the hallway answering a text

when Kelly suddenly loops her arm through mine. Then she takes my free hand, twirls me in a circle, and hugs me around the waist.

"Tuesday-night poetry!" she exclaims, which means she's been reading my texts over my shoulder. My coworker Kim texted that she wanted more hours and asked if she could pick up my shift today.

I was hoping to get in an extra-long swimming session, but I can't disappoint Kelly, so I say, "Yes! Finally!"

○)))) ● ● ((((○

Tuesday night, I'm sitting on a stained couch next to Kelly and sipping a latte. Youth-group Dave performs with his acoustic guitar, singing about how a girl unearthed flowers in the graveyard of his *soul*, and without her his life was an empty cereal *bowl*. And his chorus is, "Be my milk, be my milk, water my flowers with your milk." A lot of people in the crowd nod and close their eyes, some even mouth along, "Be my milk."

I guess it's good.

But it's also the same three chords as most of our worship songs, so I don't know if I should lift my hands to cows for their provision. I wish Jake was here so I could say that to him. I know he'd laugh. Still, it's courageous—no one could buy me enough surfboards to get me singing poetry to strangers—so I clap and cheer with everyone when Dave finishes. Kelly squeezes my knee. "He wrote that for me," she whispers. Oh no. Should I say something about her reading into things? But then Dave strolls over and wedges himself between Kelly and the edge of the couch, draping an arm around her.

"What'd ya think, babe?" he says with his slow drawl. *Babe?*

"So deep." She copies his drawl.

"It's like secular, yeah, but I think God would be like, 'Way to be in the world, not of it, so I'm proud of you, son, yeah.'"

"So proud, totally." She nudges me.

"Totes." I've never said *totes* in my life, but Kelly's never had a drawl, so I guess it's a night of firsts. When did this happen? Dave and Kelly? A small part of me's relieved. Maybe she can get her mind off Jake. Maybe she'll stop judging him.

"I love your honesty," she says. "Some of our guy friends need to hear your music. I know of one."

Dave traces the purple strip of hair peeking through Kelly's messy blond bun. "In the world, not of it."

How did he know about that? Two years ago, Kelly wanted to do something to feel like she was relatable. It's cute, her purple strip of hair. I love it. For her, it's crazy wild. Her parents okayed it, as long as she didn't get any piercings. She told everyone she did it for fun. Only I knew the truth. "It's for God," she told me. "See? I'm in the world, not of the world." I was sworn to secrecy. But now, Dave is clearly in on the secret.

"I'm gonna get some water," I say, and wish for the millionth time that I'd given Jake my number. I'm dying to tell him about this. Would he get why I'm a little bummed that Kelly just put milk-flower Dave on the same level as me? Kelly and I have been secret keepers for years. How can a guy she just started hanging out with suddenly be more important?

When I'm pouring water at the counter, I look up at the bulletin board of people selling bikes, looking for roommates, and giving away kittens. A full-color flyer peeks from underneath a car for sale, with just the word *surf* visible. I wiggle it out and scan the details, my heart thumping.

ALL WAVE JUNIOR OPEN. MANHATTAN BEACH PIER. NEW COED DIVISION! ENTRY FEE $100. There's a website and a phone number. It's the surf competition that girl Alix told me about.

Was this from you, God? Did you want me to find this?

"Hey, sorry, miss, but you can't post that." One of the baristas points at the flyer. "The bulletin board's for nonprofits and personal ads only. Community board. No company listings or for-profit orgs. Sorry."

I nod and fold the flyer, jamming it into my pocket.

The rest of the week, I keep it with me, reaching for it constantly to feel the wrinkled paper folds.

Every night I go swimming, but it's so dissatisfying now. I want to ride, and even though I body surf, every wave that crashes over me reminds me that I'm *in* the wave rather than *on* it. Still, I do the one hundred pop-ups every day, one hundred lunges, one hundred squats, and I run on the beach for fifteen minutes in the sand.

By Friday, every muscle in my body aches, and I'm waddling like a geriatric duck. On my way to first period, Lydia appears and slaps my sore butt. The crinkled flyer falls out of my back pocket, and she snatches it. "What's this?" She holds it out of my reach. "Coed competition?" She screams an expletive in Spanish. "Lovette! You're signing up?"

"No," I say.

"¡Sí!" she screams back. "You have the flyer! You can't deny it. All Wave Junior Open. That's why Jake's making the workout schedule for you."

"Jake's just trying to encourage me to tell my parents. That's all."

She reaches for the crucifix around her neck.

I hold up a hand. "Please don't make me kiss Jesus on the cross."

"Fine." She kisses it herself. The one-minute bell rings, and I grab the flyer from her hand.

"Do NOT tell anyone. No one, Lyds."

She fakes zipping her lips and locking them with an imaginary key, but when she's halfway down the hall, she turns and shouts, "I'm so proud of you! You're gonna win the entire thing and get a surfing sponsorship and tour the world in your bikini!"

"Lydia!" I shout. *Shut up!* But she misunderstands.

"Okay, fine! Not a bikini. A one-piece. They're coming back!"

Chapter Sixteen

In the cafeteria later that day, Cecilia Grayson and her ponytail swing into my personal space while I'm mid-bite into my every-day-Dad-made PB&J.

This is weird for two reasons: One, Cecilia Grayson's a soccer diva. Two, Cecilia Grayson doesn't visit my side of the cafeteria (see number one).

In the beach cities, outside of surfing, soccer's big, like, *big* big, the way lacrosse is big on the East Coast or the way my father's big on clipping coupons and pointing out how much money he saves by serving me PB&Js. *Every. Lunch. Of. My. Life.*

The Caroltown Cougars is a club team that has been together since the girls stopped wearing Pull-Ups, and somehow they've morphed into girls who believe they're on the World Cup team with million-dollar contracts. They're all in amazing shape and wear their club sweats every Thursday, even when it's not a game day. They've even designated a part of the cafeteria as "the Club Sports" section, and they cross those lines, well, never.

Cecilia's hot-pink and black nylon pants *swish-swish* through the crowds and stop at my table. Two of her soccer-diva clones flank her in the same outfit. It's like the Pink Ladies meets hip-hop America.

"Why would Lydia say you're competing in the All Wave Junior Open?" She narrows her eyes and whips her ponytail in a helicopter spin.

I turn to Lydia, who's suddenly stiff as cardboard. *Lydia!* I lick the peanut butter from the roof of my mouth and search for the closest fire exits.

Lydia stands so she's eye to eye with the Cougars. "Because maybe she *is* competing in it."

I clear my throat. "Uh, hello? I'm right here. And no, I'm not."

Lydia mumbles, "Yes, you are."

My friends wait on my cue to back one of us up, but they're not sure who, because we're saying two different things.

Jake doesn't wait. "What's it to you?"

"Home wrecker!" Cecilia yells at me, not Jake.

"Wait," Jake interjects, "is this about the Disney prince?" He's trying to lighten the mood, which is good because my underarms are sweating again. "The guy who uses selfie mode on his phone as a mirror?"

"Who doesn't do that?" Cecilia quips. From the table, Niles and Kaj both raise a hand.

"Look," I say, "I'm not trying to compete, and I'm not trying to steal Trevor."

"Oh really?" Cecilia snarls. "Then why's *Lovette Taylor* on the list of coed competitors when I looked it up online?"

"What?" I look at my friends, and they jump into gear.

"Back off, Cecilia," Kaj says. "Maybe it's a typo."

"Maybe you're making it up," Kelly snaps.

Niles says, "Maybe you can't read."

Lydia barks, "Or maybe it's because she knows she can kick your boyfriend's ass all over the waves!"

"Lydia," I say.

Cecilia laughs in short, exaggerated bursts. "Trevor says you quit back in junior high because you were too scared. You can't *possibly* think that you have a chance in this competition. You only signed up to get closer to him."

A tempest starts in my belly as she says, "You can't *possibly* think that you have a chance . . ." Why's this so hard to imagine? I was good. *Really* good. And it was never about the competition.

I think of the feeling when Jake and I rode the waves at night. It was like God had built me for that moment. Maybe He's built me for a lot of things—things way bigger than surfing—but that night, in that moment, I knew I was doing what I was designed to do. Nowhere in my life have I felt more complete, more at peace with Him, than when I'm surfing. God wants to do something through it. I don't know what, but He's in it.

I remove the scrunched flyer from my back pocket and unfold it, hold it up for her soccer tribe. I slam it down on the table in front of my friends. Their mouths open into perfect *O*s.

Niles says, "Oh my god, you really did sign up."

Kelly gasps. "Are you essing me?"

"Why not?" I blurt, and it's so loud that the rest of the cafeteria is now at full attention. "But not for Trevor," I say to Cecilia. My heart's pumping with so much adrenaline, I'm ready to fight in a boxing match or flee from a bear. "It's for God. It's because when I surf, I know God's proud. And yes, I'm signed up, and yes, I'm doing it, because I'm *supposed* to do it."

My table cheers and whoops. Niles says, "Hell yeah, you are." Jake's strangely quiet, scrutinizing me.

Cecilia closes her eyes. When she opens them at me, there's fire. "You're done, Taylor."

I don't even know what to say. I've never been called by my last name. That's like a team-sports thing, I think. And I'm *done*?

"Oh, she's just getting started!" Lydia yells as Cecilia backs away. I wish Lydia wouldn't make this worse, but her blood's boiling. She rattles off a host of words in Spanish, all swear words, I'm sure.

"You better lace up," Cecilia says through gritted teeth, and once again, I don't know how to respond. I mean, I don't even own cleats. Cecilia turns, whipping one of her friends in the face with her ponytail. The three girls swish back to the rest of their team, the crowds parting.

"Reowwwrrr," Lydia growls.

I could punch her, but Jake says, "You told your parents?"

He thinks I did, I can tell by the small smile lifting the corners of his mouth, saying, *"See? I told you it would be okay."* It feels so unbelievably good, and I want it to continue and never end. I smile and say, "I was going to surprise you." Then I actually glare at Lydia for spoiling my big surprise.

"Oops," Lydia says, and she means it, which makes me feel bad. I feel worse when she snags me aside on our way to sixth period. "I'm so sorry I ruined your surprise. I saw the flyer fall out of your pocket, and we all know how you've never stopped loving surfing, but you're too much of a pansy to do anything about it, so Kaj and I signed you up. I didn't know you'd have the guts to do it yourself, but I get it now. The surprise. I'd do anything for my guy, too."

"Jake's not my guy."

"Whatever you say. All I know is in two years, I've never gotten you on the dance floor that quickly at the Venue. And in the past month, you glow like you're pregnant, but unless you're the Virgin Mary come back again, you're definitely not pregnant. And your parents stole your surfboard in seventh grade. That was it. Done deal. Over. Terminado. Four of your best friends couldn't convince you to get back on a board. Now you're surprising Jake with surf competitions?"

I can't explain to her how wrong she is. How my parents would never let me surf. *Still* will never let me surf. And also, how I did this for me, not for Jake. Instead I say, "He's just a friend, Lyds."

"Mentirosa, and okay. You say so. But if you ever break up with Jesus—"

"I'm not breaking up with Jesus."

"Isn't Jesus, like, polyamorous?"

"No! I mean, yes. But not like that."

"Just saying, if Jesus will share, then—"

"Lydia, no!"

"Okay! Okay!" She kisses both of my cheeks and prances away toward her Spanish for native speakers class.

I'm unlocking my bike after school when I hear a familiar

"Hey! Want a ride?" I look up to see my brother next to a shiny silver Toyota Tundra pickup, my parents' gift to him when he graduated eleventh grade for the second time.

"Matty!" I swerve in and out of students, pushing my bike until I reach the curb. Matt lifts the bike into his truck bed, then pulls me into a hug and swings me around. He feels so much older—he's filled out since he left for college. He got so thin after the accident. Even through rehab, it was tough for him to keep on weight, but now I look at him and it's like nothing happened. Well, there are little reminders.

When Matt sets me down, I notice Jake about fifteen feet away, watching us. I wave him over. "Matt, this is Jake. He just moved here. Jake—my brother, Matt."

"Your brother," Jake repeats, and there's this brief moment where he closes his eyes and laughs at himself. *Was Jake jealous?* He shakes Matt's hand and says, "Heard a lot about you."

"That so? Hey, you need a ride too?"

Jake smiles. "Nah, got my own ride. But nice to meet you."

"Yeah, same. I'm sure I'll see you around." Matt winks at me in front of Jake, and I just about die.

On the car ride home, he asks me, "That your boyfriend? Mom told me about him."

"No, and Mom's bananas, you know that."

"Well I have a girlfriend."

"What?!"

"Yeah." He taps the steering wheel. "Since the first week of school. Brooke."

He fiddles with the satellite radio, and I wait for him to say more. "And?"

"What were we talking about?"

His short-term memory won't ever be perfect, and once in a while, he loses his train of thought. Another reminder of the accident. He knows when it happens and usually tries to cover by saying he's not interested in talking about that anymore, but really, he's forgotten what *that* is. With me, he doesn't care, because he knows I don't think it's a big deal. "You were telling me about Brooke," I prompt.

"She has amazing boobs."

"Ew! You're so gross." I flick his shoulder. I know he's just trying to embarrass me.

He laughs and turns up the music. We nod in rhythm to it for a while, and then he says, "You wanna go to a movie tomorrow?"

"Maybe. I'm volunteering at Hope Fills with my youth group for the day. So afterward?"

He makes a throwing-up sound. "Tell me you're not still going to Bible Thumpers Anonymous."

My brother's not a fan of God, to put it lightly. He thinks it's all a big joke, and that humans "made up the concept of God to give meaning for certain things in life that have no satisfying answers." His words exactly, which sound like they were stolen from someone's Twitter and recited like a Bible memory verse. He hates when I talk to him about it. We get along better if I don't, but I can't help myself sometimes, especially when he's a jerk about it. But no matter what, I always feel like the dumb, bratty little sister afterward.

"My youth group's called Revive, and yes, we're making sandwiches for the poor tomorrow. How dare we? I mean, gosh, we're such horrible people."

"Why're you being so defensive?"

"I'm not! You are!" I shout, and there it is. In less than five minutes, he's pushed all the buttons to make me act the six-year-old he's convinced I still am.

He lifts his eyebrows and turns up the music. I wish this was one of his short-term-memory moments, so he'd just forget that whole conversation, but when we get home, he opens the back of the truck bed and lifts my bike out. "You're welcome," he says before turning and walking inside.

Chapter Seventeen

I don't meet up with Lydia on Friday night since my brother's home and it's Mom's birthday. After dinner, Mom pops popcorn, Dad gets the board games out, and we play a cutthroat game of Settlers of Catan. My brother wins, of course. He builds his final road and turns over the longest road card for the final points to reach ten.

I don't reveal I had a victory point hiding with all my soldier cards. I'd rather see my parents' faces whenever Matt wins at something—the kid they thought would never win again.

"Hey, close game," he says. "You had nine!"

My parents say, "Awwww!" at the same time and with the same number of Ws. I wonder if I'll ever have a marriage like theirs, where I'll know how many seconds my husband takes to say a word.

It's weird to see them now and think back to when they almost didn't make it. The nights following Matt's accident . . . the fights. I never knew how badly two people could argue when they hadn't slept in a month and their kid's life was on the line. The blaming. The accusing. It was ugly.

Matt wasn't supposed to wake up. So when he did . . . I

think they felt they were given another chance. With Matt. With each other.

Pretty sure they felt that it was their life's job to keep Matt and me away from the one thing that took Matt down and almost wrecked their marriage. My friends think it's stupid that my parents keep me out of the ocean. But they'd never question it if they had lived through it.

Afterward, we watch a movie. My parents laugh and throw popcorn at each other like middle-schoolers, and Dad pulls Mom's feet into his lap on the couch. It's the Matty Magic: He makes my parents come alive in a way I'll never be able to. But I wouldn't want an accident to make that happen. *I understand, Jesus. I swear I do.* But still I wish I could make my parents light up the way they do when Matt walks into the room.

○))) ➒ ● ❨ ❨ ((○

Saturday morning, Kelly honks her horn at 7:00 a.m. When I walk outside, Dave's climbing into the back seat for me. I say, "Hey, Dave," like we always carpool. *They're driving places together now?* Kelly remembers my latte, and as she hands it to me, her fingers squeeze a secret "Thanks for not making a big deal out of Dave."

We're driving to Hope Fills, a homeless outreach center about fifteen miles east toward downtown LA. We're quiet, sipping our hot drinks and squinting at the morning sun.

Dave yawns loudly. "I heard you signed up for the Watermans surf thing."

"Yep."

"Cool."

We keep sipping.

"So why . . ." Kelly trails off. She drinks from her mocha again and glides into the carpool lane.

"Good move, babe," Dave drawls from the back seat.

Kelly looks stuck on her last thought. Her forehead's wrinkled.

"What?" I ask. "You okay?"

"Yeah, fine. It's nothing." She turns the music up, some new Christian song that apparently Dave knows because he leans between us and says, "This is so hard to play," and his muscles strain as his left hand shifts to all the chords on his air guitar.

When we arrive at Hope Fills, Jake gives me a fist bump and then disappears outside to work on unloading supplies. I'm slightly bummed he's not in the sandwich group, but I know Kelly doesn't feel the same. Inside the giant warehouse and elbow deep in cold cuts, she says, "Why did you want to surprise Jake by signing up for the surf competition?"

It comes out like the burst of mustard she's just squeezed onto a whole row of bread slices, and I know she's been dying to ask me since the car ride. I follow her down the assembly line, laying two cold cuts per slice. Dave follows with lettuce, and Candy, our adult leader, slaps a clean piece of bread on top. Behind her are the ziplock-bag stuffers.

"Um," I start, fumbling with three slices of meat stuck together. "I wanted to surf again. I'm ready."

"That's fine. And praise God that He's healed you and gotten you ready. But—"

"Praise God, indeed," Candy interjects, conveniently overhearing as usual, with no idea what we're talking about.

"But," Kelly says again, shaking the mustard, "what does Jake have to do with that?"

I peel more meat apart and load up the bread. "He, uh, he's been sort of encouraging me to get back on my board."

She snorts like I'm ridiculous.

"Listen, Kelly, he's not actually dating Hannah anymore. They just talk as friends."

She taps the mustard on the table before continuing. "Coulda fooled me."

I've gotta try a different route. "Look, even if he messed up with the way he acted toward you, we mess up all the time, Kells. You know that. We love a God who knows that, too, and thank GOD He doesn't treat us like our sins deserve." I ignore the *mmms* and *mm-hmms* Candy's adding as she leans over Dave to hear. "We're pretty crappy to Him most of the time. But what does God choose?"

"Love," she mumbles.

"Right?" We're both in a rhythm, slapping cold cuts and moving down the rows of bread quickly. "So, I'm giving surfing another chance. Maybe you should give Jake another chance."

She pauses, and Dave bumps into me. I feel a huge piece of lettuce on my shoulder. He removes it delicately. "Maybe," she says. "I dunno. I'll pray about it." And then, "Ew! Dave! Come on, babe!" She takes the piece of lettuce off a sandwich and throws it into the trash. "That was on Lovette's shoulder!"

"Three-second rule," he says.

"No," Kelly and I say simultaneously and then giggle. It reminds me of my parents last night, how they spoke in unison, and I wondered about my future husband. I love moments like this, when God shows me that He heard me— He knows what I want—so He gives me little mini versions, like my friendship with Kelly, as gifts along the way.

○))) ● ● (((○

It's five o'clock when we finish packing the lunches into the trucks that deliver to tent city, Skid Row, and the Los Angeles overpasses where the homeless congregate. The sunset's orange and yellow through the hazy sky, reflecting off the distant skyscrapers.

Kelly, Dave, and I are walking back to Kelly's car when Jake appears.

"Hey!" I say. "Where've you been?"

"Brett had me on dumpster duty most of the day."

"Gross."

"Yeah. Good thing we don't hug."

I laugh. "See? God's so good to me. Maybe He put the no-hugging rule in my heart because He knew this day would come."

He chuckles. "Good one." He pulls something out of his jacket pocket. "Hey, catch."

It bounces off my stomach, but I snag it. "Ow!"

"What *is* that?" Kelly asks, looking at the fist-size gray clump in my hands.

"Sex Wax," Dave says, and I'm surprised he knows.

Kelly's alarmed. "Sex?"

"That's the name," Dave says. "It's surf wax."

She scrunches her nose. "Looks like pigeon poop."

This pigeon poop feels like a diamond ring. I know what Jake means by it.

"We should start practicing Monday." His hair's sweaty, and he has grease stains on his shirt and grime under his eye, but I've never wanted to hug him more than I do right now. Instead, I wrap my fingers around the wax. He sees my tight grip, and it's like he understands. He smiles. "Old Man Mike's. Six in the morning."

"Six in the morning," I repeat.

Kelly claps once. "Okay, time to go." Her tone's a little rude, so I mouth, *Love, remember?*

She rolls her eyes. "Thanks, Jake, for your gift of wax." Her words are clunky, but she's trying. Well, almost. She still doesn't wave at him as we exit the parking lot.

○)))) ● ((((○

When I get home that evening, Matt's already left with some old high-school friends to shoot pool somewhere. I sleep with the ball of wax on my pillow, kneading it and feeling the grains of sand from previous use. *"Do you really hate dating, Jesus?"* I say, staring at the ceiling. *"I mean, of course you don't, but I promised you I wouldn't date, so I shouldn't go back on that, right?"*

I think of Jephthah in the Bible, the warrior who rashly told God that if God gave him victory, he would sacrifice the first thing that walked out of his courtyard, assuming it would be an animal. But when he returned, who walked out first but his dancing daughter to say, "Yay, Dad!"

Talk about a buzzkill.

I whisper my prayers that night, as if talking at full volume is too bold—too much like Jephthah. "God, are you holding me to something I swore off in seventh grade? Are you teaching me to watch my commitments? Are you, like, 'So you swore you wouldn't date? Aha! Well, then, may I present to you . . . drumroll, please . . . walking now through Jephthah's gates: Jayyyyke Evans, the hottest and most amazing guy you'll ever meet in your life!'"

I search the night sky through my blinds. "You're not like that, are you, God? Can I change my mind? I don't think I hate dating anymore. I still won't have sex, of course, not a chance. But it's okay to hang out with someone you like more than a friend, right?" I remember the first night, when I asked if he and Hannah still talked. *"Every day,"* he said. "Never mind," I tell God. "I can't match what they have." I mutter an *amen* and turn away from the window.

○))) ● ● ● ● ((○

Sunday morning, Matt has to leave early to drive back up north, so he comes into my room to say bye. I reach my arms up for a hug, but as he leans down, his eyes flicker to my mattress. Before I can react, he grabs the ball of wax.

"What's this?" he asks, even though he totally knows what it is. What he really means is, *"What are you doing with surf wax?"*

"Um, it's Jake's," I say quickly.

He nods like he gets it. "I love it when Brooke leaves behind one of her shirts in my bed."

"Ew! Matty!"

"What? She smells nice." He sits down on the edge of my bed. "Real talk. Don't do anything stupid, okay?"

"I'm not having sex."

"I don't care about that." He holds up the piece of wax. "I mean this. Our parents would shit a brick if you ever went back out there."

I prop myself up on my elbows and look at him earnestly. "Why am I being punished for what happened to you?"

"Punished? Don't be selfish. They're so good to you."

"Says the guy who gets a new car and his full tuition paid."

"I'm in college."

"Did you have to ride a bike everywhere as a senior? Or work a day of your life in high school?"

He stands up. "Wow. Just wow, Lovette." I've struck a nerve, but I don't know why. I'm annoyed with my parents, not him. "Yeah, I did work," he says, facing my window. "I had a job at the hospital for a year and a half learning how to say words like *balloon* and *Pop-Tart* all over again. And no, I didn't ride a bike everywhere because, guess what? I lost all. Of. My. Balance."

I'm the worst. "I'm sorry! I didn't mean that." But he's already at my bedroom door. I sit up in bed. "Please don't leave mad." He stops. Glares at me from the doorway. "Look," I try again. "I'm sorry. Please."

"Can't you find another sport?"

"What if God's made me for *this* sport?"

He looks like I told him two plus two equals five. "God"—he puts *God* in air quotes—"has nothing to do with this."

"Or everything."

He groans and throws his head back. "Talking to you's like running on a hamster wheel. How about this? Next time I come visit, if I see so much as a grain of sand in the house, I'm telling Mom and Dad." He slaps the doorframe. "See you next month."

A few seconds later, the front door slams behind him, and I throw myself face-first into my pillow and scream.

Chapter Eighteen

Monday morning at 6:00 a.m. isn't exactly romantic.

For the millionth time I lose my balance, plunking like a boulder into the wave, my ankle tugged by my leash through the white water until so much seawater shoots up my nose that I gag.

I emerge, sputtering and coughing, and grab hold of my board. Jake doesn't ask if I'm okay. He's sitting on his board away from the break, arms folded. "Again," he says, just loudly enough that it bounces off the surface of the water, his tone colder than my numb hands. Even though I can't see his eyes from the glare of the sun, I know they aren't twinkling.

I don't know what's wrong. Back in elementary school, I never thought about balance when I surfed. Now, it consumes my every thought: *Don't fall off, don't fall off, don't fall off.* I'm wobbly and disconnected from my board. I'm nervous that Jake's watching, and I can't seem to replicate how easily I rode that first night. Granted, the surf was calmer, but I'm supposed to be good. I *was* good. What happened?

I paddle out and turn my board for the next wave. I stroke hard and feel my board catch, take a quick look down the line to see how it's breaking, and pop up. The tip starts nose-diving, and I try to correct by stepping back, but it's too late. The nose of my board's diving down, I'm catapulting forward, and the board's shooting back up like an arrow, sailing through the air above me as I crash into the water. Again. I strike the water with my fist and pull myself back onto my board.

"What was that?" says Jake, who's paddled up beside me.

"I dunno," I mumble.

"You don't know? Since when do you stand so forward?"

"Since maybe five minutes ago!"

"Why'd you do it?"

Why'd I do it? What kind of a dumb question is that? "Maybe I was just dying to pitch myself forward and look like an idiot."

He gives a half smile, not amused by my sarcasm. "Well, now that you've gotten it out of your system, go back out there and do something different."

I inhale slowly through my nose. I hear the edge in his voice. He's frustrated watching me, too. Whatever.

Every time I mess up, I do worse the next time. That's how my brother used to be, not me. Some days Dad would say to him, "You gotta be okay not being okay." Matt would make a dumb move, overcorrect on a cutback—nothing even that big—but he would get so frustrated that the rest of his time out there, he'd look like a beginner.

I remember once Dad said, "Look at your sister. She doesn't get nervous."

"She's ten," Matt said, annoyed.

"No. She just doesn't care what people think. You'll get yourself hurt if you start becoming a head case."

The irony.

"Hey!" Jake interrupts my memory. "You just missed a perfectly good set!"

I'm over it. I see a little wave forming, and I paddle to catch it, but it rolls right under me and dies. "Seriously?" he shouts. "Why'd you go for that one? Read the wave!"

I remember praying to Jesus to help me lose feelings for Jake. He's good at answering. If I'm ever struggling with feelings for someone in the future, I'll make them my coach. It's an instant cure.

Instead of standing, I ride the next wave on my belly and hop off in the shallow water, ripping my leash off and slapping it onto my board. I lift my board and walk onto the dry sand. When Jake catches up to me, he says, "We still have fifteen minutes."

I shake my head. "I need to rinse off in the beach showers and look at my physics notes before school."

He doesn't buy it. "So that's it?"

"Yeah, that's it."

"What's going on with you today?"

"Me?" I can't believe him. "You're the one barking like a sea lion."

"I was coaching."

"Yeah, well, your coaching sucks."

"You had a bad day."

"Ya think?"

He doesn't fight back. "Fine then. Tomorrow." I'm heading for the showers when he calls out, "Lovette? If I seem edgy, it's just—"

I turn to him. Hug my board. "What?"

He shakes his head. Of course he's changed his mind.

"Call Hannah later," I say, stomping away from him through the sand. "I'm sure you can tell *her*."

Tomorrow isn't any better, or the next day. Every morning we go out for forty-five minutes, and every day I get worse. My legs are shaky, I'm scared on every pop-up, and the second that I feel slightly off balance, I dive off my board into the still-crashing wave. Jake's instructions get shorter and snippier as the week continues. At school, we don't talk much. I don't know what's gotten into him, but he's moody this week, and even my friends notice. At lunch on Tuesday, Kaj tells a story about accidentally dropping his cheeseburger out the window last night when he was adjusting his side mirror.

Everyone's laughing except for Jake, who's kind of staring off at a corner of the cafeteria. Kaj stops mid-story and asks, "You okay, bro?"

Jake looks at him and smiles. "Yeah, why?"

Kaj shrugs, not pushing it, and I'm thankful because Jake's clearly not okay, but he's definitely not ready to share. Whenever he picks me up in the morning, he turns up the music, and we drive in silence to the ocean. On Thursday, I ask him about arriving to my house ten minutes late. He says one word, "Traffic."

"From Redondo?"

"Been driving up from the base this week."

He sounds like he doesn't want to talk about it, but I can't help it. "Why?"

He's quiet for a long time, gnawing on his lower lip. "Had to stay with my dad for a few days." Obviously he had to stay with his dad if he was driving up from the base. But *why*? Did his aunt have company for the week? Or was it something with his dad? He looks like he might talk about it, but then he looks away and out the window.

It does explain his tired eyes. Getting to my house at 6:00 a.m. means for the past couple of days, he's been leaving before 5:00 a.m., which means waking up in the fours, which is practically the middle of the night. No wonder he's been cranky. It's still not okay. I didn't ask him to lose sleep and come early. Just because I stink at surfing, it doesn't give him the right to yell at me, no matter how bad other things in his life are. And by Thursday, it's mostly yelling.

"What the hell was that?" he shouts after I pull out of a perfectly cresting wave.

"I haven't done this in five years!" I yell back.

He paddles up to me so he can yell in my face. "So?"

"So my body's five inches taller. Everything feels wrong!"

"It didn't the other night!"

"Maybe I got lucky!"

"Or maybe you just tried harder!"

"I *AM* trying!"

"Bullshit!"

His curse word shocks me into silence, and he can tell. His face softens, but mine doesn't.

"I obviously don't remember how to surf," I say coldly.

"Yes, you do." His words are tender, and it's the first time I've heard him talk nicely to me all week.

"What do you know?" I snap.

His eyes flicker, and the moment's gone. "You're right. What *do* I know?" This time, it's Jake who gets out of the water first. Our session is over, at least if I plan on getting a ride to school.

I know there's so much churning inside of him. I know he's not just mad at my crappy surfing. But as long as he stays locked up, there's not much I can do except be a punching bag. I guess I should be thankful it's showing up now rather than later. I still think of him during my quiet times in the morning, but my prayers have changed to, *Thank you so much, God, for revealing this to me early on in our friendship.*

Friday morning, he doesn't show up. I wait outside my house for thirty minutes before I get a text from Lydia.

Jake says to tell you he's not coming. Why doesn't he have your #?!?!

I still haven't given him my cell number, which is weird because everyone else has it—all my guy friends—but with Jake, it feels like a bigger deal. After this week, I'm glad he doesn't have it.

It only took four days before he gave up. That must be a record somewhere. I'm about to get my bike when Lydia texts that she's on her way with Kaj to pick me up.

On the way to school, Lydia asks, "So what's up with your novio this week?"

"He's not my boyfriend."

Kaj jokes, "You not putting out or something?"

"He's not my boyfriend," I repeat. "And there's just a lot going on with him."

"Like?"

"I wouldn't know. He only talks to his ex about it."

They don't say anything to that, and I'm thankful, because I don't feel like explaining.

When we pull up to Lydia's usual parking spot at school, Jake's standing there waiting. Great. He's wearing sunglasses even though it's not bright out, and it reminds me of the guys who try too hard. How was I so blind to this before? Note to self: Feelings can really mess with your perception of reality. When we get out of the car, Lydia and Kaj disappear so quickly, you'd think they were fleeing a fire. Jake approaches, and I'm face-to-face with the guy who stood me up. The guy who won't share anything with me but then yells at me for all the stuff he's not sharing, pretending it's my surfing that's making him so angry. The guy who's wearing sunglasses for no reason. He doesn't take them off, either, which makes me bristle.

He says, "Sorry for not getting there this morning. I would've texted earlier, but—"

"Don't make this somehow my fault because I haven't given you my number."

He holds his hands up, palms facing me like he's surrendering. "Whoa."

I immediately regret snapping at him. I'm just frustrated after a week of surfing horribly while watching someone I care about feel miserable and being unable to do anything about it. I'm embarrassed that he matters so much. Without warning, my eyes fill, but I blink back the tears. I refuse to let him make me cry.

In a moment he's cupping my cheeks. "Hey, hey. Heyyyyy. What's wrong?"

"What's wrong?" I yell, pulling his hands off my face. "I'm horrible at surfing. You know it. I know it. And I'm only getting worse, and all you do is yell at me like I'm *doing it on purpose.* I know there's other stuff happening, but you won't tell me a thing, and then you say we're great friends, but friends are honest, okay? Now you won't even talk to me at school or in the car, and you're making it look like it's because I stink at surfing, but maybe it's because you realized I'm never going to be someone you can share things with." He takes a step back, and it only upsets me more. "So I'm sorry I'm not who you thought I was, but you aren't either! I thought you were nice, and you're kind of a jerk! No, you *are* a jerk! And then you don't even show up to take me to school, but you don't tell me why. So fine. Don't apologize. Don't let me in. Wear your stupid sunglasses." Even I know my words sound childish, but the whole week of frustration vomits out of me.

He looks down at his feet and shoves a hand into a pocket. With the other hand, he takes off his sunglasses, breathing evenly for a few beats before looking up at me. When he does, I gasp. A purplish-black hue forms a half halo under his right eye from the bridge of his nose to his temple.

"You really want in on this?" he says gruffly.

Chapter Nineteen

His eye looks awful. "Jesus," I say, without even thinking that I'm taking God's name in vain.

"He already knows." Jake smirks at his bad joke.

I don't know what to say. Everything sounds inadequate or stupid. *"Can I pray for you?"* feels pretentious, but I don't know why since prayer is supposed to be my go-to. *"I'm so sorry"* sounds lame, like he lost a life in Fortnite or jumped into the ocean with his iPhone in his boardshorts. Even calling it like it is, *"That's awful. What happened?"* sounds like, duh. Obvious much?

We look at each other for a long time. I think of all my rules with guys—no hand-holding, no flirting, no touching, no hugging face-to-face. For years, I felt good about them. Like God was proud. That was *me.* But now, everything I fought for because it felt right suddenly feels wrong. A side hug would be patronizing, and I've never thought that before.

There's this—I don't know how to explain it other than a tug at my heart, and I'm assuming it's from God because it goes against every standard I've set. I follow that tug, and it leads me forward a step, so close to Jake I can feel his warm breath caressing the top of my hair. I lift my arms, encircling them around him, and it feels right. Good. True. There's nothing impure in the action, and I truly think it's what Jesus would do right here.

He flinches when I first touch him, knowing I don't do this. I feel his arms creep up my sides and move to my back. He squeezes and I squeeze back, and he buries his face in my neck. A one-syllable sob escapes from his lips. He clears his throat and breathes deeply. We hold on to each other, not moving, not releasing, and this single act says more than the most beautiful prayer ever spoken in the history of the world.

From the side of the portable classrooms across the quad, where she's hiding from us, I hear Lydia shout, "Breast to breast! You did it!"

They obviously don't know the situation, as Kaj, next to her, yells, "Full frontal, Lovette! Didn't know you had it in you!"

Jake and I erupt in muffled laughter, him giggling into my neck and me into his chest. His shoulders are broad and warm, and I have a brief moment when I think how nice it would be to lie on his chest more often. I push that thought away and remember why we're hugging.

I start to pull away, but he pulls me back in. He says into my ear, "I can't deal with school today."

And again, I feel a switch—this disregard for my rules—and I'm okay with it. "Then let's not."

He pulls back so he can look at me with a raised eyebrow.

I keep my arms looped around his waist. "You have a car, and I have a perfect attendance record. What's one day?"

I don't know what happened to him last night, but I know it's bad, and I remember what God showed me five years ago when I was at a low point.

"You sure?" He knows I'm not a ditcher.

"Never been more." I release from our hug and lift my chin toward the parking lot. "I need to take you somewhere."

Because I live in a prime vacation spot, no one notices when two teenagers are at the beach instead of school. This morning, I have Jake drive to the streets above Highland Avenue in North Manhattan. We park on the top of Thirty-fourth, where all the locals find street parking without the two-hour meters. We walk down the hill in comfortable silence, but our thoughts drag our feet and slow our steps.

As we turn south on Highland, I glance up at the purplish black of his cheek and eyebrow. "You wanna talk about it?"

He shakes his head.

"Hannah know?"

He sighs deeply, and I don't know if it's out of annoyance with me or longing for her. "Yeah," he admits.

I know I can't compete with their history. But still. My heart hurts that she gets to know things I don't.

"What I have here is good," he explains. "We sit at lunch, and it's good to feel normal. No reason to mess it up by bringing my shit to the table."

"Might be better than my peanut-butter-and-jelly sandwiches."

He laughs and throws his arm around me; well, around my neck so it's more of a headlock, and I feel like a little sister. It's both exhilarating and heartbreaking. I'm the *friend*. Again, why am I unhappy with that? It's what I told him: I don't date. We can only be friends.

Jake looks up at the street sign as we reach Twenty-eighth. "We heading to Old Man Mike's?"

I shake my head.

At Twenty-seventh and Highland, we arrive at Bruce's Beach. I take him to the middle of the two steep slopes of grass, and we walk on the level sidewalk separating the upper slope from the lower. I lead him up the slope diagonally, until we reach the third tree from the left. I crouch down and pat the grass in front of a large root. "Here."

"You brought me to a tree?" He's joking, but he sobers when he sees my face.

"Welcome to my seventh-grade home."

Chapter Twenty

I rub my fingers through the blades of grass, press on the soft dirt. Jake sits beside me.

"Before the accident, I used to come here to check the surf. Get a grip on the thing that was way bigger than me. You can see the lines, the current, even riptides from here. It's where I'd wax my board, talk to Mike before my coaching sesh, dry off afterward."

He scans the span of ocean. "Great spot."

I've never shared this with anyone, but it's time. He knows I didn't only bring him here to show him some grassy hills. "Mom and Dad weren't so awesome to me the year Matt was in rehab." I keep my eyes to the sky, pull up grass with my fingernails. Easier to share if I pretend I'm talking to myself. "Like it was as if I hadn't been born."

I lie down, feeling the cool grass against my neck. Jake lies next to me, the slope so steep, it's like we're in propped-up lounge chairs. The sky and the ocean blend at the horizon, light blue against deep blue, God's ombré. Our arms touch, and I feel guilty and right at the same time. I always imagined the first moment I'd be lying on my back next to a guy would be different. Somehow it's not a big deal with Jake.

"I know my parents were just doing their best, and I'm sure their heads were scrambled eggs wondering if they'd lost their only son. All that mattered was making sure he was okay. But it still sucked."

"No shit," he mumbles, and I know he's talking about his own family. He curls his index finger around mine, locking us together. I squeeze his finger, and he squeezes back.

"This became my place," I continue. "Even my church when it wasn't a Wednesday or Sunday. I needed a place I could feel God all the time, not just two days a week."

His face looks troubled. "Can I ask you something?" There's a new edge to his voice, and he pulls his finger away. "You said your parents were absent— Don't you ever wonder why God didn't take care of you if He loved you so much?" He sits up, brushes the bits of grass off his back.

His black eye contrasts with the sunshine, and I know this burst of anger is about him and not me. He's wondering where God was last night, or maybe where He is right now. I don't blame him. Faith starts out so simple. Lots of guitar songs and jumping around. Shouting that the love of God is better than mangoes and papayas. Jesus is fun! God rocks! God loves you! So many exclamation points, and everything makes sense. And then one day life punches you in the face, and you have to decide whether God loves you when nothing makes sense.

I choose my words carefully, knowing any cookie-cutter answers will be more like acid than lotion. "One time this family from church walked by with their dog. Asked me to their block-party barbecue. People on vacation would ask for directions to restaurants. Locals would ask me about the surf. Mike would pop in, crack a beer, talk about the waves. Kelly's dad would drive by on his way home from work. Give me a ride to youth group or their house for dinner. One time I napped midday and woke up with a plaid blanket on me. There was something about this spot. No matter what, I never felt alone." A skateboarder flies down the asphalt on Twenty-seventh, braking by making sharp, skidding turns. "And it reminded me that I may not see it right now. Or maybe not ever. But it doesn't mean God's not at work. And it doesn't mean He's not good, just because I get the short end of the stick. Besides, he didn't leave me hanging. I didn't see it then, but I do now."

"You really think God took care of you?" Doubt drips from every word.

"I do." There's nothing I know more. "Not the way I wanted, but yeah. He did. I'm still here. I'm okay."

Another skateboarder flies past, braking in big, sweeping carves. His friend stands at the bottom of the hill, clapping and saying "Niiice," every time he slows by dragging the back of his board through a turn.

"You ride?" Jake asks, distracted or maybe wanting to change the subject before he argues with me.

"Skateboard? Nah, not really."

"I thought those were your skateboards at Old Man Mike's."

"No. His. He wouldn't care if I borrowed them, but I just never thought about it. I guess I could. It's supposed to be a lot like surfing."

"It is," he agrees. Recognition dawns on his face, and he

bolts to his feet. I flinch at his sudden movement. "That's it!"

"What's . . . it?"

"You can't train in the water all the time. But you can train on land. Skateboards. Come on!"

He pulls me up by my hand, and before I even know what's happening, I'm jogging down toward the Strand, toward Old Man Mike's.

I was hoping if I were honest, he'd open up. But it worked as great as gripping an unwaxed board.

We get to the alley and open the gate to Mike's side yard. Mike's sliding door is open, and he pops his head out. "Hey, kid," he says. The smell of weed wafts toward us. Deep crow's feet mark his leathery face—a life of a lot of laughter and way too much sun.

"Hey, Mike. This is Jake."

"We've met." They nod at each other. I forgot Jake had to find my wetsuit the night he took me out with the light-up boards. Wonder what they talked about. Mike probably didn't ask any questions. He was my first surfing coach when I was six, coaching me and Matt up until I was twelve, when Matt went down. He never asked why I stopped taking lessons. I'm sure he assumed it was because of the trauma. We didn't talk much that year, but one day he saw me sitting on the grass at Bruce's Beach. After that, it was like God gave him "Lovette Radar." Somehow he knew when I was there—he'd walk up and toss me a granola bar, then sit and drink a beer. He wouldn't talk, other than pointing out the tide or a swell coming in from the south. One day during my eighth-grade year, he brought a wetsuit to my usual spot. "It's about your

size," was all he said. The tag was still on it. "Hate to see it go
to waste." It had been a year since Matty's accident, but that
was the first time I cried about everything. I sat on the upper
grass hill and bawled. He didn't say anything or pat me on
the shoulder. Mike's not like that. He just stood over me with
his arms crossed, looking out at the ocean. When I was done,
he said, "I'm gonna hang it on my gate. You ever want to get
back out there, you know where to find it." Two weeks later,
I got the nerve to put it on, and a day after that, I started
swimming again. Soon he started leaving extra towels out.

"You heading out?" Mike points at Jake's two surfboards,
as if I'd never stopped surfing. It's what I love about him. No
questions. "It's kinda flat. You should wait until four thirty
or so. Mid-tide should be good."

"Actually," Jake says, "could we borrow your skateboards?"

Mike kneels down, grunting from age and inflexibility, and
reaches under one of the lounge chairs for the skateboards.
"Have at them. Used to ride with my wife." Mike's wife died a
long time ago, before I met him. I never hear much about her.

"Thanks, Mike," I say. "And thanks for letting us keep the
surfboards here."

"You kidding? Was wondering how long it'd be before
you hopped back on. You were meant to ride, kid. Glad your
boyfriend convinced you."

"Oh," I start, my face flushing. "He's not—"

"Yeah, me too," Jake finishes for me, and I try not to stare.

Mike spins the wheel of one of the skateboards. "These
boards are SmoothStar—shorter length than longboards.
The front trucks turn more than your normal truck, but the

back is fixed. Acts like surfboard fins."

"Thanks, man," Jake says, like they're old friends, and Mike's eyes do the crinkly thing I love as his face cracks into a rusty smile. Jake takes the boards, and Mike disappears back inside, shutting his sliding glass door.

Chapter Twenty-One

I don't say a word until we're out on the Strand and riding our boards south toward Hermosa Beach. "So you told Old Man Mike I was your girlfriend?"

"No," he says. "I asked him if I could store the boards for 'Lovette,' and I think he assumed. Who cares, right?"

Hannah, I want to say, but he pumps and goes faster, end of discussion. I pump to keep up and the wind whips through us, blowing away my concerns and his anger about whatever happened the night before. Our bodies undulate with the boards like seaweed with the current, flowing in sync to the rhythm and tilt of the wheels over the sidewalk.

Mike was right. These skateboards are incredible. So smooth, it's like I'm on a wave.

"How's it feel?" he asks.

"Exceptionally amazing."

"Exceptionally?" He throws his head back, laughing. "Who says that?"

I give him a friendly shove. "Lots of people." He shoves me back, and I fall off the skateboard but luckily land flat-footed and running. The board keeps gliding next to me, and I hop back on, pumping to catch up.

"Nice recovery. Here's the thing," Jake says as we glide side by side. "Once you pop up on a wave, you've only got a few seconds to perfect a move that you haven't done in years. But with skateboarding, it's like you have an endless wave in front of you." He gestures grandly to the boardwalk ahead of us. "The cement is your ocean."

My heart leaps. All the discouragement I felt the last time I was in the water disappears under the four wheels of my new ride. Jake's right. I can practice carving turns and rail-to-rail transitions, and I do, rocking from toe edge to heel edge and again, over and over. It's flat ground, not a steep wave, but it's balance that I need to work on.

It's like Jake can read my mind. "We're gonna do this all the way down the Strand. Practice your board-body technique. The only thing you're missing when you're surfing is your balance and your muscle memory. Doing the same thing over and over until it comes naturally." He sounds like a kid opening Christmas presents—he's practically squealing at this breakthrough—and my body pumps with adrenaline in response.

He coaches me as we continue down the flat stretch, the million-dollar mansions on our left, the sound of the surf one hundred yards to our right. My friends and I have a game where we pretend we've won the "house lottery"—and instead of a million dollars, we're given one house on the Strand. We each get to pick one, and we're not allowed to choose the same. Once someone chooses theirs, they have dibs on it. I explain this game to Jake, but he waves me off. "Think about your toe pressure," he says. "Pay attention to how your ankles flex, and when. Control it. Make sure your hips are centered over the board. Feel where your center of gravity is. Play with your balance." I forget about my silly house-lottery game and do what he says. It works. I feel the things he points out in ways that I couldn't on a wave.

He looks over his shoulder at me, grinning. "Copy me." And like two five-year-olds, we engage in a skateboarding version of follow the leader. He makes a swooping carve to the left, and I mimic it. He lowers his body, working with gravity and physics to swoop back to the right. I crouch down and do the same.

"Catch up," he says, and I ride up next to him. "Stay on rail for ten." And then he makes ten turns in a row where he is never on the base of his board. He stays on his rails—right side and left side—the entire time, and I follow, carving back and forth with my board. It's gorgeous—the way we flow side by side as we make serpentine curves—and people move to the curb to watch our synchronized dance. He slows when we reach a water fountain and stops to take a drink.

I'm breathless from it all.

"How'd that feel?" he says.

"Unreal."

"You just needed to remember."

It's true. I felt it all coming back as I made turn after turn, dropping low and leaning my body with the carve. It was like my muscles were waking up after a five-year-long hibernation and remembering what they were supposed to do.

I take a long drink of water from the fountain, and in my periphery, I can see him looking at me. I raise my head, wipe my lips with the back of my hand. "What?"

He smiles. "Nothing. The way you light up when you ride—I wish you could see it."

This day was supposed to be about him, and he's somehow made it about me again, which feels amazing, but underneath his sunglasses, there's a glaring black-and-purple reminder of something more important than the surf competition. "Your eye," I say, and he winces at the word. "What happened?"

"Come on, Lovette." He shakes his head. A couple strolls by with their three dogs, the littlest pausing to sniff Jake's leg.

"Please," I say.

He turns toward one of the mansions and examines it. Even through the glasses, I can see his eyes blinking. Maybe he's deciding what he can tell me. He turns back my direction and shakes his head slightly, like he's pulling himself out of a trance.

"Today was"—he pauses—"*exceptionally* better than I expected." He grins at his use of the word, and everything in me warms. "Can't we keep it that way?"

"I guess?" It comes out as a question because I have no choice. He doesn't want to share.

"This one," he says, pointing to the mansion he was looking at. "Your house-lottery game. I'd pick this one." So he was listening.

"It's nice," I agree. "I like the brick." There's only brick on one wall of the house. The rest is a dark navy-blue wood.

"Yeah, me too. And the attention to detail. Check out the windows." They're perfectly framed with white wood, contrasting the dark wood of the house. It still has a beachy feel, not sterile like some of the more modern builds out here.

"Looks cozy," I agree. "Only you can't see inside." The windows are covered with a dark tint.

"Exactly." He turns to me then, his eyes suddenly serious. "If you saw inside, you may not want it for your lottery house." Again, the saying things without saying things.

I step forward, and we lock eyes. "What if it was the worst inside, and I didn't care?"

His eyes flicker, and he's just a friend again. He takes a step back. "Well, then you can't, because I already picked it. Not allowed to pick the same one. *Your* rules."

He kicks onto his skateboard, facing back toward Bruce's Beach. "Come on!" he shouts behind him. "Keep up!" We ride back to where we started, but the whole way back, we try not to strike a foot on the ground. Instead, we build momentum with tic-tacs, swinging the front of the board from the left to the right to the left with small kick turns, imitating "pumping down the line" in the water on a shortboard. In only a few hours, I feel as if I've ridden ten thousand waves.

The next week, we skate every day after school, sometimes as fas as the Redondo Beach Pier. Niles says to him once at lunch, "Nice shiner." He wiggles a finger at Jake's eye. "What'd you do—drop in on her wave?"

"Surfboard to the face," Jake says, and he doesn't make eye contact with me.

Kaj ribs him. "Can't keep up?"

The boys laugh. "No one can," Jake says, which is an even bigger lie than the surfboard to the face. I haven't even been back out on the water since my flopping charade two weeks ago. Jake's been trying to build my confidence back up through all our skateboarding. It's been fun, but I can't help but think of how far behind I am. The other girls competing in my age group have five more years of waves under their belts.

The following week, Jake and I continue our pattern. He shows up before school, we skate to school, and then after school, he skates with me to work. He must skate back to his car after he drops me off, because it's always gone from the front of my house when I get home at night. We even download the FriendFinder app so we can find each other and still meet up when traffic isn't his friend or I have to stay after school to finish an assignment.

In just a few weeks, my friends have gotten used to seeing Jake and me together. No one says anything. In the mornings, they start waiting for us at the corner of the quad, where we arrive on our skateboards. Kelly's polite, but her face is in her phone a lot these days texting Dave, and when she looks at Jake or me, I notice that she tugs on her single strip of purple hair, pulls it down hard in front of her face so she can stare at it and not us. Maybe I'm just imagining it.

At youth group on Wednesday, we're in our small groups, talking about boundaries. Why does God set boundaries? What boundaries do you set for yourself? Things like that. I notice Kelly fidgeting with my hands more than usual and looking at me like she wants to say something.

Back in the youth room, Pastor Brett gives a great sermon, well, minus the cringeworthy slang. "God knows that we are dust," he says. "He knows how He formed us. Nothing is TMI to God." Some of us snicker. Leave it to Pastor Brett to find a way to slip "TMI" into a sermon. "But because He built us and He's like, 'What up, G. I know your biz,' then He also knows what's best for us. And if He loves us—which we believe He does—then when He tells us *not* to do something, it's out of love for us, not because He's some cosmic killjoy. He knows what will ultimately make us feel whole. He knows what will keep us from emptiness and shame. So any boundary that He sets for us in His word is ultimately for our freedom, not for our captivity. Not to hold us down or to suffocate us. He's not trying to yuck our yum. It's the opposite. That's why Paul says in Galatians, 'It is for freedom that Christ has set us free.'"

We reach for the hands next to us and close in prayer, but Kelly holds on to mine after we say "amen."

"Wow. God seriously loves you so much," Kelly whispers.

"Thanks," I whisper back.

"That's why He led Brett to give that talk just for you."

My head cocks to the side. "For me?"

"Def. Both Dave and I have been concerned for your heart." Her hand feels clammy, and I slide mine off of hers. "I've told Dave how you've given up everything you've stood for. And then tonight, this talk on boundaries? It's like a total answer to prayer."

I'm struck into silence, and luckily, Jake rescues me. "Hey, Tony Hawk," he says, handing me my skateboard. "You ready to take on the church hill?"

My head feels wobbly as I nod. Kelly squeezes my hand with a goodbye and skips off to find Dave fingerpicking his guitar on one of the couches.

Chapter Twenty-Two

At dinner on Friday, Dad goes through his usual checklist. Did I clock in ten minutes before work? Did I make my bed with hospital corners? Yes and yes. He air high-fives me across the table. He asks if I'm doing more than what the teachers assign, and when I tell him I've been studying my ACT math, he draws a graph on a napkin. I don't need any help, really, but I act surprised and impressed when he shows me slope-intercept form. He clicks the pen loudly and drops it like a mic. It clatters onto his plate next to his peas and chicken, and my mother scolds, "Honey!"

Mom shares about her latest home designs, and just when I think it's a normal Friday, she asks me how swimming at the Y is going. I ignore her mischievous grin and instead pass the potatoes to Dad. I gather my courage and say, "Speaking of swimming, did you hear they're having a local surf competition in February?"

Dad scowls. "Not run by a professional organization?"

My parents are never an easy audience with anything surf related, but I thought this would be an easy in. "It's run by the community. Some local surfers got together and are putting the proceeds into our beaches."

"Parking tickets can pay for that."

"Parking tickets cover Hermosa's summer concerts on the pier," I counter. "But this will go into keeping the beaches clean, sand maintenance, extra trash cans. It's a good cause."

"Run by a bunch of locals?" Mom says, which is basically what my dad said.

Dad stabs at his peas. "That doesn't sound safe."

Mom waves her fork at me. "Sounds unsafe if you ask me."

It's like we're in the Grand Canyon of echoes. Shoot. Both are jabbing at their food, and I've barely mentioned surfing. Not even surfing *plus me*. I pour a glass of milk.

"So when's Matt driving home for Thanksgiving?"

Friday night at the Venue, there's no Jake. No Kaj, either. Just the good ol' days of me, Lydia, Uncle Joe, and a lot of dishes and poorly understood Spanish. I'm getting better, though. I can't speak it, but I'm understanding more. Tonight Lydia is telling Uncle Joe about her latest fight with Kaj, which sounds remarkably similar to last time. Words in every fight: mentiroso (liar), tonto (dummy), pendejo (coward and/or pubic hair—actually, a lot of other meanings, too, but those are the kindest).

Tonight she ends with an easy one: El burro sabe más que él (The burro knows more than him).

"Ay, mija," Uncle Joe says, handing her a highball glass to rinse. "You're so hard on him."

When she says *no*, she holds on to the *N* for a long time

like she's winding up with a big gust of wind for her *O*. "Nnnn-oh! He's un burro."

Uncle Joe asks her the same question every week. "So you gonna break up?"

"Por supuesto que no. Of course not." She says it in both languages for emphasis, as if Uncle Joe is the burro. "Es tan patético, que resulta entrañable." That one goes over my head, but she doesn't translate. "Speaking of breaking up, where's Jake?"

"He had to be back at the base."

"What's the latest?"

"We're surfing Monday! He says I'm ready."

"I meant what's the latest with you and him?" She bounces her hip into mine.

I shake my head, thinking of Kelly at youth group, and try to focus on drying silverware. "Nothing. We're friends."

"Mentirosa, but okay."

"Really. He still talks to his ex, and I don't date. It works out great that way."

She clucks her tongue. "Hay días tontos y tontos todos los días."

"What?"

"Lydia!" Uncle Joe chides. He shakes his head at her.

What's that supposed to mean?

"Nothing." She reaches for a clean dishrag. "Tell me about surfing."

I'm giddy just thinking about it. "We're hitting the water before school. He's picking me up at five thirty."

She crosses herself.

"What's that for?" I ask.

"That's an ungodly hour."

I throw some soapsuds at her, and she tells me we should FaceTime him from the dance floor. I say my phone's dead because I don't feel like explaining why I still haven't given Jake my number. It feels like a big deal. I almost asked for it the day he showed up with a black eye, but that would've seemed like I was getting it just to check on him. Which I totally would've been.

I know he's not my boyfriend, but the truth is, I feel like we have something better than a relationship. I like that when we have a moment together, nobody gets to experience it except me and him. And God. There're no texts, no pictures, no forwards or retweets or screen captures. It's just ours. And somehow that feels more special.

It's refreshing to be with Lydia when lately Kelly's felt judgy. She never used to feel that way, and I don't know if it's me or her who's changed. "Lyds, do you think I'm different?"

She narrows her eyes. "I feel like this is one of those questions that I'm going to be in trouble no matter what I answer. Are you trying to be different?"

"Yes. No. Maybe. I dunno!" I set down a coffee cup. "Kelly says I'm not creating good boundaries between me and Jake."

"Girl, you're like Alcatraz. Where's she getting her info?"

"I dunno. Jesus?"

"Don't you talk to Him, too?"

"Yeah, but it doesn't mean I can't make mistakes."

"Aaaaah," she says and points an index finger up like a light bulb just dinged over her head. "Maybe *she* wanted to be the one making mistakes with Jake?" She does a little hip shake, which makes me giggle.

"No, she has a boyfriend now, remember?"

"Right. Dave from youth group. Well, then maybe she's just on her period." Lydia's phone lights up, and she smiles ear to ear. But when she picks it up, she acts angry. "Give me one reason I shouldn't hang up right now."

I know that's the last I'll get of Lydia tonight. She and Kaj will be at it over the phone, their anger building in volume, until she stalks off to the dance floor to shake it out of her or he shows up to kiss it out of her.

When I asked Lydia if I was different, she didn't answer. Which means I am. Maybe as I'm getting closer to Jake, I'm getting further from God. Lydia wouldn't know. She likes God and all, but He *stays on the cross*, so to speak. They don't talk much. Maybe Kelly's being judgy, but it doesn't mean she's wrong.

○))) ● ● ● ● ● (((○

I forget all of that by Monday morning when I hear Jake's car humming outside for me. I prance out the front door like a deer, leaping into his passenger seat.

"Let's do this," he says and cranks up the music.

At Old Man Mike's, we slide into our wetsuits in record time. School starts in two hours, and I want as much time on the water as I can get. I'm nervous, but more from excitement than from fear. Jake takes one of the LED longboards for himself, but instead of handing me the other, he motions at

Mike's shortboard. "Do you think he'd mind?"

I grin. I love Jake's confidence in me. "I think he'd love it."

○))) ● ● ● (((○

Down at the shoreline, I strap on my leash and start toward the water, but Jake holds me back by the elbow. "Aren't you forgetting something?"

I check Mike's board. It looks waxed.

"Every time we go in the water, you either bow your head or look up at the sky for a few seconds."

Oh my gosh. He's right. I've never gone in the water without praying first. I've never forgotten. Like, ever.

His comment is a wave that knocks me down. I stand my board upright next to me and lean my cheek against it. "Maybe Kelly's right about you."

"Me?"

I didn't mean for it to sound that way. "Well, not you. Me. Kelly doesn't think I'm setting good boundaries with you."

"Does it matter what Kelly thinks?"

"No. But what if she's right?" I lower my voice, embarrassed. "What if I can't think of God *and* you? Like, I always pick one over the other?"

"Well, then stop." He puts an arm around both me and my board. It's friend-like, but whirlpools swirl in my stomach. "All I meant was that you always pray before you get in the water. So you forgot. Big deal. It's not because of me. Think about it. We've been skateboarding for the past two weeks every day until we both had blisters on our blisters."

I lift one foot out of the sand and wiggle my toes. A couple Band-Aids wiggle back.

"And now you're getting back in. To *surf.*"

He's right. I'm nervous. Excited. A lot of things. I say a silent apology to God for overlooking Him. I look out at the ocean and speak aloud. "Jesus, please go with us out there today. And thanks for this. *All* of it." I squeeze Jake's arm, so he knows I'm thanking God for him, not just the ocean. As an amen, I stand up, but Jake stays sitting for a minute. I wait, watching the direction of the break, until I hear him shuffling to stand.

He tucks his board under his armpit.

We sprint at the water.

The waves thunder in the quiet morning, small breakers with intimidating voices, but I pierce my board through each as I paddle out. There's no time to think before a glorious set comes my way. I see the bumps of water building as they head for me, and I flip my board around and go.

My arms strain to keep up, but just when I think I've missed it, I feel the mountain rising below and propelling me forward. It's small, but it's breaking cleanly, and I'm lined up in perfect position.

I pop up, and for a split second—the second when I hold my breath because God stops time—my board hangs on top of a hill of ocean, and then drops eggshell light, with a speed that pushes the air out of my lungs and forces me to breathe again.

I don't jump off this time but instead attack it like it belongs to me. My stance is familiar now. I've lived like this for the past two weeks on a skateboard, and I have no problem keeping my bare feet glued to the waxy base. I carve back and forth, creating a wake through the sloping face just like all those tic-tacs I did from the pier to Twenty-sixth Street. Strands of wet hair whip into my wide open mouth, and I can taste the seawater dripping off the ends from the wind.

Jake whoops for me after I kick out of the wave. His clapping echoes across the surface. "Attagirl!" he shouts.

He rides, too, and because it's a small surf day, he looks effortless on his longboard. We switch boards a couple times just for fun. For almost two hours we keep at it, never tiring, cheering each other on through every attempt. Even the surfers around us join in on the clapping when we catch a particularly sweet ride. The whole morning is golden.

At school, we both sprint to first period, and I slide into my seat as the tardy bell rings. When my test second period is returned to me and I tip my head down to look at it, a cupful of seawater drops out of my nose like a gushing faucet, splashing all over my test, and I giggle.

Mr. Jenkins frowns. He knows I got a C-, which normally I'd care about, but there's a puddle smearing my C- into a blur, and it reminds me of my perfect morning and perfect waves and perfect-imperfect Jake, which blots out any bad test grade.

At lunch, neither of us can shut up about our morning. How we rode smooth, like it was a lake of glass. How Jake had this one great cutback. How I pumped down the line.

"Pumped?" Kelly interjects.

"Yeah," Jake explains. "It's when you compress your stance

with each bottom carve and extend your stance with each top carve. Creates momentum. She was flying. You should've seen—"

"But not as good as when you did that perfect roundhouse cutback and then went right into an aggressive top turn."

We keep talking over each other, and our friends—well, except for Kelly—are amped by our excitement, interrupting us with questions about waves and wipeouts. They "Hell yeah!" me and pat me on the shoulder, impressed by Jake's stories. He's so proud of me, he's glowing, and it's weird to see someone reflect what I feel inside. I can't believe I'm actually out there doing it again. It feels incredible, and it's like he knows it and is pumped by it. As Jake gushes, I see Lydia trying to make eye contact. I look once, and she waggles her eyebrows. I look away, but I'm smiling, and she knows I saw. By Kelly's frown, I know she saw, too.

"Seriously," Jake says, "if we keep this up every morning until February, she's gonna be like—"

His phone vibrates, interrupting him by break-dancing all over the lunch table. He looks down, and there it is for us all to see, that caller ID name.

HANNAH

It's in all caps, no last name needed. My stomach twists.

Our entire table of six grows quiet. Everyone stares at the phone shaking and rumbling, announcing those six letters, H-A-N-N-A-H, that palindrome that says the same thing whether you read it forward or backward:

Ex-girlfriend.

This time it's Kelly who waggles her eyebrows. I don't look

in Jake's direction, but I can sense he's also looking at me. I can tell in my periphery that he looks concerned, but I keep my eyes on the phone as it dances, transfixed.

"Sorry, guys," Jake says. "I have to get this."

He takes the phone off the table and stands. I don't dare look up at any of my friends, especially when he walks away. Before his voice trails off, I know they hear his words, too.

"Hey, babe. It's okay, I'm here . . ."

Chapter Twenty-Three

"I have to go to the bathroom," I say, and with my head tucked down, I head to the bathroom so it's not a lie. After splashing cold water on my face, I look in the mirror.

"Sorry, Jesus," I whisper. "That was hard."

I want to say more to God, but there's a lump in my throat. Jake's never told me we're more than friends, but my friends treat us like we are. It's become *What are Jake and Lovette doing?* Or *Where are Jake and Lovette?* Secretly, I like how they've started to look at us. And in one phone-rattling caller ID word, they were reminded that we are *not* what they've made us. My face burns thinking of my friends' faces, jaws tight, sucking in air through clenched teeth, those saucer eyes filled with pity.

I need to get out. For the second time in less than a month, I walk off campus without looking back. I have my backpack and Mike's skateboard. Everything I need. The ocean is never closed during school hours.

I'm out in the water in no time, the ripples of waves slapping and licking the edges of the board. I'm on the longboard today. I wanted something steady, something solid that I could rest my whole body on. It's more like lying on a table. Sturdy. Reliable. I sigh, and my stomach sinks deeper against the hard fiberglass. My board is in its "no-no" position, parallel to the shoreline, but I'm out beyond the lineup so I don't have to worry about being sideswiped.

I'm embarrassed that I feel empty in the rib cage, like hollow and achy. Strangely, that makes me think of the second book in *Twilight*, how Edward left Bella, and from October to January, an entire eight pages were left blank to signify that nothing happened. Literally nothing was worth anything outside of Bella's relationship with Edward. Life was over if she couldn't have her man. I remember how girls swooned, and I rolled my eyes. *Ohmygosh, Jesus, am I turning into Bella?*

This prayer makes me laugh out loud, and I feel a little better. I guess outside of Jesus, everything would be about finding the perfect guy. The perfect job. The perfect image. But there's more to this life. There's more to me. God's taught me that, and I can't un-know it. Why do my feelings try to make me forget? I groan and prop up on my elbows.

"What do you think about all this?" I ask Him, my voice bouncing lightly off the lapping waves. "Are you getting me out of something before it gets worse? I didn't feel crummy about guy-girl stuff before I met Jake. Maybe if I stop talking to him, I'll feel better. Maybe that's what you want."

But if I stop talking to Jake, that feels petty, like I'm someone dramatic who'll ask him for a glass of water and then pour it on his head and say, *"That's what you did to my heart!"* or slam his locker closed when he opens it and yell, *"Thanks for doing the same to me!"* I grin imagining it, and there's a part of me that wishes I could be that person for a day.

I slide my elbows off and place my left ear against the wet board, and it makes a few suction cup noises as I settle. My eyes focus on the horizon, the light bluish white against the dark water, and I feel His presence so close as I stare at His handiwork.

The word *handiwork* is in the Bible, I remember. "For we are God's handiwork, created in Christ Jesus to do good works, which God prepared in advance for us to do."

My hands trace the smooth curves of the board. The guy who shaped this board was meticulous—I know that without ever asking him. I know he took great care. His handiwork is the only evidence I need.

This makes me smile. I'm God's surfboard. He's shaping me. And the smallest imbalance or rough edge, He's going to find. And He won't settle until I ride perfectly.

But then, is Jake just a rough edge? Or is he part of the finished product? What if he's the rough edge, and God's taking the sandpaper to him, rubbing him off and out of my life?

Oh my gosh, I *am* Bella.

I'm not in the mood for catching waves, but I paddle around saying the second part of that verse as if it's a song on repeat—how God has created me to do good works for Him—and a boyfriend is unnecessary. I don't need to be an uneven board. I don't need Jake. I don't.

When I get home Monday evening, Mom is already there. Morning migraine, she informs me.

"Your boyfriend stopped by after school. Where were you?"

"I had some things to do," I say. "And he's not my boyfriend."

"Well, I hope you're not sleeping with a stranger!" She laughs, and my jaw drops.

"I'm *not* sleeping with him!"

"Okay, that's your story, but I thought maybe you were called in to work, so I sent him there. I imagine that's why the school called, wondering why you weren't in sixth period."

"Oh."

I fiddle with my backpack, pulling it off my shoulders. She watches me, waiting for more. "Jake seems nice. Your father invited him to dinner on Friday."

I cringe. "Mom!" This is horrible. He cannot come over. "I have to work Friday," I say, and make a mental note to ask Kim for a shift switch.

Mom pouts her lips. "Oh, that's too bad. You never have to work on Fridays. Well, he declined too. Why don't you invite him next week? Make sure you don't get scheduled. And while you're at it, tell Billy's Buns never to schedule you again during school, or I *will* have a talk with your manager."

I sigh. I don't have the energy to argue. I'll figure it out later. "Okay, sounds good."

I shuffle to my room, snap my blinds shut, and crawl into my bed with my clothes on. *"He declined too."* I looked up at my Kelly Slater poster. He's tucked in a barrel, the fierce water circling him but not taking him over, like it's there to protect him, not take him down. "Like you," I say to God. I throw my head against my pillow. "Stay in the barrel," I remind myself as I nod off to sleep. "Jake's not your barrel."

○)))) ● ● (((○

I think Jake got the hint after Mom sent him to work to find me, and Kim told him that I wasn't scheduled that day. He's been polite, but we both have taken a step back. We say hi, and we talk at lunch with our group as if nothing happened. But a film of tension has settled at our table, like everyone sees that we're not showing up together or talking about each other, but no one wants to point it out. Everyone laughs and jokes, but their eyes shift around at one another, and no one asks what *we* are doing after school. It's back to Jake *or* Lovette. It's no longer Jake *and* Lovette.

At youth group, I avoid him during big-group game, and at the end, I leave right after the final amen of the sermon. I sit in front, and he sits in back. Kelly stays glued to me, squeezing my arm and telling me it's better this way. Dave sits on the other side of her, and it's a little weird to have her holding both of our hands.

On Friday, I work Kim's shift at Billy's Buns until eight, and then I head over to the Venue. I'm late, but Lydia doesn't seem to notice. She also doesn't bring up Jake, and for the first time in months, she doesn't complain about Kaj, which is so weird that even Uncle Joe asks if she's feeling okay. She waves him off like, *"Not now, I'll fill you in later."* Then she tips her head at me and gives Uncle Joe a shake of her head. I don't mention that I have these things called eyes and that she's as subtle as a tsunami.

Every morning I wake up at five thirty and surf, skate, or read my Bible. I fill my time as much as I can. On the water, I practice my cutbacks, my momentum building, and even after a few sessions, my surfing feels natural. But it's lost some of the joy, especially when I have a great ride and I don't hear Jake's voice yelling, "Attagirl!" or his hand slapping the water.

On our second Friday apart, I see Jake in the hallway after second period. I nod and give a quick wave. He smiles the polite way—without teeth—just lips pressed together and slightly upturned. This has happened a few times, and it seems to be our new distant way of communicating. Yesterday he even said, "How are you?" and I said, "Fine."

Progress.

After fifth period, I head to lunch. My fifth is on the far corner of campus, so I get to the lunch quad by circling around the outside of the school rather than cutting through the interior walkways. I pass a few kids and they snicker. I think it's about some inside joke, but then the next two girls laugh also as I walk by, their eyes on me and not each other. I feel for the zipper on my jeans. Nope. I look down. No toilet paper on my Chucks. An uneasy feeling is spreading upward from my toes.

A guy shouts, "Hey, Lovette, can I be your first?"

Another guy shouts, "First what?" and they both laugh.

I turn the corner and push through the double doors to the cafeteria.

Papers.

That's the first thing I see, even before all the students.

Papers, like confetti after a concert, are blowing in every direction. So many students I know and don't know, papers in their hands. All looking at me. Giggling. Shushing. This stuff only happens in movies, I think, but no. They really are all looking at me. Against the walls of the cafeteria, under the sports banners, on the backs of chairs, on the sides of the food kiosks, there are papers plastered with Scotch tape.

A guy walks by. "Don't get too close. You know what might happen."

I reach for the wall next to me and pull off one of the papers. It rips from the tape, and the top part stays on the wall, but I recognize the writing. It's my writing.

I decided back when I was twelve that I was going to wait until I was married. And not just for sex.

Oh no. I feel light-headed.

My first kiss is going to be at the altar when the pastor says, "You may kiss the bride." It's the most romantic thing I can imagine.

Cecilia. I search for her, and she's not hiding. She's standing there, her two clones with their swishing soccer sweats giving her a wide berth so she can hold the spotlight for this moment. She smiles like she's scored a winning goal, her ponytail high, her shoulders back. There's no mistaking who's behind this. She wouldn't dare let anyone else get the credit.

I look at the paper, and it's hard to read because it's shaking in my hand. Cecilia blacked out some of it with Sharpie before she made the megazillion copies. The part where I said I wasn't sure if I felt the same way anymore. She cut that out.

I read the next part without breathing:

I even signed a purity contract.

More Sharpie. Then:

Saying you've never kissed a guy sounds really dumb and embarrassing.

More Sharpie.

But it's not like people walk around asking that, so it's fine. Anyway, if you read this, Ms. Jensen, which I know you won't, no kissing and telling. Lol. Get it?

Underneath, Cecilia tried to mimic my handwriting, adding:

Everyone knows you can get pregnant from kissing.

"*That part's not me!*" I want to scream. And it doesn't even fit after my last words: *Lol. Get it?* I'm sure it all sounds ridiculous. But *that.* That part makes Jesus sound positively absurd.

After the past two weeks, this is all I can take. My eyes get glassy. *No, no, no. Blink. Hold it together, Lovette. It's a dumb prank.* I look at the carpet of papers strewn across the linoleum. This took a team of people. Cecilia didn't work alone.

Someone walks up from behind and says in my ear, "You're fine, Lovette. Just don't let her see you cry." I *was* fine. But it's Jake's voice in my ear, and he's standing right next to me, and he's saying my name as if we haven't had two full weeks of monastery silence between us. I feel his gentle touch on my waist, and it's all I can take. The tears spring forth. I whip my head 180 degrees from Cecilia, so she can't see the waterfall cascading down my cheeks.

"Aw, shit," he whispers, and I think he realizes that it's

him who's made me cry. He throws an arm around me, and I want to throw his hand off and yell at him like in the movies, but everyone is watching, so instead I burrow my face into his armpit. It doesn't smell of aftershave and soap like the books say. It smells like it's been five hours since he put on deodorant. Still, it's better than looking at Cecilia. He guides me out past the tables, our feet sliding on the paper like sneakers on an ice rink, past the kid who says that Jake should wear a condom if he's putting his arm around me. Jake only pauses enough to shoulder-check the kid, sending him stumbling backward with a middle finger in the air. He ushers me through the double doors into the parking lot, and when we're away from the world, I crumple to the curb and put my head in my hands.

Chapter Twenty-Four

My hidden face feels hot against my hands. My nose drips snot to the pavement like a long strip of taffy, which is fine because I don't plan on lifting my eyes to where Jake can see them. The strange thing is that I'm not hated at our school. I'm not popular, but I'm not hated. So to be the butt of something so calculated, so grandiose—feels shocking. Yes, planned by Cecilia, but executed by more than one person. She got others to agree to help her. That's the part that gets me.

I wonder what Jake is thinking as he rubs my back. Is he going to say we should ditch school again and go surfing?

"I can't ditch school again," I say after five minutes of curb silence.

He doesn't respond. Is he planning to tell me not to worry about what others think? Maybe he wants to remind me how I play to an audience of one—Jesus—and how nothing else should matter. Or—oh no—he's going to say something cheesy like, "Buck up, buttercup," or worse, quote *Notting Hill* when Hugh Grant's character says, "Today's newspapers will be lining tomorrow's wastepaper bin." Like, who cares? And who does care? I know this. It's just everything all together.

"My dad went to Afghanistan," his voice begins, gravelly and strained. I don't move. He's never shared specifics about his dad's deployment. "A few months in, guess someone got word that there was a soldier encampment, and the rebels came in and bombed. His best friend was in the market grabbing some food for them."

I look up from my hands, not at Jake, but out at the parking lot. I want him to know I'm listening. I clean my snotty face with the back of my sleeve. Two students are walking off campus, one lighting a cigarette as they go. I pull my knees to my chest and rest my chin on my forearms.

Jake removes his hand from my back, strokes the sidewalk open palmed. "He wasn't alive when my dad found him, but Dad carried him out, got third-degree burns on his arms from touching his best friend's skin. He only set him down when he found a little Afghani girl, six . . . maybe seven years old, who was riding her bike home from school when it happened. The wheels of her bike were melted to her leg. He held the girl until she stopped breathing."

"Oh, Jake." I have no other words. This horrible person I've envisioned his father to be fades away. Now I feel like the horrible person for thinking of him that way. "Your dad did the right thing."

He nods. "He did. Carried his friend out. Held on to a kid. But his brain doesn't give a shit. It keeps looping the scenes at night, ya know? The images. His best friend burning to death. Holding a child while she's dying and looking up at him as if to ask why, and he has no answer."

"So your black eye . . ."

He laughs gruffly. "Had to wake him up. He was gonna wake the neighbors with all that yelling. Turns out he has great aim in his sleep."

I think of how much I had assumed. "I'm so sorry."

He shakes his head. "Don't be. He's no holiday. When he first got back, he couldn't sleep. So he drank. No sleep makes you crazy. Drinking makes you ugly. Awesome combo."

"That why your parents split up?"

He finds a gravel rock and chucks it across the pavement like he's skipping stones in a pond. It bounces four times. "Yeah. Finally Mom said, enough. She couldn't live with it. I don't blame her, but I hate her for it just the same. Schools are better out here, she argued. In the end, she wanted out from anything that reminded her of him. And sadly, I'm one of those things."

"That can't be true." He stands, holds out his hand. I take it, and he pulls me up. I wipe the dirt off my backside and shake my head. "Gosh, I feel stupid for crying now."

He grabs me by the shoulders and looks at me squarely. "I didn't tell you this to make you feel bad about feeling bad. What Cecilia did sucked. Sure, my mom left me with a guy who sucker punches me in his sleep. But you were abandoned for a year while your parents took care of your brother. We all have our stuff."

"Then why—"

"Because by now, you've seen the real me, and you know my dad doesn't define me. What happened back there"—he lets go of my shoulders and offers a lazy swat of his hand toward the cafeteria—"doesn't define you."

I rub my chin, crusty with dried tears. "It's not just that. The letter. She added stuff, crossed out stuff." I feel my heart quickening again. "It makes Jesus look like a moron."

"So?"

So?

But then he adds, "You think this is the first time someone's made Him look like a moron? He'll be okay. I think He can take it."

I'm thankful for Jake's response. I can't imagine having feelings for someone who didn't care about the One I loved most. Then I remember the words of my assignment: *My first kiss is going to be at the altar when the pastor says, "You may kiss the bride." It's the most romantic thing I can imagine.*

Jake read that, and the humiliation returns. "But the other stuff," I say, my face hot again. "I'm not even sure I believe that anymore. I mean, I still don't believe in sex before marriage. But now everyone knows. Lovette's a virgin. Lovette's never kissed. Lovette's never had a boyfriend. Lovette signed a contract with God. Lovette's training to be a nun. If they see me even holding a guy's hand, they'll be like, 'See? All Christians are hypocrites.'"

He steps forward so we're face-to-face, and my breath hitches. The bell rings to go to sixth period, but I don't move. He takes my wrist gently and lifts it, places our hands palm to palm, fingers pointing toward the sky. I feel a charge like electricity from his touch. Then he opens his fingers and slowly interlocks them with mine.

He's held my hand before when he led me out to the ocean. But now with our fingers meshed, it feels intimate—like we're naked or something—and my eyes dart around before meeting his gaze. He motions to our two hands, fingers braided, palms squeezing tighter. I'm not pulling away, and he knows it.

"We're all hypocrites, Lovette. Trust me, if they don't want Jesus, it's not your hypocrisy holding them back."

He releases his hand from mine, and I almost reach for it again. Almost.

"I gotta get to sixth period," I say. Sixth period is through the cafeteria. I lick my chapped lips and reach in my pocket for my Dr Pepper ChapStick.

"I'll go with you," he says, and I almost start crying again.

"Thanks," I manage, and then I remember Jake's words: *"What happened back there doesn't define you."*

You define me, Jesus, and You don't cower. To prove it, I stand tall, shoulders back, and sling my backpack over one arm.

"Attagirl," Jake says, like I caught a good wave, and I smile.

When we push through the double doors, I slide to a stop. The cafeteria's cleared of students, except for my best friends. Niles, Kaj, Lydia, and Kelly are walking around with trash bins. Lydia is stripping every last xeroxed paper off the walls. Kaj is on his knees, shuffling a bunch into a pile. Kelly's got the tables, and Niles is cleaning the benches. They work as a team, cleaning every piece of the cruel joke. My eyes fill again, but for way better reasons than before.

"Well, hey!" Niles says as we enter. "If it isn't the lady of the hour!"

"Thanks," I cough out. They stop what they're doing and walk over. "You didn't have to."

"Of course we did," Niles says. "Any excuse to ditch Mr. Flannigan's."

Kelly wraps her arms around me and squeezes until I might pop.

Kaj adds, "Besides, we can't have you bringing down our status."

Lydia punches him in the side.

"Ow! I'd like to turn in my girlfriend for domestic abuse."

She punches him again, and he grabs her, and then they're kissing.

My heart feels full. "Seriously, thanks. You all still gonna be my friends now that I'm the most unpopular girl on campus?"

"You kidding?" Niles says. "Now that everyone knows you're a virgin, you'll have the entire senior class of guys after you."

"Gross," I say, but Niles and Kaj laugh.

"What're you doing tonight?" Lydia asks, but she knows. It's Friday.

"Going to this club called the Venue. Why, you wanna come?"

Her hips shake. "Seven thirty?"

"Right after family dinner. Which reminds me—I need to get to sixth before my family grounds me from fun."

"Go!" Kelly says and motions to the few papers still strewn about. "We got this one." She's ignored Jake this whole time, but her love for me is so palpable that I overlook it for the moment.

We get to my classroom nineteen minutes after the late

bell. Luckily, Ms. O'Toole will let it slide. I'll talk to her after class. I start to turn the door handle, then stop and turn to Jake.

"Um, do you—do you want to come to family dinner tonight?"

His dimple creases his cheek. "I thought you'd never ask."

Chapter Twenty-Five

I feel as if I'm going to puke into the meatloaf as I set it down onto the dinner table. Jake's here, sitting in Matt's usual spot, and the table is set like one of Mom's million-dollar open houses. Everyone looks at ease except me, who *just* remembered that Jake thinks I've told my parents about surfing. I'm not sure how I've pulled As in three AP classes and yet can't remember the SINGLE MOST CRITICAL PIECE OF INFORMATION THAT COULD RUIN MY LIFE. I guess I've been keeping those realities separate for so long that I forgot until right now when Jake says there's a sale at Dive N' Surf.

"Oh no," I say. I grip the sides of the table.

Jake thinks I'm talking about the sale. "I know, right? Dangerous!"

My father asks him, "Do you scuba dive?" because of course, Jake wouldn't be talking about the "surf" part of Dive N' Surf. Not in this household.

Jake's momentarily distracted from the sale, which he probably brought up because my wetsuit has a hole under one armpit. "Actually, yes." I notice how he makes eye contact and addresses my father with *yes* instead of *yeah*. Definitely a military kid. "My father taught me when I was eight."

"Good man."

"Yes. He was."

I don't miss the past tense, but Jake says it with a smile, and no one else notices. He adds, "Haven't been out recently, though. You dive?"

Dad nods. "In my early years with the Navy, I worked with dolphins—you know, training them for underwater mine location, object retrieval, swimmer detection."

"Incredible. Such intelligent creatures."

"And total assholes!" Dad laughs. He goes on to tell how the Navy puts the dolphins through drills in open water to test them. As soon as the dolphins do the drill, they're rewarded with fish back in their aquarium cages. The drill could take as little as an hour, and the dolphins know it. They also know they'll no longer be in open water once they finish the drill. So instead, they throw a party in the open water, playing and flopping around. They know what they have to do, but if they don't feel like it, which is every time, they play. I imagine my dad and his buddies out in the open water climbing back on the boats, grumbling and cursing at the dolphins as they switch out their tanks because the dolphins are taking their "damn sweet time frolicking." When they finally get hungry, they'll do the drill. By that time, Dad and his buddies are furious that it's taken seven hours to do a one-hour assignment. The worst part is, they still have to reward the dolphins, or as my dad calls them, "the smug SOBs," with buckets of fish for a job "most inefficiently done."

I've heard this story a zillion times—and Dad uses the

same phrases every time—but it still makes me laugh the way he tells it. I always think my dad looks younger when he talks about his enlisted days. Before the conversation dies and we can go back to surfing sales, I say, "These are lovely." Jake brought flowers (for Mom, not me) and she placed them on the table in a crystal vase I've never seen before, which doesn't surprise me. Mom works with a realtor staging homes for open houses. She designs the rooms from a warehouse of furniture so that when people come by, they think, *I could sit in this cozy chair and think about my life and feel perfect and intelligent. Why haven't I bought this house yet?*

"Oh, yes!" Mom adds. She beams at the flowers, then Jake. "I hope you rub off on my husband."

Dad chuckles, but I remember him bringing flowers home to Mom when I was a kid. Like, a lot. Then, when the accident happened, we received so many flowers, our house looked like a Rose Parade float. I wonder if flowers remind them of that painful time. Come to think of it, I haven't seen a petal in our home since Matt left rehab.

I've just gotta make it through dessert without any ocean talk. The rest of dinner, I flood Mom with questions about her home decorating so she can share with Jake what she does. So far so good. It tickles her that she's the focus, I can tell, but Dad interjects as he clears the plates and brings out the brownies.

"So Lovette tells us that you lived in Hawaii?"

"Yessir. Originally from here, but we were stationed there for five years when my dad was deployed eighteen months and then another eighteen."

"And now your father is stationed—?"

"Pendleton. I live with my aunt in Manhattan during the weekdays."

"Are there no schools there? Oceanside High?" Dad says it nicely, but I want to crawl under the table.

"Dad!"

"What? What'd I say?"

Jake pauses and picks at a brownie, deciding how he can answer. He doesn't look bothered when he finally says, "It's temporary. It's nice for my aunt, who lives by herself. My dad's schedule's pretty packed during the week, so it works out."

"Well!" says Mom, who's noticed that my eyes are screaming, *Please don't ask about his mom please don't please don't.* "We better clear the table so you can get to the Venue on time." She tilts her head at Jake. "It was so lovely to finally meet Lovette's boyfriend."

"Mom!"

Jake smiles. "It was lovely to meet you, too." Man, he's good. I'm dying, my insides curling in on themselves, sweaty armpits, the works, and he's all dimply and charming.

We're standing up to leave when Jake adds, "Maybe you could come watch us surf sometime."

No.

Please no.

No, no, no, *no.*

My mouth opens to a capital *O* and stays there. Dad stops mid-step, and Mom grips her empty plate, arms extended, like we're holding still for Jake to snap a family action photo. Only no one's smiling.

A dawning realization comes over Jake as his eyes land on me last. "If, that is, Lovette ever gets back out there."

Everything clicks back to life. "Oh," Mom says, "Lovette didn't tell you? I just assumed, since you've been so intimate."

"Mom!" *Jesus, couldn't you have given me a mom who says normal things?*

"She's a no-go for the water," Dad finishes. "Ocean, that is. You seen her in the pool? Regular fish." He salutes me like trout and bass are saving lives.

"Our son had an accident a few years back," Mom continues, setting down the plate. "We feel it's best if she—"

"She's a darn good swimmer." Dad isn't as ready to open up about the family secrets. "Don't know if she tells you how much she practices at the Y pool after work. I'm sure you know." He wipes the table with a napkin, which I've seen him do, well, never. "I tell her every year to go out for the swim team. But she always says no time left between her job and school."

"The ocean's . . . unpredictable." Mom wrings her hands.

"Of course," Jake agrees.

"But we love that you surf," Mom adds. "Nothing against that of course."

"Great sport," Dad says. "It's just not for Lovette."

Jake smiles. "I remember she used to be good."

"Jake remembers when I used to surf in sixth grade," I blurt. *He's not remembering last month and the killer heel edge I carved.*

"Ah," is all my father wants to say to that.

Mom says, "She always wanted to be like her brother."

"Shame," Jake says. "I remember being out on the waves with her and the other guys. Never saw someone who loved the sport more. Never watched her brother ride, but"—he pauses to put his jacket on—"she lit up the ocean without his help. That's for sure." Mom looks at me like I'm a stranger in her daughter's skin. She never considered that I liked surfing. It was my brother's thing. Dad's smile turns tight. He's at his limit, and Jake picks up on it. "Good night, Mr. and Mrs. Taylor. Thank you for your hospitality."

We don't talk the whole drive to the Venue. Jake has the music on full blast, and it bounces in my rib cage and hurts my ears. No room for other noises. Voices. Explanations. He doesn't want one, he informs me by the bass pounding in my skull. We park in the back near the service entrance. Finally I disconnect his phone from the speakers. The music jolts to a stop.

"I'm sorry," I start. He doesn't move. "I tried. But you saw them. It's impossible. There's no way . . ." His eyes stare out through the windshield, giving me no indication that he's listening. "If I told them, I'd never even be able to get away with swimming at night anymore. They'd be all over me to make sure I stayed away. I can't imagine losing the ocean. It's like a part of me would die. I couldn't risk it."

"So you lied to me?" He still won't look at me.

"Not exactly. You just assumed I told them. And I didn't have the heart—you were so excited—and I guess I didn't want that to go away." I reach out and touch his arm, but he flinches. I return my hand to my lap, a little confused that he's so irritated by this. "Maybe you didn't know what I was risking. It's the place where I feel closest to myself. And where I see God the most. Like, sometimes it's like He's *literally* out there with me in the water. I couldn't chance losing it all."

His voice is eerily calm. "I had every idea what you were risking. I know it was a shit ton of a big deal. Possibly losing what you love most. Leaving things is hard. That's why I was so impressed when you did it." He swallows. The next words are difficult. "You changed me by it." My insides warm at hearing that, but he turns away, like he's embarrassed by those words, and looks out of the driver's-side window. "I was like, if Lovette can face up to this, then maybe I can man up and—I mean, you were the *whole* reason—" He doesn't finish. He rakes his hand through his hair, pulls at it in sharp tugs. He hits the steering wheel, and it makes me jump. "You should go." And that's when I realize he's not coming.

"You're not being fair." I shift in my seat so I can face him. "You didn't correct my mom when she called you my boyfriend."

"Neither did you."

"I correct her every day! It's not like you told the truth."

"Why does it matter?"

"Because it's the truth!"

"Are you hearing yourself?"

I throw my head back against the headrest. "I'm just saying I'm not the only one lying."

"I'll drive back right now and tell your mom we're not dating. It doesn't matter to her. We're talking about things that matter."

"My mom thinks you're my boyfriend, and maybe that

doesn't matter. But you think it wouldn't matter to Hannah?"
I don't even know why I said that. I'm not concerned about
Hannah's feelings. But he's being totally unfair, and it's the
only ammunition I can think of. By the look on his face, it
worked. I see the way I've stunned him, and for one lousy
moment, I revel in it. I get out of the car and slam the door
for effect. He rolls down the window.

"I wouldn't know, Lovette." This makes me stop mid-turn.
I look back, and his laser eyes bore into me as he says, "I
stopped talking with her two weeks ago. Right after someone
taught me the reward was worth the risk."

He peels out of the parking lot, leaving me reeling.

Chapter Twenty-Six

"What happened?"

Lydia hands me a soapy stack of plates to rinse. This is at least the tenth time she's asked, and every time I say nothing. I'm not sure what I feel. I go between frustration with myself and anger at him. Why didn't Jake tell me about Hannah? It's been two weeks! For the past hour and a half, Lydia's been eyeing me with squinty suspicion, waiting for me to dish the dirt on why Jake's not here.

"He's fine. I'm fine. It's fine."

"I heard his tires screeching."

"Maybe he was in a hurry."

"Then you accelerate. You don't slam the gas pedal."

"Maybe he had a cramp in his foot."

"Or a churro up his butt."

"Lyds, it's nothing."

"Mentirosa."

Jake already called me a liar, but hearing it in another language just compounds the misery, like now all Spanish-speaking countries have also sided with Team Jake.

Uncle Joe is outside unpacking the delivery truck, and I wish he'd come back so she'd stop harassing me. He has a way of changing the subject and getting it back to Spanish phrases.

"Look!" I say, yanking my hands from the too-hot water. "I didn't tell my parents that I'm surfing again."

Lydia's hand dangles the sponge midair. "I thought you did."

"So did he."

"That's why he's mad?"

"Well, kind of." I swallow. "It's the reason he stopped talking to Hannah."

The sponge plops into the sink. Lydia claps her hands together and smears them across her mouth. Soap bubbles float in front of her wide eyes. "Sweet Jesus . . ."

She sees me frown, but it's not because she said His name in vain. Still, she points a finger up. "And, Oh Lady, Mother of Him."

"Lydia, stop." I wipe my hands on a towel and head for the service entrance. "I need some air."

○))) ● (((○

Outside, I look up. "Sorry," I say. "Sorry for so much."

I should trust God enough to tell my parents. And so what if they cut me off from the ocean? Well, then, they cut me off. I can suffer being a land mammal for a couple of years. God suffered the cross.

"Sheesh!" I say out loud. Talk about a rough comparison game. "You win," I say, half joking. I know God doesn't want me to just do the minimum. It's easy to do easy things for

God. He wants me to do the right thing in the face of hard things. And this, for me, is a hard thing.

I think back to my morning watching the surfers, when I felt God ask me, *"Do you love the ocean more than Me?"* Was I in love with the created thing more than the Creator? I remember being appalled. I'd never deny Him before giving up the ocean. But aren't I denying Him by lying to my parents? Doing something against God to keep doing what I want?

I saw the hurt in Jake's eyes, and I get why God says that He *hates* lying. It hurts people. It puts people in unfair positions: *"I stopped talking with her two weeks ago. Right after someone taught me the reward was worth the risk."*

Two weeks. Again, a surge of righteous anger rockets through me. Why am I the bad guy? Why am I the one accused of keeping secrets?

"You're the one who brought him into my life," I accuse the starless sky, and I know it sounds bratty. "All I'm saying is, my parents told me not to surf. I listened to them before I met Jake. Okay, fine, I was swimming, but that's not the point! I didn't ask to meet Jake! I was doing fine!"

I don't think I've ever been mad at God. Not when Matt was in a coma for a month, not when my parents were MIA for the eleven months after, not even when they got him a pimp-my-ride car and me a used bike. But now I'm annoyed with God, like He should know better.

"See?" I say and fold my arms. "See what Jake's doing?" And what I mean is, *See what You did by bringing him into my life?*

I stomp back into the Venue. The club is starting to pick up, and the music echoes in my ears and chest. "There you are!" I hear Lydia say from the dark hallway near the restrooms, but it's me who grabs her by the elbow and leads her to the dance floor. I feel this energy and frustration pulsing through me, and I don't feel like standing like a pole tonight. In the middle of the floor, I close my eyes, letting the music take over my emotions. Lydia squeals in delight and grabs me by the hands. Together we salsa and twirl and shake, and in three songs my shirt is drenched and my hair is sopping wet.

"Ooooh! Someone's been hiding those hips!"

I have to admit, I get why Lydia loves this. During the fourth song, however, a strong arm intercepts me.

Jake.

Jake, who should almost be back to Camp Pendleton by now.

He tries to lead me away, but I dig my sneakers into the slippery floor. His eyes pinball between me and Lydia.

"Come on," he says, his voice gentle but firm. "You're drunk."

His warm hand feels good against me, which makes me angrier. I laugh. "I am many things, Jake Evans, but drunk is not one of them."

He looks at Lydia. "Help me out."

She shakes her head. "She's sober."

His eyes turn furious. "Then what the hell, Lydia! You text me that she's in trouble, so I flip around when I'm over halfway to San Diego, breaking every traffic rule to get here, and she's fine?"

"She's most definitely not fine."

"Lydia!" I'm horrified. "You *texted* him?"

She ignores me and says to Jake, "In the ten years that I've known her, I've never seen her like that. It's, like, te caga en su leche."

Before I can translate, he snaps, "I didn't *crap in her milk*! Why don't you ask her what she lied about?"

I retort, "No, Lydia. Why don't you ask him what *he* lied about?"

He turns to me. "What?" He lets go of my arm. "You can't be serious!"

"Two weeks!" I shout over the speakers, and I'm glad for the music because I want to yell anyway. I'm shoving down the other emotions—the ones that whisper how he drove an hour back here to check on me. No. He doesn't get to be self-righteous about this. I want him to get out of my face, and I want him to put his arms around me, and I hate that I feel so many things that contradict one another. "You cut off Hannah two weeks ago, and you hid it from me!"

"Hid it fro— You wouldn't talk to me!"

"You embarrassed me in front of my friends."

"Because her name showed up on my cell?"

"You answered!"

"That's what you do with a phone call!"

"And you called her 'babe'!"

"She was crying!"

"Because you told her not to call anymore?" Lydia interjects.

"No! Because her dad was deployed!"

I can't exactly make fun of that, so I stay silent and glower.

Lydia breaks the tension with her giggle.

"What!" both Jake and I snap at her.

"You two look like me and Kaj arguing on the dance floor."
It's true. We've been waving our arms around and shouting
while the rest of the clubbers do their best to ignore and dance
around us. He motions with his head, and we walk to the bar.
Lydia follows, not wanting to miss one moment of this.

"When did you cut things off?" I ask.

"Same day she called. Later that night." He talks like
we're discussing the tide charts. "I realized we were using
each other." Then he adds, "Hannah and me. For so long we
needed each other, ya know, we understood what the other
was feeling. But my dad's not gonna be deployed anymore,
and Hannah lives across an ocean. Our lives are different.
Sure, we cared about each other, but how do you move on
if you keep calling each other every time things get shitty?"

Lydia whistles an intake of breath. "You cut her off the
night her dad was deployed?"

He glares at her. "There's never a good time for hard
things." Then he turns his glare to me. "I'm not about
dragging something out and leading her on. That would be
lying." He digs those last words into me and twists. "And
someone taught me to face things head-on."

"You lied to me for two weeks!"

"You avoided me for two weeks! You didn't give me the
chance to be honest. And why does it matter? What the hell
would change if you knew?"

"I just would know!" I realize how ridiculous that sounds
the second I say it, and it makes me huff. Some strands of hair

are wrapped around my sweaty face and stuck to the sides of my mouth, but I don't swipe them away.

"You don't even date. It *doesn't* matter."

"Don't put that on me. It wouldn't matter to you if I *did* date!"

"Like hell it wouldn't!"

Lydia whistles again. I blink. Jake looks like he can't believe he said it either. I feel all my defenses go down. This changes things.

"But I promised God . . ." I trail off weakly.

"You know, when I was four," he starts, but this time his tone is soft, "I told a girl that I didn't like her because I only liked trains and dinosaurs." This makes me smile—I can't help it—and he gently nudges my shoe with his. "You think He doesn't know that your mind is changing about things? You were twelve. Give yourself a break."

"True," I admit, "but He doesn't change. I know He doesn't want me having sex."

He laughs and drops his head back, exasperated. "God! I'm not asking you to."

I fold my arms. Think everything over. My knees are weak, and my throat is so busy swallowing all the butterflies, it's hard to talk. I manage to gulp out, "Fine."

He pauses. Squints his eyes like I blurred out of focus. Then he opens them again. "Fine?"

"Yeah. Fine." He tilts his head, and his dimple creases like a solo parenthesis. He's smiling, but with only half of his face, and somehow it feels better than a full smile. It means he knows what this means.

Lydia puts a hand on both of our shoulders, and at first

I think it's to interrupt, but maybe it's to hold her up. She looks confused. "¿Cómo fue? Did you just become girlfriend and boyfriend right now?"

I smile, my eyes never leaving Jake's. "Es posible."

He smiles back. "It's more than possible, mannequin." He reaches for my hand—interlocks only his index finger with mine—and I squeeze, and it's as exhilarating as I imagine a kiss would be. My knees become rubber. He looks down at our fingers. "Is this allowed?"

"I don't know. We should make a list."

"A list?"

I've made lists before when it comes to my future husband. All the qualities I want. *Loves the Lord, confident, makes me laugh, athletic, at least 6'2", wears a watch, wants to build houses in Mexico, bilingual, loves dogs, left-handed.* Okay, so I've been specific, but I figured if God had a decade to work on him, then I didn't need to skimp. But, gosh, I've never made a list of what I should and shouldn't *do* with a boyfriend, because in my wildest dreams, I never imagined a boyfriend as part of God's plan. Is it?

"We have to make a list," I repeat.

"Like a to-do list?"

Lydia waggles her eyebrows. "You got a lotta boxes to check off, Jake!"

"Ew! Lydia, no." I smack her arm. "Like a list of what we can and can't do. What God is not okay with. I'm not giving Him up for you."

"I don't want you to." He squeezes my finger again, and I almost fall over.

I look into his brown eyes, darker than the night against his sandy, floppy hair. They seem to pierce right into my soul, like they know I'm freaked out and excited and that I love maraschino cherries and hate wet socks. And weirdly, I can see that he's feeling some of the same—the excited and freaked-out part. I don't know about the wet socks, but in a month or so maybe I'll know, and that erases the fear. He's giving me the green light to get to know the things that others don't. And for the first time in my life, I don't want to think about my future husband. I want to think of Jake. I want to think of all of him, and I can't wait for tomorrow because tomorrow means I'll know more about him than I did today. Than I do right now. My heart does some tic-tacs, building momentum.

"A list," he repeats. "Okay. We'll make a list." He nods once. "But first, you have to do something you've never done before."

He leans in slow. My heart plummets, and Lydia's eyes go wide. His cheek touches mine, and it's soft and warm.

I feel the breath of his whisper as it tickles my ear. "You need to give me your phone number."

Chapter Twenty-Seven

"I can't believe you don't like Nutella," Jake says. "We might have to break up already."

My phone is wedged between my head and the pillow, and my ear is hot from two hours of talking. I'm guessing it's midnight from where the moon is outside my window—but I don't want to take my phone away from my ear to check the time.

It's Sunday night. I should be asleep. But I want tonight to be like last night, when he hung up only after he knew I'd fallen asleep. Jake wasn't at church today—he never comes on Sundays—but it feels like an eternity, not two days, since I've seen him. Even though we talked on the phone Friday and Saturday nights until our throats were hoarse from whispering. Even though we texted endless emojis and memes during the day while I worked on my million school projects. It's not enough. I want to feel his shoulder and how it barely brushes mine when he stuffs his hands into his jeans pockets—how before, he made it look like an accident, but now he leans in and keeps us connected, like when he walked me to my bike on Friday night.

"Nutella is gross, says the girl who eats crushed bug guts." I can hear his smile in his voice, the big one that creases both his cheeks with dimples. "Good thing we don't kiss." Last night he asked me my favorite dessert. And when I told him red-velvet cake, he explained how the dye's made from grinding up cochineal insects with water. I didn't believe him, so I searched it on my phone. When I told him afterward that I didn't lose my appetite, and I'd eat them anyway, because it turns out those insects are delicious, he laughed and said, "That's hot."

My insides skip even when he's joking. I'm feeling things in the past two days I didn't know lived inside of me. Before, sure, my heart would quicken when he was around. Now, when I talk to him, I feel like my heart is going to leap out and onto the phone separating us. It worries me. It thrills me. It worries me that it thrills me.

"Speaking of kissing," I say, "we need to talk about this list."

"Ahhh," Jake says. "The list." He hums Darth Vader's "The Imperial March." "Okay, let's do this. Do you want to write it down so it's official?"

"Ugh. I don't want to turn the lights on."

"What are you, fifty years old? Write it on your phone."

I whisper, "Then I have to put you on speaker."

He chuckles. "I'll do it." I hear him rummaging. "Okay. I found Post-its. Ready, go."

I take a deep breath. He's being playful about this, and it's making me grin, but I can see my Bible on my nightstand that I haven't opened for the past two nights, and it sobers me. "Number one. No sex."

"Oh, come on," Jake says. "Does that even need to go on the list? Isn't that, like, a given? You're wasting trees."

"It all needs to go on the list."

"Apparently saving the environment isn't on your list."

"Jake! Be serious."

"Okay. Sex. Got it."

"*No* sex."

"Right. That's what I meant."

"Wait," I say, and I don't know why I haven't thought to ask this. "Have you had sex before?"

Silence.

"Jake?"

"Come on, Lovette." I hear something on his side of the phone shuffling, like he's shifting in his bed.

"Hannah?" I press.

Silence again, and I feel like I'm going to throw up.

"Look," he says, and I can tell he's not smiling through the phone anymore. "You set a pretty high bar. It's not a bad bar. It's just—I don't think my past would make the cut, and I'm not sure I'm comfortable talking about it." I start to protest, but he clarifies, "Yet. Not comfortable *yet.* Here's what I know about us—not me and Hannah, but me and you. You don't want to have sex outside of marriage, right?"

"Yeah," I murmur.

"Okay, then. I can promise you I will never put you in that position. But you gotta promise me that when I start sharing about my past, you won't judge me for it. That fair?"

I think of the verse "I—yes, I alone—will blot out your sins for my own sake and will never think of them again." God doesn't judge me, even when He has a right to. I swallow. "Yeah, but . . ." I trail off.

I want to ask so much more, but he cuts me off. "Number two."

"Fine," I say. "Number two. No kissing."

He's quiet again, and I hear him blowing "ch" sounds through full cheeks, like he's contemplating. "Can I ask why?" he finally asks.

"I want it to be with my husband."

"So it's true."

"What's true?"

"The paper Cecilia made copies of. Your essay. Part of me thought she made stuff up."

My cheeks burn. "She did! She added things."

"But not that thing."

I hesitate. "No." How do I put this into words? "One day, God's going to bring me His best." I stop. "Not that you're not His best. It's just—I mean, hopefully I'll be the best to that guy, too." I groan. Why is this so hard to verbalize?

"You believe your husband is going to kick ass and that he's worth saving every kiss for."

How does he do that? "Yes. Exactly."

"And you want your man to know that you believed in God enough to hold out for him because you knew he'd be worth it."

"It's like you're in my head." He laughs, and it brings my thoughts back together. "So why have all these intimate memories with someone who's not my husband?"

"Then what are we doing?" he says, and it's soft, almost romantic.

"I don't know," I murmur and press the phone closer. I'm afraid he'll want to hang up, to end things right here.

"I like you," he says, unashamed. Relief floods through me. "I like making memories with you. If I don't end up being your husband, are you gonna be embarrassed about this some day? About us?"

"No!" I blurt out. "I love us!" Then I gasp because I don't know why I said that, and I wasn't thinking, but it just came out. "I mean—"

He chuckles under his breath, and I remember how it felt when his lips tickled my ear at the Venue, when he asked for my phone number. "Good," he says, with the tone that tells me one corner of his mouth is turned up enough to dent one cheek. "I love us too."

He exhales loudly through the phone. "All right then, no kissing. God."

I giggle. "I hope you're talking to Him and not using His name in vain."

"Oh, I'll be talking to Him all right. I'll be begging Him for some serious self-control."

I ignore that. "Great! Number three. Everything in between kissing and sex."

He whistles the sound of a cartoon bomb dropping from the sky. "Damn, you bring it."

"Maybe I should make that number two."

"Make what number two?"

"The stuff in between."

"I'm sorry. I don't know what this *stuff in between* is. I think you're going to have to specify."

Blood rushes to my face again. How can he do that so many times in one conversation? I lower my voice. "You are *not* making me say it. You know. The *stuff.*"

"Between kissing and sex? Lots of words come between *kissing* and *sex* in the dictionary. Like *mac and cheese.* Can we eat mac and cheese together? Does that need to be a husband-only memory?"

"Stop! You're totally making fun. Look, clothes stay on, hands stay off. If that's too hard for you to comprehend, then maybe you should rethink college."

He groans. "College apps. Don't remind me."

I've been putting off the future. The present has been enough. "You applying for local?"

"Maybe . . . ," he trails off. "Hey, don't change the subject. We're making a list here."

I laugh. "Do you wear a watch?" I wince as soon as I say it. How do these things come out of my mouth before I think?

"Huh? Uh, yeah. My diver's watch. You've seen it. Why?"

I think back to my husband list. *Wears a watch. 6'2". Makes me laugh.* "Just curious," I say, biting my bottom lip with my teeth to keep from smiling too wide.

"Do you have a number four?" he asks.

I don't, but I should. I need to make sure I can do this boyfriend thing and not lose sight of God. "How about—no dark rooms alone together?"

"Okay, probably a good idea. 'See numbers one through three.' Are we done with our rule book?"

"For now," I say.

"Good. How about we make a schedule for surfing?"

"Yes!"

"You tell your parents yet?"

"I'm still surfing, so . . . no."

He sighs, but his words are gentle. "It's only gonna get harder the more you wait."

"Are you honest with your parents about everything?"

He's quiet for a handful of awkward heartbeats. Finally, I hear his voice. "So I'll pick you up at six in the morning?"

I exhale and it comes out as a one-syllable laugh. "No. I need to work on leg strength. I'll bike to Mike's and meet you at six forty."

○))) ● (((○

I fall asleep around 3:00 a.m., my 6:00 a.m. alarm blaring way too early. I text him that I'm skipping surfing this morning, hit the snooze, and then pedal to school on wobbly legs, so tired that I don't even think about the repercussions of Cecilia's prank.

It doesn't hit me until Tuesday, when somebody has taped a blown-up condom on my locker. I'm so shocked, I can only stare at it. Lydia arrives, rips it off, and holds it high above her head. She shouts in a voice that could cut glass: "Who's the boy with the small penis who donated his condom as a flotation device for my chihuahua?"

The crowd of students laughs, and I wrap my arms around her. "Thank you," I whisper.

"They're all tontos. I got you."

I wish I was strong like her. I don't normally feel weak, but ever since Cecilia did that last week, I've felt like I have a "Kick me" sign taped to my back. *Take this, please,* I say to God. *Help me not feel dumb.*

In English class, Cecilia smirks like she's won some contest. At first, I think it'll get better if I wait it out, but as each day passes, I find myself dreading her smirk more and more. If she walks by my desk, I look at the bulletin board. It feels like she's taller than I remember, and her sweats swish louder when she walks.

Our whole friend group has been especially nice—I wonder if they notice how dumb I feel—and Niles even offers me his Hot Cheetos, which might as well be his firstborn. Kelly's been affectionate, putting her head on my shoulder at lunch, playing with my hair when she talks to me, the usual Kelly stuff.

Lydia slaps me on the butt when she notices me slouching, and it works. I stand tall. "Tontos," she reminds me, and I smile. It's amazing how the right word from a friend can be a perfect answer to prayer.

Jake makes sure I'm okay in his own quiet "new boyfriend" way. Nobody can really tell that anything is different, but I know. He doesn't even hold my hand as he walks me to class, but his shoulder stays connected to mine, gently bumping me on purpose here and there just so I'll look up at him, and he always looks back at me in a way that makes me feel like I'm the star of a TV show.

○) 〉 ﻝ ● ﴾ ﴾ ﴾ ○

The following Wednesday night at youth group, Kelly pulls me into the bathroom.

"Listen, I've felt God's conviction all week and this has

been on my heart, like, every second." She grabs both my hands and then scrunches her eyes like it's painful to speak. When she opens them, she says, "Lydia's starting rumors about you."

I cock my head to the side. "Really?"

"Yeah. She told our whole friend group that you and Jake were dating. And I tried to tell her that you don't date, but she called me some name in Spanish, so she's clearly out to get you."

"We *are* dating."

Her hands drop from mine. "But." She shakes her head like she's waking up from a bad dream. "I thought." Her mouth opens and her lower jaw shifts to the side. "But I was going to date him."

I'm thoroughly confused. "You have a boyfriend."

"Well, uh, yeah! *Now* I do. But back then. And you can't date someone who your best friend dated."

"Wait. You never dated him."

"Duh. He had a girlfriend."

"They broke up."

"TFTI!"

Thanks for the invite? Invite to date him? I'm so lost. "I didn't know you'd want to date him if you were with Dave!"

"I don't!" She blows out a exasperated groan. "But I *could* have! Like, before, when I almost did."

"But you didn't."

"Probably only because he didn't pray about it. Anyway, it means you can't. Friend code."

This surge of protection swells in my chest. It hasn't even been a week, but I don't like anyone telling me I can't be with

Jake. I've always been honest with Kelly. I take her hands in mine, the way she would, and tell her with sincere eyes and a loving voice, "I'm already dating him, Kells. And I don't think 'friend code' is in the Bible."

"Uh, yeah it is . . . Proverbs . . . 'Though one may be overpowered, two can defend themselves. A cord of three strands is not quickly broken.'"

I'm pretty sure that has nothing to do with friend code. "What? Who's the third strand?"

"We are, you and me! We're three strands!"

"Kelly, that makes no sense."

She scrunches her face, and I think she sees it too. "Okay, whatever. Look, if you date Jake, you won't be able to give your husband everything like you wanted to."

Ouch. That took a turn. I pause, rubbing my eyes with the backs of my wrists.

"I know." I link my fingers in the side loops of her jeans. "I actually think it'll be okay. I'm being careful."

I see the inner wrestling match contorting her face. But she looks at my fingers looped in her jeans and relents. She smiles weakly. "I hope so. It's *your* future you're forever altering."

"Geez, Kell."

"I'll pray."

"Thank you."

But as we walk out of the bathroom, she adds, "I'm sure you've seen his Insta."

She knows I'm on social media maybe once a month, so I don't know why she said that, but we're back in the youth room and sitting down for Brett's talk before I can respond.

Chapter Twenty-Eight

I never check Instagram. I forget about it as the next two weeks fall into a rhythm of workouts, homework, job, and surfing. Mondays and Thursdays I bike to the beach, do a leg-and-arm workout on the sand, and have my morning Bible study. After work, Jake meets me at Mike's, and we surf at night. Tuesdays and Wednesdays, we surf before school. After work on Tuesdays, I run the six miles home from Billy's Buns. And Wednesday nights, we meet at youth group and smile at each other from across the room. During worship and Brett's talk, Jake sits next to me and our arms touch, elbows to wrists. Sometimes I remember the sermons. Other times, I'm too focused on smoothing my arm hairs from standing on end from his touch. I know he notices. He keeps his eyes down during worship, his eyelashes brushing his cheeks, and it looks like he's praying, but he's really hiding his smile. His dimples give him away.

Jake coaches me in a way that would make Old Man Mike proud. Out on the water, he'll watch me free surf for a few sets and then point out where I'm weak, giving me drills to improve them.

One night, about two weeks into our training plan, we've borrowed Mike's shortboards to work on connecting turns. The moon isn't full, but the night is clear and the crescent reflects off the white of our surfboards, making them bright against the dark ocean. We're past the break, straddling our boards as the water laps softly, tap-tapping against our wetsuited thighs. "So, you're doing great on your basic rail turn," he says, using his hand to demonstrate what my board is doing while I ride. "You know how to place your weight on the outside rail down the wave and then the inside rail on the way back up."

"But I can't turn to head down the line without slowing down."

"Exactly. Your rhythm is off. You're compressing your stance at the bottom carve, but you're not extending enough at the top carve."

"Really? I feel like I am."

"You're on your haunches like a bunny rabbit."

I splash him. "So then what?"

"So when you do the top carve next time, try a soul arch, just to get the feel of extending."

"A soul arch?" I say. "On the top of a wave? I'll totally fall!"

"That's the point. I want you to fall."

"Why?"

"You're afraid to."

I sit up straighter on my board. "No, I'm not."

"Well, something in you is. Maybe you need to get your brother out of your mind."

I never thought I was thinking about Matt. But maybe I am. Maybe something in me *is* afraid I'll fall like him.

"It could happen," I say. "A head injury like my brother's. I mean, I know it was a freak thing. But it could happen."

He shakes his head. "Not the way you surf. Besides, your brother fell forward, and his board hit his head from behind. Remember for this drill you're falling *away* from the board. Above it. The board can't smack you from behind if it's in front of you."

"That's if I finish my turn. If I don't, I'll fall backward down the wave, and the board will be above me."

"Well, then, finish your turn."

Annoyed, I twirl my legs in fast eggbeaters and turn my board, then flop onto my stomach to paddle for the waves.

I catch my first attempt, riding down the line to the left. After my bottom side turn, I ride back up the wave, and at the top, I try for a soul arch. I extend tall, but I haven't finished my turn, so I end up panicking and leaping behind the wave. I dive headfirst and feel the leash tug at my ankle hard as my board gets pounded by the wave.

"Again!" I hear him shout as soon as I surface.

The second time, I complete the turn and start to arch my back and tip my chin to the sky, but I lose my balance and back flop.

When I pull myself back onto my board, I swallow a mouthful of seawater, and it makes me cough and gag a little. I blow snot out of my nose and wipe it away with my hands.

"Again!" I hear from across the water.

The third time I don't complete a soul arch, but I feel my

legs straighten, my knees almost locked, and I get what he means about extending my body. I'm tall and leaning, so I attempt the topside turn. I'm on the outside rail, and there's such little surface area of the board in the water that I fly down the face of the wave. I feel the bottom of the board slap the water, and I bend my knees to absorb the shock and create some drag to ride it out.

I pump a fist in the air at the bottom, and I hear him whooping behind me. I just connected my first rail-to-rail turn, bottom side and top side.

He paddles up next to me. "That was sick!" He holds up a forearm, and I tap it with mine. I'm grinning so big my cheeks hurt, even though my teeth are chattering.

"Come on," he says. "Let's get you warm." He means a shower back at my house, but I honestly feel warmer when he's peeling me out of my wetsuit at Old Man Mike's and wrapping me in a towel.

○)))) ● ((((○

It's been three weeks since we started dating, and I'm wondering if anyone else besides our friend group notices. He calls me "Lovey" sometimes instead of Lovette, and I guess that's something, but I've called Kim my coworker "Kimmie" or "Kimber" and nobody assumes we're an item. Before, I didn't want others to notice, but now, I'm dying to tell everyone. I want to wear a sign every time we're together that says "I'm with him." We talk on the phone, we surf, and we walk to classes together, but other than that, it looks like we're just buddies. That used to make me feel relieved, but now, it bums me out if I'm totally honest. We definitely hug more, and he'll throw an arm around me sometimes after a good surf session, but it's brief because it's not like he can do that when we're carrying our boards from the beach.

On November 10 at youth group, Brett announces the annual lock-in scheduled for February. This year, our theme is Six-Sport Saturday, and before we lock ourselves in the church for the night, we'll be outside doing six sports over the course of one day. Our first sport will be skiing or snowboarding up at our local ski resort, Mt. High. I wonder if Jake looks as good when he's snowboarding as he does when he's surfing.

During big-group game, all fifty of us have a balloon tied to both ankles, and we're hopping around the room like one-legged kangaroos trying to stomp on one another's balloons. Once both of our balloons are popped, we're out, and tonight it's girls against guys. Dave and Jake team up against me, and I'm sprinting on one foot across the thin layer of carpet. Dave lands on one of my balloons with two feet, making a loud firecracker sound when the latex explodes under his weight, and I see my chance to stomp on one of his balloons with my other foot. Unfortunately, it was a setup. Jake surprises me from behind and pops my last remaining balloon as I stomp down on Dave's. Dave sacrifices only one of his balloons, but I'm out.

They high-five each other and take off to corner another girl. On the sidelines, Kelly waves me over. "They team up on you too?" she says. "Gah! Why didn't we think of that?"

"I know, right? They're like pack animals. Find the defenseless one."

She rubs her hands on her jeans, then reaches her arms high and stretches, like she's trying to look casual. "So I take it things are still good with Jake?"

"Yeah. Really good. He's great."

She's quiet after that, and then we're dismissed to small groups. Tonight's topic is about the danger of gossip.

Some girls are sharing about the horrible gossip at their schools. Jill says how this girl at her school, Jenny Kitchins, had an STD and how someone posted about it online in the school's math chat room.

"That's horrible," Christa says. "Wait. Jenny Kitchins from Green Elementary?"

"Yes!" Krista (with a *K*) responds. "I heard the same thing. Can you believe it?"

"Do you know what kind of STD?"

"Girls!" our group leader Candy interrupts. "We're talking about how gossip can be *damaging*. We don't need to know details."

"I only wanted to know so I could pray for her," Christa says.

Kelly tilts her mouth toward my ear. She whispers, "You never looked at his Insta, did you?"

"I totally forgot." This feels like more gossip. I try to shift the topic. "How're you and Dave?"

"Good. We're praying about God's leading right now."

I'm not sure what this means, so I say, "I'm glad. How long have you been dating now?"

"We're not."

"You're not?"

"No. We're courting."

"Ohhh," I say, nodding like I know the difference. Are Jake and I *courting*? Should we be?

Candy has us end by reading Paul's words to the Ephesian church: "Do not let any unwholesome talk come out of your mouths, but only what is helpful for building others up according to their needs, that it may benefit those who listen."

Wow. I love that verse. I'll have to memorize it when I get a chance. I wonder how different school would look if everyone listened to Paul's words.

○)))) ● ● (((○

Maybe Kelly didn't really hear the verse because immediately after Brett's sermon and closing prayer, she says innocently, "Jake, do you have an Instagram?"

Jake's sitting on the other side of me, and he pulls out his phone. "Pretty sure you follow me," he says to her.

Caught, Kelly backpedals. "Right. But Lovette doesn't."

Jake chuckles to himself. He can see right through her words.

"It's okay," I say. I don't want him to think I'm part of this, but Jake unlocks his phone, opens the app, and hands it to me. Kelly's mouth drops open. He smiles. "Go ahead."

I feel him watching as I scroll through photos of his life in Hawaii. I click on the most recent upload: a pic of a girl in a bikini. She's freckled, and her hair falls over the front of her tanned shoulders in sticky saltwater strands. She looks like she's clipped from a magazine.

best view in #oahu

My stomach feels hollow when I read his caption. I scroll down and click on another. It's Jake and a bunch of guys in front of a place called Joe's Coffee Shop.

bros before Joes

Another with the guys in boardshorts and bare chests, up on some rock, their arms draped over one another.

#summatime

Jake's finger reaches over and taps a thumbnail that I saw but didn't have the nerve to click. There, in full screen now, are Jake and Hannah on a beach towel. It's a selfie—I can see Jake's long arm as it holds the camera away from them— and they're kissing at sunset. I cancel out of it, my stomach turning. Jake reaches over and clicks back on it.

"Scroll down to the date," he says.

I do. I see the year.

"Fourteen months ago," he says.

"But you haven't deleted any," Kelly says, but a little hesitant now. This obviously isn't going according to her plan.

He doesn't seem fazed, but he clicks on the most recent photo. It's the one of Hannah looking into the camera. The cute bikini, perfect salty hair, and dancing freckles one.

"This was my last post," he says, his eyes on me even though Kelly's with us. "It was taken almost twelve months ago to the day. I haven't posted on Insta in a year. Lost interest. And all this"—he waves his phone at me—"it's my past. It's a good one. I don't regret that I dated Hannah. No reason to erase her."

"She's pretty," I admit.

He nods. "She is."

He puts the phone back in his pocket. Dave appears from nowhere. "Hey, babe," he says to Kelly. "You listen to my latest song I put up on SoundCloud?"

"Hi!" She jumps up. "No, but let's do that right now."

"Actually me and Randy are having a jam session. You wanna come listen?"

She leads the way, pulling him behind her. He looks back and waves with his free hand.

There's a Ping-Pong game behind us with a lot of shouting and laughing. The music from the speakers blares, a punk Christian band with too many horns, and we can hear Randy's and Dave's guitars in the corner as they start strumming. Jake leans close. "I'll shout you out on Snap, Insta, Twitter, tumblr, Facebook. You want me to do that?"

I shake my head, but I'm smiling again. "I'd never see it."

"Yeah, me neither." He takes my hand and places it face down on top of his hand, palm to palm. His fingers extend a good inch longer than mine. "So why don't we start with the stuff that matters to *us*."

He shifts his hand and laces his fingers between mine, gently squeezing. We're holding hands. Oh my gosh, we're in youth group and we're holding hands. He catches me biting my lip.

"Oh no, is this on the list?"

"No, but . . ." I look around. No one seems to notice. Do I care if they notice? Should I?

"Good." He squeezes my hand with his, and I squeeze back. He guides me with his eyes to look at our hands, my right and his left, our fingers tightly intertwined, and I wonder if he's thinking what I'm thinking, that our fingers fit perfectly— like God made them that way. His thumb rubs the inside of my wrist, and it makes me inhale sharply.

"You okay?" he asks.

"Of course," I whisper. My wrist still tingles. "Kelly holds my hand, but . . ." I feel my cheeks grow warm. "This feels different."

He smiles. "It better."

Chapter Twenty-Nine

The next week at school, Jake and I walk down the halls as a two-man army, locking hands. I think of the verse Kelly recited a few weeks back at youth group: *"Though one may be overpowered, two can defend themselves."* I feel stronger somehow when I'm linked to Jake, and the new curious glances make me stand a little taller. When a tenth-grader named Gus yells across the hall, "I thought you didn't touch guys, Lovette!" I gasp, removing my hand from Jake's and grabbing my wrist with my other hand. "Oh no!" I shriek, staring at it like it's diseased now. Then I look at Gus and laugh. It throws him off his game. He blinks and turns away. When I return my hand to Jake's, he squeezes.

Lydia catches up to us from behind and slaps me on the butt. "That's right," she says, head nodding toward where Gus stood a few moments ago. "Tontos."

I wish that God was enough for me to get over my embarrassment—to stand tall regardless of the lies (and truths) Cecilia spread about me—but I think of Moses in battle holding the staff of God, and how as long as he held up his hands, the Israelites were winning, but when he'd lower his hands, the Israelites would start losing. But old Moses got tired, so they gave him this rock to sit on, and then Aaron and Hur literally held his hands up for him, and thus became the coolest wingmen in history. It reminds me that God gets it. He knows we get tired, and that sometimes others need to "hold up our hands." Or in Jake's case, just hold our hand.

The Wednesday before Thanksgiving, youth group is canceled, and my parents are out shopping after work. It's a perfect time to hit the water in the afternoon, especially since I won't be going that much in the next few days. Not with my brother home and watching me like a hawk. Jake texts that he'll be late, which makes sense. I barely saw him at school even though I know he was there. He wasn't at our usual meeting spots during passing period or at lunch, and I finally found him tucked away in the library working on college apps. He minimized his screen when I walked up, so I joked, "You don't have to be embarrassed about watching Harry Styles videos. He's a good singer." This got a smile out of him. He stood and gave me a hug and a sorry.

"Just didn't want to bring you down with all this," he said. "I'm way behind on these apps, which is totally my fault." He looked more stressed than I've ever seen him. I mean, he still has until November 30, but by the look on his face, he's just started a couple of them.

At three thirty, I splash out into the water alone, enjoying the rare windless afternoon. Stomach to my board, I arch my back and tip my chin to the sky, closing my eyes and thinking a simple but genuine, *Thanks. It's perfect.* The sun beats down on my neoprene, and I soak in the heat on my back, dipping my hands in the cold almost-December water.

There's a cluster of about five or six guys on the north side of Lifeguard Tower 27, so I paddle over to them to get a surf report. "How is it?" I ask when I'm in earshot.

An older forty-something guy answers, "Pretty flat, but a good set here and there."

"Well, well, well." I know that voice.

Trevor Walker.

He's behind two other guys, and he paddles around them and flips his wet hair back so he can see me better, or maybe to show off his pretty hair. "Hey, Trev," I say and offer a mini wave hello.

"The Legend is back on her wave rider."

"That's the rumor," I say, and look back at the horizon.

"Speaking of rumors, heard you signed up for the All Wave Junior Open."

I nod.

"Babe, I'd take you out any night of the week. Always thought you were cute."

I feel my eyebrows crowd against each other. Huh?

"It's all right. Cecilia told me you signed up. I told her about your crush back when we were in JGs."

My crush? Junior Guards? On *him?*

There are so many things wrong with this conversation, but I don't have words. My mouth clicks open, but someone yells, "Outside!" and we see the set coming in. I turn and paddle, but Trevor is on my side ten feet away. He sees me paddling for it, but he doesn't pull out. I pop to my feet and bark out a warning. No response. He never even looks back. He does a roundhouse turn, comes off the bottom, and a collision is imminent. I kick out, but the lip of the wave smacks me in the chest, and my board is sucked over the falls, nearly pulling me over as well. Adrenaline is pulsing through me. It takes me a minute to retrieve my board, but eventually I heave myself back on and meet him as he's paddling back out to his pack of boys.

"What the heck, Trevor? You snaked my wave."

"Hey, can't help it if you can't keep up."

"Can't kee— You fully knew that was my wave."

He laughs like I have no clue. "Hardly."

"You do that at All Wave, and you'll lose points."

"We'll see."

Another set is coming, and he turns to paddle for it, so I wait for him to disappear. I catch the second wave clean and quick, and I feel the weightless plunging drop of my stomach as I race down the wall and turn hard onto my inside rail, soaring back up. Maybe it's the adrenaline or the annoyance, but I'm not paying attention, and I surf right up the lip and catch some unexpected air, back flopping behind the wave.

Trevor paddles up. "A little rusty, huh?" He sits up onto his board. "I could work with you." The way he says it hints at more. I can't believe he's still trying.

"You have a girlfriend, remember?"

He shrugs as an answer. Unreal.

"Well I have a boyfriend," I say, and pop myself up to sitting. "He's on his way."

Trevor searches the expanse of the beach. It's empty today. "That so?"

"Yeah, he's just late. Actually, thanks for reminding me. I

should probably go check on him."

"Good luck with that," he says. I paddle away from him, but I hear his voice as he regroups with his guys, "Not nearly as cute as the freshman I hooked up with last week, but she's got mad skills on that board."

The comment about the freshman he "hooked up with" echoes in my brain as I catch a small one-footer, riding down the line as it angles for the shore. I don't turn or try anything fancy. I'm too busy thinking back to all those papers stuck to the school walls, strewn across the floors, stuck to the bottoms of sneakers sticky with soda. All that effort. The venom in Cecilia as she changed my essay and made it into something else entirely. I remember in that moment asking God why. Well, now I know.

I pad across the sandy beach, lugging my surfboard under my armpit.

It doesn't make it right. But in a strange way, Trevor's comment shifted the pity I felt for myself to Cecilia.

I shrug off my wetsuit and grab my phone from under the towels on one of Mike's lawn chairs.

There's a text from Jake: *Sorry can't make it*

He's been absent all day. I know he was busy with college apps, but he's gone completely MIA from all conversation.

I type: *U ok*

Yah just getting these apps done

I can't imagine the stress—deciding where to spend the next four years, what major to pursue, wondering if it's the right one. I've still got a year, but he's going through it all right now.

Sorry. How's it going?

Eh

Tomorrow?

We're supposed to meet up in the morning at the church to make Thanksgiving baskets for the poor.

There's a pause. Then his text appears.

Sorry. Deadlines

I get it

I do. But I don't get a chance to even show that concern, because he hasn't been around. Which makes me worry that there's something more going on. And then he responds.

See you Monday

Monday? Two months ago, this would've been normal. But not seeing each other for the next four days feels like, well, like something's wrong. I call him but it goes straight to voicemail, which means he pressed Ignore.

An uneasy feeling settles in the pit of my stomach, but I text back: *Kk*

It's after eight when Matt arrives and gets settled in. Mom and Dad are in the kitchen banging around, getting all the pots and pans in order for Thanksgiving, and of course, joking and laughing way more than usual. The Golden Child appears in my doorway as I'm folding my clean laundry.

"Hey."

"Hey," I say. "Thought you might be home. Mom and Dad are way too chipper."

He grins. "They're just happy we're all together."

"Yeah, okay, keep telling yourself that."

"Whoa, what's up with you?"

I sit down on my bed. "Sorry. My boyfriend's not responding to my texts. He was supposed to show up today to take me sur—" I stop myself just in time. "Somewhere, but he bailed."

"There another girl?"

"Matt!" He always knows what to say to push my buttons. "He's just stressed with college apps. And we were supposed to make Thanksgiving baskets tomorrow at church, but he just texted no." I toss the phone onto my bed.

"They gonna preach at this basket thing?"

"What? No. We're boxing up food and lugging fifteen-pound turkeys across a parking lot."

"I'll go."

My mouth opens but no words come out. My brother is offering to go to church? Mom and Dad have never even mentioned joining me on a Sunday. I've asked. Mom says, "That's more *your* thing," and then pats me on the shoulder as if I've done something adorable. Dad gives a quick shake of his head like someone asked an inappropriate question in public. "But we're proud of you," he always adds, and it makes me feel like I've joined my high school's ROTC or something. "It's good to live by rules. Keeps your head straight and your life in order."

My parents see church as rules. My brother sees it as a joke. I see it as the opposite of both, but nothing I say to them ever has much of an impact, so I gave up a long time ago and just do my own thing.

"Yeah, okay, sure," I say. "But it's seven in the morning."

He freezes, the words shocking his system. He takes a huge

mouthful of air and forces out a squeaky, "Sounds great."

He pats the top of my bedroom doorframe as a goodbye but then pauses.

"You go swimming tonight?"

I grab my wet hair. "The YMCA has a pool."

"Saltwater pool?"

"No. Chlorine."

"Hm." He doesn't blink when he says, "You have sand on your forehead."

"Oh," I say. I used Mike's hose to rinse off, but when I wipe above my eyebrow, flecks of sand rain down. Oh no.

"Must be from my towel," I say.

He taps the top of my doorframe again and then turns to go. "Yeah, okay, keep telling yourself that."

Chapter Thirty

The church parking lot glows in the early morning light, reflecting a light pink on the bright-white tables. There are ten rows, each five tables long, and volunteers are lined up wherever they can find a spot. Matty and I park ourselves in one of the lines at the canned-yams station.

"Damn!" he says, yawning, and I look around to make sure nobody heard. It makes me nervous that the one time I bring him to church, the single crotchety old lady with cats and gnarled fingers is going to find him and tell him to watch his language.

"What?" I ask, opening a box full of canned crushed pineapple.

"This is like a well-oiled machine."

It's true. We're here to make hundreds of boxes for the poor. Prior to us arriving, volunteers stacked food next to different areas of the tables: rolls, stuffing, cranberries, and everything else. At the beginning of the line, volunteers have empty boxes ready to be filled. At the end, volunteers are waiting to carry the full boxes to the trucks, which will then be delivered to downtown LA.

As a box gets passed to us, already full of green beans and powdered mashed potatoes, we add a can of yams, a can of crushed pineapple, and a bag of marshmallows, then slide the box down the line.

Pastor Brett is nearby opening boxes of marshmallow bags and tossing them to our table. Matt snags some bags midair, but others drop through his hands as his timing isn't quite perfect anymore. Brett joins us a short while in and shakes Matt's hand.

"Hey, I'm Brett. You must be the brother," he says.

Matt smiles and shakes his hand.

"Don't worry, though," Brett adds, and I cringe, knowing a punch line is coming. "I didn't believe any of it. I said, 'Nah, I bet he's a good guy.'"

Matt laughs. "Surprised she even talked about me. If it's bad, it's probably true."

"Nah, nah, all good."

We fall into line, stuffing bags and cans into boxes. Brett and Matt start talking sports and basketball trades, which becomes white noise until I hear my name.

"I don't know, Lovette, what do you think?"

"Hmm?"

"Marvel or DC Comics?"

I'm holding a can of yams, and it hovers above a box before the person next to me nudges me to drop it. "Aren't they the same?"

The guys tilt their chins down and crease their brows in unison. They frown like I've let them down at life.

"How are we related?" my brother says.

"Are you even saved?" Brett jokes, and for some reason, this gets the biggest laugh out of my brother.

"Look," I say, throwing a can into the next box. "If you said, peas or pea soup, sunrises or sunsets, Crest or Colgate, I've got you."

"Why would we care about toothpaste?" my brother says. Brett nods like they're best buds.

"You just gave me a choice between a fake thing or a fake thing!"

"And you should know where you stand."

"Amen," Brett adds.

I laugh. "I swear comic-book people are so weird. Give me a real thing. Manchester United or Arsenal. Angels or Dodgers."

"Don't you dare say Angels," Matt says, throwing a pack of marshmallows at my head. "Okay, I've got one you can answer. Longboard or shortboard?"

I glare at him. I know he's hoping to catch me off guard. "I wouldn't know."

"Just asking what you like. Not what you ride."

He's trying to imply that I'm being defensive, but I stay calm and say, "Longboards are designed to turn on their tails, whereas shortboards are more for rail-to-rail turns. So it would depend on what you're looking to do."

Someone hollers, "That's a wrap," and it's time to clean up, so I escape the conversation. Before we leave, Brett shakes Matt's hand. "It's good to finally meet the guy we prayed for. Glad to see you're doing okay."

"Getting by. Thanks. Appreciate it."

There's no awkwardness about Brett saying he prayed for him. How does Brett do that? Every time I mention God, Matt looks as if I've asked him to scratch his nails against a chalkboard for fun.

○)))) ● ● ((((○

On the drive home, a text lights up on Matt's phone. An email notification. He clicks on it, and I see the first line, but pretend like I don't. Matt flips his phone over, then looks at me, but I turn my head out the window.

He doesn't have the music on, and we sit quietly for a few miles. I bet he's wondering how much of the email I saw, but instead he says, "When you went to the bathroom before we left, I was talking to Brett about your new boyfriend."

I cough and shut my eyes. "You didn't! Matt, I haven't told him that Jake and I are dating."

"Well, he knew."

Did Jake already tell Brett about us? Weird. Brett didn't lecture me or give me the disappointed Kelly look. He didn't even act like he knew.

Matt taps the steering wheel. "He says Jake's been working with you out on the water." My breath lodges in my throat. Before, Matt had no solid proof, other than sand in my hair and a chunk of wax in my room. Now he has my boyfriend and my pastor talking about it. "Says you're getting pretty good at your rail-to-rail turns." My brother's voice has become a tightwire. "That true? You connecting them?"

He waits for an answer. I gulp. "One or two."

"Impressive." He doesn't sound impressed. "I'm sure Mom and Dad would love to hear about that."

He's not gonna pull a big-brother move like this. "It's Thanksgiving."

"You can wait till tomorrow morning. But first thing."

"Fine," I huff. "I'll tell them. And while I'm at it, I'll mention your email notification." He looks at me, all bravado gone. "When were you planning on telling them?" I ask.

He waits a beat. When he finally speaks, his voice is flat. "After Christmas. Once everything's in order."

After Matt woke up from his coma, he was on medications to prevent seizures and blood coagulation. The doctor said air travel could lower his seizure threshold. It would be rare, but flying could initiate seizing. That was almost five years ago, but the "no fly" rule has stayed in effect.

I don't think our parents would appreciate seeing: *Congratulations, your application has been officially accepted for next semester's Study Abroad.*

"Don't," is all he says. "Not yet."

"Then don't take away the one thing I love in life."

His eyes narrow. "The one thing you love? After Mom and Dad nearly divorced over it. After I almost—"

"I loved it before all that happened."

He throws his head back and laughs with perfect big-brother mockery. "You only love it because Mom and Dad tell you not to."

"Not true!"

"Oh, come on. You've always been that way. Mom put you in dance. You said you only wanted to surf. Dad signed you up for Girl Scouts. You quit. They told you to focus on school. You got a job. You never listen. You do what you want."

I can tell he's just mad that he doesn't have the upper hand, but still. "You've been away for three years. You have no idea who I am now."

"Oh, because you go to church now? Doing another thing so you can look better than us?"

"That's not why I go!"

In our driveway, he slams on the brakes, and he's out of the car before I can unbuckle my seatbelt. "Matt, please," I say, running after him toward the front door. "I love surfing. It's like . . ." I think for a second of how to put it. "A lifeline. I love it like the air I breathe. You don't know what it's done for me."

"Have you seen what it did to me?"

"I'm not you! God built us differently."

"Damn straight."

He pushes open the door and whisks by my mother, who's bringing a dish of cranberries to the dining-room table. She has earbuds in and so she doesn't hear him when he adds, "Completely different."

I follow him, shouting, "And I've never been more thankful for that than I am right now!"

Mom takes out her earbuds, figuring that's the reason I'm shouting. She wipes her hands on her apron. "Are we sharing what we're thankful for?"

○)))) ● ((((○

Dad blesses the meal, thanking no one in particular, but saying that it's good to have another healthy and happy year together. Mom and Dad look at Matt when they lift their glasses.

As we eat, our parents are so consumed by the preparations

and the togetherness that they're oblivious to Matt and I steaming. We fill our cheeks with stuffing, cranberries, and turkey until there's no way we could talk without choking.

Mom tells us about her latest beachfront property that she's decorating with blues and creams, and how the house has two washers and dryers. She waves a knife in the air before slicing her yam. "Two of each. Can you believe it?"

Dad shares about the guy at Rotary who keeps ripping farts during the meetings.

Mom covers her lips with one hand and shakes with laughter. "Doesn't he get embarrassed?"

Dad shovels green-bean casserole in his mouth and says, "He thinks they're silent. Only thing worse than his gas is his hearing."

"Speaking of hearing," Mom says, sipping her pinot grigio, "did you hear from Jake? Is he having Thanksgiving with his aunt or down at the base?"

I focus on my food. "Um, I don't know. He's been busy."

"Busy with another girl?" Matt knows it's a mean thing to say. He smiles through his mouthful of mashed potatoes.

"No," I say, but it reminds me of how Jake minimized his screen in the library. "He's working on college apps."

"Good for him," Dad adds. "You can tell a military son from a mile away. Keeps the girls at bay until he gets his business done."

I cock my head to the side.

Matt almost spits his drink. "Dad said *girls*. As in more than one."

"Just an expression, Matty," Dad says, but chuckles along with him.

As we finish our meal and dig into our pumpkin pie, Mom says, "Why don't we go around and share what we're thankful for?"

The rest of us groan, but Mom shakes a finger. "It's not gonna kill you. I'll start. I'm thankful for a job where I get to make people happy with my designs, a husband who is still handsome after twenty years of marriage . . . and maybe some bottles of wine." They laugh like they've told that joke before. "My son who's overcome so much, and my daughter who's exploring a new season in her life"—and then whispers loudly—*"with a boyfriend."*

She winks at me when she says "new season," and then Matt says, "Gross," and Dad clears his throat. They're all implying sex, which is weird upon weird, not to mention that I haven't even kissed Jake.

Dad changes the subject. "I'm thankful for a retirement that pays for smart kids like mine to go to college, so they can get rich and put me up in an old people's home on a yacht someday." He lifts his wine to Matt.

Matt lifts his glass. "I'm thankful nobody in this family surfs anymore."

My parents laugh, and Mom says, "Good riddance!"

Dad adds, "God, horrible sport. Even the culture when you step back and look at it."

I can't believe my brother took a shot like that. I look down at my shaking hands. Mom says, "Lovette?"

I lift my apple cider. "I'm thankful that Matt stays close to home for college, because he knows that Mom and Dad would both have seizures if he ever hopped on an airplane."

"Poor choice of words, Lovette," Mom chides. "But yes. We're grateful for in-state scholarships."

If Matt's eyes were daggers, I'd be bleeding from multiple wounds.

We toast and drink. My brother clears his plate to the kitchen, but Mom says, "Stop. Your father and I will take care of the dishes."

"Thanks," he says. "May I be excused? I promised my girlfriend I'd call her." He heads toward his room. "I'm not too busy for her."

"Next semester you might be!" I yell as he closes his bedroom door. I ignore my parents' questioning looks and help them clear the table. They don't stop me the way they stopped Matt.

While overstuffing our dishwasher, I text Jake: *What's wrong?*

Happy Thanksgiving, he texts back.

Really?

What?

I haven't heard from you all day. Basically all week.

Been busy.

So you've said

What's that mean?

WHAT'S GOING ON? I write in all caps and set my phone down to clean. I accidentally chip a wineglass as I rinse it in the sink. My finger bleeds, and I suck on it. My mouth tastes of blood and Palmolive. I spit into the sink, pink foam all over the dishes. Finally he responds.

Nothing

It took him that long to write *nothing*?

He must be typing with his elbows, because I type with my uninjured hand faster: *Over us so soon?*

There's a long pause. Too long.

Then: *Why would you say that*

I write, *Why didn't you answer the question*

. . .

I see the three dots. I know he's writing. I wipe down the counters.

. . .

I start the dishwasher and return the china to the cabinet.

. . .

And then the dots disappear. He changed his mind. I rush up to my room, close the door, and flop onto my bed. So that's it. Maybe the rules felt like too much. Maybe he wants to find someone more open to the things he used to have with Hannah. Kissing. Other things more than kissing. My heart feels hollowed out, but I have no tears. Part of me is a little angry. Why couldn't he just come out and say it?

Twenty minutes later, my body still a lifeless lump on my bed, I feel a buzz in my pocket.

Come outside

I take the stairs two at a time and run out the front door. His car is haphazardly parked in my driveway. He stands there, fists stuffed in his jeans pockets.

I lower my eyes to the cracks in the pavement. "We're breaking up, aren't we?"

Chapter Thirty-One

He stiffens. "Why would you say that?"

"Why won't you answer the question?" I look at him, and the moment he sees the empty expression in my eyes, everything in him slackens.

His hands come out of his pockets, and he closes the distance between us.

He looks at me face-to-face, less than a surfboard fin apart. His eyes are pained with sincerity. "No. We're not breaking up. That's the last thing I wanna do right now."

I feel like I've had a surfboard leash wound up around my neck and shoulders, and it's suddenly been untangled. As much as I fight to resist, two tears escape, fat and hot, crisscrossing down my cheeks. He brings his thumbs up to wipe them away, but a couple more follow.

"Please don't tell me these are because of me."

I sniff. "Not all of them."

He wipes the wet strands of hair out of my face and tucks them behind my ears.

My body feels like an injury, limp and tired. "You didn't text. You didn't call. When I tried, it went straight to voicemail. You're about to make all these big decisions about your future, and I don't even know where you're applying. You're not walking me to class, you're not sitting by me at lunch, and when I track you down at school, you minimize your screen like you don't want me to see it. What am I supposed to think?"

"You're right," he acknowledges. "I get it. I've had a lot on my mind."

A strange sound escapes my lips, like a staccato whimper. "You can't retreat every time things get hard. I don't know if this is how boyfriends work, but it felt better before I had one."

He drops his head.

New tears leak out, and these ones I wipe away. "And then tonight, we all had to share what we were thankful for, and my parents were thankful for my brother, and my brother was thankful to throw me under the bus, and no one was really thankful for me—"

He interrupts to mutter, "*I'm* thankful for you."

"No, stop, I'm not looking for affirmation. I'm fine. What I mean is—when I look at how they look at me, I'm pretty sure I'm the worst example ever for God. They think God's a freak because of how I show Him."

"Whoa. Swim back to the shallow end. That's not true."

"It feels true!"

"Spoken like a true nonbeliever."

"Hey!"

"Hey nothing. I thought as Christians we're not supposed to rely on our feelings, because feelings can trick you. That whole verse in Jeremiah—the heart is a mess whatever whatever verse."

I crack a smile despite my tears. "'The heart is deceitful above all things. Who can trust it?'"

"Exactly. So when feelings get tricky, what do we rely on?"

"The word of God."

"And what does the word of God say?"

"That I'm loved."

"Enough to die for."

I think of all the stuff he's been going through and the ways he closes people off when he's afraid to share. "Do you believe it? All the stuff you just said?"

He lifts and drops one shoulder. Then the other. Separately. "Somewhat." He cups his hands around my cheeks, and my knees wobble like a newborn deer's. "But you do. And you make me believe it more."

He leans closer, his lips inches from mine, and my eyes widen but I don't pull away. I can't. He's the first to realize, to shake himself out of his trance. He turns his face away and then nuzzles into my neck. His arms wrap around me, one across my shoulder blades and the other on the small of my back. My fingers trace his back, our stomachs pressed hard against each other like we can't get close enough, and then I tighten my arms as if by doing so we can merge into one person. That's how close I want to be to him.

"You undo me," he whispers into my ear.

"I don't know what that means," I whisper back, and he laughs into my neck and the hot air feels like a million butterfly kisses. Goose bumps travel across my body like wildfire, rampant and uncontrolled. I steady myself by breathing in his scent. Still nothing like the books say—no

Dove for Men or Snuggle dryer sheets—but it's unmistakably better. Something undeniably "Jake" mixed with the freshness of a recent shower. "Can we stay like this forever?"

I never imagined that the closeness of human touch could feel like this, like something that's been inside you all along gets woken up, and you never knew it was sleeping.

I think that's what it was like with Jesus. How I didn't know I was missing something until He came into my heart, and suddenly I was like, "Hey, I've been missing you all along." It's scary how similar the spiritual can be to the physical.

That thought startles me, and I leap back from Jake.

"Whoa!" he says. "What's wrong?"

Keeping a foot away from him is helpful. I shake my head from my drunken stupor and remember why he's here tonight.

"Why?" I ask, and he sticks his chin out and questions me with his eyes. "Why the no calls and texts? Why the secrecy?"

It's like he remembers too. His neck becomes elastic, and his head tips back to the sky. He lifts it up and forward to look at me.

"Can we go for a drive?"

The wind slaps our faces through the rolled-down windows as we head toward the ocean. The air is loud, luckily, so we don't have to be. He slips his hand lightly onto the top of my knee, testing my reaction with a nervous glance. I reach a hand around his bicep and squeeze. *Yes, I'm okay with this.*

Downtown Manhattan Beach is a ghost town, so quiet we can hear our flip-flops slapping the clean sidewalks. The Kettle, a twenty-four-hour diner where most of the local college kids pull all-nighters tucked away in leather booths, is the only place open. A few families are inside, enjoying their nontraditional no-one-has-to-cook-or-clean Thanksgiving feasts.

"Where are we going?"

He keeps his eyes fixed on the dark ocean's horizon as if he's watching the orangey sun that set an hour ago.

A few minutes later, we stop in the middle of the sandy beach at a pair of swings. Away from the traffic noise, here with our feet in the sand, the waves are louder, creating a calming background music. The chains are rusty from wet salt and damp air, but we kick our shoes off and sit on the creaky seats facing opposite directions so we can look at each other.

Our legs are touching, and they start to lazily swing back and forth. It feels natural, but still, it makes me forget why we're here. I pretend it's no big deal, but we might as well be making out. I never want to stop swinging my legs. Like ever. I want to be a pendulum for Halloween.

He grips the chains with his hands and tips his head back, drinking in a long breath. When he brings his head up, he says, "My mom wants me to apply to the University of Hawaii."

"You spoke with her?"

"Briefly."

"How was it?"

His jaw tightens. Still sitting, he moves his feet in a circle, turning his swing, twirling the chain above him. He releases his feet and his swing spins, whipping him in a circle one direction and then back the other until it teeter-totters to a gentle rock back and forth.

"According to her, great."

"Why?"

His teeth clamp down hard. "Well, I submitted my application."

"Oh."

A ball forms in my gut and grows. The worry about next year has been marinating, but I've kept it tucked in the back of my head. Him going to college. What that will mean for us. I'm only a junior, but for him, that's less than a year away.

"You can't go to a college here?"

"Don't qualify for in-state tuition. Not after only three months."

"But when you start in the fall."

"Still under a year."

"But"—I'm gripping the sand with my toes—"But." I tug at my hair with one hand. "But you moved away. You're not in-state there either."

"I will be if I move back in time."

My stomach turns to water and I spring to my feet. The swing rattles and dangles behind me. "What?" I choke out.

He jumps to his feet too, faces me, tries to calm me with his eyes. He knows what's erupting inside of me, the realization of what this means. "Easy," he says. "No one's moving away just yet. I haven't even been accepted."

"But if you are?"

His silence is the answer I don't want. I slump down to the sand, and rest my head and arms on my knees. I hear him ease down to the sand in front of me.

"Hey."

I don't look up. I feel his bare feet reach around my hips and pull me closer to him.

"Heyyyy."

I peer up at him, and his deep brown eyes are rich with apology. "*That's* why I avoided you all week. I've been a trainwreck. Confused. Pissed. Frustrated. All the things. Didn't know how to tell you. Knew I needed to. Didn't want to. I decided I'd keep it from you, but you're so damn honest about everything. You look at me sometimes, and I *want* to tell you things." His next words are strangled. "I want to tell you everything."

He's looking at me, and it's intense. It's a way he's not supposed to be looking at me if we're gonna hold to our list. Then his eyes flicker like he's thinking of the list too. He exhales slowly.

"So why didn't you?"

"My parents, my future, my past, my thoughts about God—it's never a mess I want to bring you into. But every now and then, you knock the wind out of me, and—"

"Stop." I can't do this. I can't start thinking these thoughts, because there's something deep in me that knows what he's talking about, and I feel drawn to it more than the waves, and sometimes more than God, and it's more dangerous than surfing. It distracts me from the issue at hand. "What you did wasn't okay."

"I'm sorry," he says. "I'm sorry I left you hanging. You're right. You're my girl." Again, my body electrifies. "And you deserve to know it all, even the bad."

When he looks at me with that unblinking stare, caresses the inside of my wrist with his thumb, talks to me with that low growl, I feel weird things in my body and they feel wonderful and terrible at the same time. They make me want to ball up that list, tie it to an anchor, and drop it in the middle of the Bermuda Triangle so I can throw him down on the sand right here and make out with him.

With my clothes on, but still.

Clothes off starts with clothes on. And I'm embarrassed that he's confessing about his mom and college and honesty, and in my mind, I'm rolling around on a beach with him.

"What are you thinking?" he asks, tracing a finger across my forearm.

I can't speak. There's no chance I'm going to lie, but there's less chance I'm going to be honest. I shake my head and he misunderstands.

"No more keeping stuff from you. Promise."

I'm so relieved hearing those words, that it takes a minute to realize he just referred to his thoughts about God as a mess, right next to the mess of his dysfunctional family. It reminds me of an earlier time, when he questioned, "Don't you ever wonder why God didn't take care of you if He loved you so much?" Have I been wrong in thinking he loves God? I know what the Bible says. If we're not looking in the same direction in our faith, then it's not a direction I'm supposed to go.

But my heart's already there.

Chapter Thirty-Two

Four. He's applied to four universities, and only one is within driving distance from here. He wants to double major in accounting and communications and get his master's in business. When I ask these questions, he's honest, but I can hear the strain in his voice. The thoughts of his future worry him, so I don't add to the stress by telling him how much they worry me too. Do we have an expiration date? College is a big deal—far bigger than us—but my heart is having trouble accepting that.

The thought of him moving away next year makes me want to curl up and dissolve into sea foam. And then there are other thoughts creeping in. How maybe he appreciates my love for God but doesn't *share* it. I don't want to have to mute God every time Jake and I hang out. That's not freedom. But letting go of Jake doesn't feel freeing, either. My thoughts are a brain hurricane, swirling and whipping around in every direction.

I know Jake's noticed that I've been a little stuck in my own head, but he's been kind and respectful of the fact that I don't want to talk about it. He, of all people, understands that. Every time we've gone surfing these past couple weeks, he's asked me at least once while the waves licked our boards between sets, "You sure you're okay?" It's the perfect question, because yes, I'm okay. Okay means average. Okay means not great but not horrible. And truly, I'm not horrible. I'm just confused. And if I don't deal with it, then I can stay at that flat area beyond the break—not catching waves but not being tumbled. Safe waters. So I nod each time he checks to see if I'm "okay."

He hasn't pushed it, and I haven't either.

"Your brother coming home for Christmas break?" he says one morning a little after dawn. We're paddling out, and I have to duck-dive a wave before I can answer. I pop up with a quick gasp. The water is colder now that it's mid-December.

"Good question."

I tell him how Matt was accepted into a study-abroad program, and how that involves flying, and the whole seizures and no-flying thing. I'm pretty sure he told my parents before he went back to college after Thanksgiving, because I heard muffled arguing late that night. The next day, Mom didn't talk much and her face was puffy and swollen. She told me it was a migraine, but if that's true, then she's had the longest migraine in the history of America. Since Matt went back to school, she shuffles from room to room like she's trying to sweep the floors with her socks.

I tell Jake about this as we surf, so I think he assumes that's why I've just been "okay" these past few weeks.

Mom still asks about my day when I see her, but her smiles look pained—like she's constipated and needs prunes—and when I answer, "Not great. We had a test," she answers, "That's nice," and shuffles along.

Dad's been consistent with his salutes, so that's comforting. I think he knows I sense the tension. He'll add a smile if Mom doesn't look up when she walks by like a human Swiffer, as if to say, "Don't fret, kid. She just likes clean floors."

The silver lining about this is that I've been able to head out early and come back late, and no one's been asking questions. I've spent more time on the water than I have the past couple months combined, and I feel comfortable riding the waves now, even in the rougher winter surf.

Jake and I work on form, and I rarely take out the longboard. My shortboard tricks need work, but they're getting there. This morning before school when I catch a wave that lines up perfectly, Jake reminds me I'm standing too upright, or as he calls it, "cruisy."

I argue, "I was still going pretty fast."

"For a sea turtle, sure."

I cup a handful of water and splash him.

"It's true! If your board's flat, then your ride's gonna be flat. Think about minimizing your board's contact with the water. Rail to rail. Rail to rail. Compress, extend, compress, extend. It's like you become a spring—up, down, up, down—as you ride down the line. You'll generate better momentum."

"Got it." I love these moments, when we can lose ourselves in what we love. There's no drama—no parents saying no or friends disappointed in me or worries about God or about dating or how far is too far? There's just us, our boards, and an endless expanse of God's perfect deep-blue majesty.

I look down the line. It's a left, forming perfectly, and I paddle and glance to make sure my timing is lined up with the wave.

"Yes!" Jake hollers, and a second later I'm up and on my board's rail. I feel myself accelerate as I try to cut laterally down the line. I hear Jake's voice in my head: "Rail to rail, rail to rail." I carve back and forth, one side of my board to the other, with a slight shifting of my body weight. My board undulates faster and faster until I'm pumping and racing, the cold winter air whipping my hair across my face. It gets too fast, and I panic and bail, but it's okay. It felt glorious.

Jake swims over and meets me with a forearm-to-forearm bump. "You see any cops out here?"

My face pinches in confusion. "No, why?"

"'Cause you can't afford a speeding ticket right now," he says, grinning. Oh my gosh, that was so cheesy and I laugh so loud, it bounces off the water and magnifies in the morning air. If only all my worries about Jake and God were like surfing, so black-and-white, so easy to answer by following one set of directions. But my feelings for him send me every which way, dragging my toes in the water or leaning too far back, compressing when I should extend, or vice versa, and all the while I'm plugging my ears with my index fingers so I can't hear my heavenly coach, who keeps reminding me that at some point, Jake and I need to talk.

○))) ● ● (((○

On the day before Christmas break, Jake's holding my hand like he does every day at school during passing periods. I used to look forward to it, the linking of our fingers, and the thrilling sensation it sent from my rib cage to my lower stomach. It was a drop on a roller coaster every time for the first few weeks. But since Thanksgiving, these thoughts about him leaving for college—not to mention our faith issues—have consumed me. I feel guilty holding his hand, but if I refused, it would look like I was being dramatic or causing a scene. Part of me wonders why we're moving forward if he's moving away so soon. And I know I can be straightforward and bring up the whole God thing, but I keep waiting, hoping that I'll see a glimmer of his love for Jesus in something that he says.

When we ride in a car or sit next to each other at lunch, he'll put a hand on my thigh. It never travels upward, just rests there, a simple reminder of *Hey, we're in all of this together, even this sitting thing.* But every time it happens, it makes me ask myself if we're *really* in this together. Is it the three of us? Or just two? On a few occasions when we're alone, he's pulled me close as we hug good night, held me there to breathe in the scent of me, and we nuzzle, all ears and cheeks and necks, never face-to-face, but it still feels forbidden and wild, and it makes me take in gallons of air afterward. Those are the worst moments, because they feel the best, and I never once want to stop to talk about our faith or our future.

○))) ● ● (((○

Today, right there next to the east-wing lockers and before we hit the double doors to the outside lunch area, he digs his heels into the linoleum hallway mid-step. Before I can say "about face," he's whipped me around and we're eye to eye.

"Whoa!"

He doesn't respond, just searches me with his eyes.

I ask, "You okay?"

"Me? That's what I've been asking you for the past three weeks."

"I've told you I'm okay."

"Are *we* okay?"

I pause. "Yes?"

"Is that a question?" He holds my hand up, my fingers linked in his. "See this? This used to grip me like I was a lifeline. Now your hand is a floppy dead fish every time I reach for it. You're the one who called me out on being honest."

He waits, knowing me well enough to know it's me this time who's holding back.

"I like you," I start, but then stop when I see this slight doubt creasing his eyebrows, making his eyes bigger and browner than normal. It makes me think of a deer. "You know that much," I say louder than I intend. A few students stop to look. The novelty of Cecilia's prank has worn off, but the gossip paparazzi are still on high alert, hoping I can give them something more to keep the talk going. I grip both of his hands and say quieter, "Jake, I like you in a way that scares me." I feel his hands relax a little. "But—" I look around. More curious eyes have stopped to see if this is going to be social-media worthy. There's no way I can talk to him here about the future of us.

He's the opposite, so unaware that we have an audience. He releases my hands and pulls me into a full embrace. We're wrapped around each other in public, fully hugging with our entire bodies, and this time it's not because he's got a black eye or because Jesus is telling me to. It's because I want to, and Jake wants to, and so here we are.

"You had me worried," he whispers in my ear, and it feels like silk. "Look, I'm scared too. But we'll figure it out, okay?"

I nod into his neck, then promise God and myself that I'll talk to Jake sometime during Christmas break about all of this.

○))) ● (((○

At lunch, Niles holds up a Coke. "I'd like to propose a toast." We hold up our waters and Capri Suns and sodas. "Lovette finally rubbed Jake's chesticles in public."

"Hear hear!" the guys shout. Everyone cheers. Well, everyone but Kelly, who puts down her kombucha and frowns.

"Ew!" I giggle, throwing a balled napkin at him. "Not when you put it that way!"

"Saw you two right before we headed into lunch. Well done and I'm proud. Our little girl is growing up." He holds up an open hand.

"I am *not* high-fiving you for anyone's chesticles. It's called a 'hug,' okay?"

"I thought you only did that hip-hugging church thing."

"Okay, fine. It was more than a side hug. We were facing each other."

"Full frontal *again*?" Kaj says, like he did when he first saw us weeks back. The guys laugh, and I shake my head. They find the grossest things so hilarious.

"Woo, girl! I told you!" Lydia teases. "Breast to breast is the best!" She does a little breast shimmy with her shoulders. "What's next?"

"I mean, we'll have to check the to-do list," I joke.

Jake holds up a finger. "We *did* make a list," he confirms.

Kelly excuses herself to the bathroom, but I'm the only one who sees her scowl. We talk the rest of lunch about our Christmas plans. Niles, who hates the snow, is heading Back East with his family, where they received four feet of new powder. Lydia is having the family come stay with them, which means she has to share her bed with not one but two cousins. Kaj is going away for a few days but only to Riverside, where his grandparents live with two cats.

"I thought you were allergic," I say.

"Oh, I am," Kaj answers. "My eyeballs will be swollen shut."

"You're gonna be so sexy," Lydia coos. He scrunches his eyes and puckers his lips, searching with flailing hands for Lydia's face.

I wonder when my brother's coming home. I haven't heard a peep about it from my parents, and I'm afraid to ask. And lurking in the back of the cat allergies and bed sharing is a conversation with a boyfriend that might result in a breakup. Pretty sure breast to breast wouldn't solve any of that.

Chapter Thirty-Three

Matt arrives home on the first weekend of Christmas break, but aside from extra footsteps through the house in the middle of the night, I barely notice the difference. He's out with friends all the time. I leave early every morning for a run followed by a ride on my skateboard or bike, depending on the day. When I get back right before lunch, he's usually just left. I work at Billy's Buns until nine, and whether I surf at night or come straight home, he's not back until well after I'm asleep.

The house feels like the floors are made of tightropes. Matt came home with an anger that has him shut off, and by the way my parents tread around him carefully, I'm almost positive now that the muffled argument I heard back at Thanksgiving was about studying abroad. I do my best to stay out of everyone's way, but I'm pretty sure he thinks that this all is somehow my fault. He sees me once in a while walking out of the bathroom when he's walking in, and I can feel his seething resentment, as if he hates me for breathing.

We get an unexpected storm that lasts two days, keeping me out of the water and off the sidewalks, so I actually visit the YMCA, pay for the day pass, and swim laps in the pool until my arms ache. I don't shower afterward but go straight home to sit with my parents on the couch, my chlorine-drenched body emitting proof of my pool time.

Kelly finally texted me a day ago and asked if we could meet for lunch. It'll be good to catch up. Even though we see each other at school and youth group, we haven't talked much lately. We used to hang out all the time—getting acai bowls at Paradise Bowls or surfboard-shaped cookies at Beckers in Manhattan Beach, and then walking up and down Manhattan Beach Boulevard, stopping at the boutique stores and trying on shirts we'd never buy, or browsing the teen section at the independent bookstore Pages. I've asked her to get together, but she keeps saying she's busy, so my heart does a little hopscotch skip when I get the text inviting me to lunch tomorrow. She does add, *You're coming alone, right?*

I text back *yes* and do my best to ignore the subtext, *Jake's not invited.* I get it. She wants it girls only. Jake's been stuck down in Camp Pendleton, anyway. His father found him a temporary job over Christmas break at the base's credit union because, according to his dad, "Nothing good can come from an eighteen-year-old with free time."

We text every day, joking about nothing and everything. I've been able to read my Bible over the break without the school thing interfering, and it's been so good for my spirit. But it also makes me more concerned about me and Jake. It's weighing on me, so before bed one night, I text, *What are you doing for christmas*

Surviving

Lol can you get away

Once he passes out

He means his dad, but he sends me a gif of a kid seat belted in a car and screaming, then fainting.

K. I look up at the Hume Lake photo on my wall—me smiling so wide with my arms around Kelly, me full to the brim with camp food and Jesus. With shaky fingers, I add, *We need to talk*

About???

I don't even know where to start, so I pick the most obvious.

Sex

Are you having sex??!!

Lol, very funny. About moving away. God too.

What about God?

Dunno. Never hear you talk about Him.

So?

Ugh. Sometimes I hate texting. This would be better as a face-to-face, but I couldn't get myself to open my mouth before the break. This deserves a real conversation, not simply a Bible and a praying-hands emoji. I don't answer. Instead, I write,

Tired. Just thoughts. Zzzz. don't forget to pray

He gives a thumbs-up emoji.

Thumbs-up that he'll pray, or thumbs-up that he'll forget? I don't know how we can text so much and say so little. I look out at the night sky through my window. I don't have words tonight for God. Instead, I shrug my shoulders at Him, like, *Yep, I know. Lousy attempt.*

I know His mercies are new every morning, but when I

wake up the following day, I wonder if He gets frustrated that I'm such a wuss and He has to give me so many of these mercies because I don't step it up more. How hard is it to pick up a phone, call Jake, and say, "When you leave for college, are we breaking up? And by the way, what do you believe about Jesus?"

Instead, I pick up my skateboard and take off toward the ocean. The air is clean and crisp, the past two days of rain tamping down and clearing out the smog and haze. As I skate to Hermosa, I think of my year after Matt's accident when my parents were always gone. When loneliness got like a weight on my chest and I'd talk to God like He was my best friend. If I was in my bedroom with my blinds tight, He was sitting at my desk chair. If I reheated lasagna from the dish Mom left me, He'd sit across from me at the dinner table. When I'd walk the streets of Manhattan and Hermosa, I always left enough room on the sidewalk to the right of me. I memorized Bible verses, which was my way of imagining Him talking back to me.

"Heyyy," I say to God now. I ride to the edge of the sidewalk, imagining Him rolling up next to me. I bump over the sidewalk cracks, tic-tacking to build momentum. A man with five dogs pulls them out of nipping zone of my wheels. A lady with a stroller squints at me, like she might recognize me, but then realizes she doesn't. She looks away and rolls her stroller over my imaginary skateboarding Jesus.

"She just flattened you like a pancake," I joke. A couple holding hands looks at me, and I realize I should keep my prayers in my head for now.

I take Rosecrans west three miles, which spits me out in El Porto, the tip of North Manhattan. The waves are washed out today with early winds, and the only people out there are the tourists with the foam longboards and thick wetsuits who don't know any better. I lose myself in the sound of my whirring wheels, skating south toward Hermosa, and stop at the pull-up bars at the bottom of Twenty-sixth at Bruce's Beach. I do a couple of pull-ups next to a chiseled shirtless college guy.

"Not bad," someone behind me says. I turn to see the girl who I ran into at El Porto that morning a while back, when surfing still felt like a far-off dream.

"Thanks," I say. "Alix with an *I*, right? Last time I saw you, I could barely do one of these."

She jumps for a pull-up bar and does a few knees to chest. "Yeah, I've seen you out there a couple times since then. You're pretty good."

My face warms at the compliment. "Oh! I signed up for the All Wave Junior Open, like you suggested."

"Great!" she says, and she means it. "Too bad today's so sucky out there. I'd totally invite you out with me."

"You have your wetsuit?"

She nods.

"Mine's at my friend Mike's just a couple streets up. We could do an open-water swim to the pier."

"Let's do it. Meet you down at the lifeguard tower in ten?"

I pick up my skateboard and run up to Old Man Mike's. I slither into my wetsuit and check my watch. It's 9:33 a.m. Plenty of time before lunch.

Alix goes to Mira Costa, the surf dominators of the entire South Bay, and she's on varsity, which is funny to me that they have enough surfers to fill varsity, JV, and frosh/soph teams. We don't even have enough girls at my school who could make a C squad, much less varsity. As we swim, we talk about the surf competition. Alix says they're trying out a new coed division but she totally thinks it's going to be dominated by the guys because there aren't enough girls our age at the same level. I learn that she plays lacrosse, has two little brothers, and hates seafood. Once she lost her bikini top in a wave, and since then, she wears a rash guard even when she's swimming in the dead of summer. Flip-flops make her toes cramp, so usually she walks barefoot from her car to the beach. We backstroke and front stroke and sidestroke, and although it's cold and windy, the wetsuit and constant swimming keep us buoyant and warm. I tell her about Matt's accident and how I'm back surfing again after four years off. "Cool, cool," she says. She learns about Jake and how I work at a sandwich shop and think Kelly Slater is super hot, even though he's old.

Manhattan Beach Pier is between Eleventh and Twelfth Street, so by the time we return after swimming past the break and hanging a left, it's about two miles round trip. When we crawl out of the water back at Twenty-sixth, my shoulders are tight and my lungs feel bruised in my rib cage from the deep breathing. We exchange numbers and promise to get a quick practice in before our competition in February.

I was planning on getting in a swim or a run anyway, but this was an unexpected surprise. I can't wait to tell Jake. After I wriggle out of my wetsuit, hose my body down, and dry off with one of Mike's towels, I snap up my board and continue my trek, skating past Manhattan Beach Pier where I just swam, past the public bathrooms, past the house that Mom points out every time she sees it, where they filmed the exterior shots of *Beverly Hills, 90210*, some show she watched in high school. I'm early for my lunch, so I ride past Martha's Grill and stop at Hermosa Pier for a drink of water.

"Will you take our picture?" a father asks me. I snap a photo of him, his wife, and toddler in front of the big bronzed statue of Tim Kelly. Tim's crouched down on a surfboard, just before standing, or maybe getting ready for a trick. Tim was this amazing surfer back in the '60s, but he died at twenty-four, and it jarred the surfing community. We heard about him all the time as Junior Guards because supposedly he was also this "legendary" lifeguard. I imagine him saving children out of the mouths of seals, punching sharks in the eyes. There have been so many surfers in the world, even in Manhattan Beach, and yet Tim is the one who has a statue memorializing him. That always strikes me. I feel connected to him somehow, but I never know why. Some days I'll stop and stare at him for minutes. I'll always get close enough to touch him, to take a hand and stroke the bronze edge of his back as he crouches down, his eyes captivated by a wave and his future. The weird thing is that he died in a car accident. Not on the water, attempting a maverick wave, or out rescuing people from a sinking boat.

My phone vibrates in my pocket. When I remove it, Jake's name is lighting up my screen. "Hi!" I answer.

"Where are you?"

"Hermosa. Where are you?"

"Your house. I'll come meet you."

Disappointment floods me. "I can't. I promised Kelly I'd meet her at Martha's for lunch." Something in my gut tells me if I showed up with Jake at my hip, she wouldn't be pleased. This is Kelly-and-Lovette-only time.

"Okay, afterward. You don't have to be at work till three, right?" he says.

"Yes, but I thought you had work."

He coughs in my ear. "I've developed this one-day cold."

I laugh. "Okay, I'll text you when we get the bill."

At 12:55 p.m., I stroll up to the outdoor patio area of Martha's. Kelly's been there for a bit, I can tell by the glasses of water at our table. Two are half empty, condensation dripping down the sides. I tilt my head. Two of *three* glasses. She waves me over.

Next to her, Dave gives me a solemn nod.

Chapter Thirty-Four

The outside tables of Martha's 22nd Street Grill are covered by an awning and fenced in by a waist-high steel railing that doubles as a dog-hitching post for the patrons who bring their rescues, which is pretty much everyone in the South Bay. To the east is Hermosa Avenue and the lunchtime cycling traffic, and to the west is the boardwalk, the sand, and the endless blue ocean looking bright against the grim faces of Kelly and Dave.

"Hope I'm not late," I say, walking through the gate. "I was with Alix, and—"

"Alex? A date?"

"What? No, Alix with an *I*. Girl. Super-good surfer—oh, she's competing in the Open too. We talked forever ago, but I ran into her today so we ended up hanging out and exchanging numbers and— You guys okay?" Their faces look paralyzed.

"Well," Kelly hesitates. Dave touches her shoulder and nods at her to go on. "That's what we were going to ask you."

"Me?" My mind is racing. "You mean the thing with Cecilia?" Kelly winces.

"Oh." I sit down. "Yeah, I'm okay. Guess I cared more about

people's opinions than I thought I did. But I'm pretty much over it. I overheard her boyfriend on the water, and I get why she did all that to me. Doesn't make it okay, but God gave me a little perspective, and that's good."

I'm trying to speak their language, and it works because Dave points an index finger lazily up to heaven and drawls, "Hashtag truth." His eyes are half closed, like he's praying. Or stoned. I stifle a giggle.

Kelly adds, "Amen," which sounds extreme, even coming from her. She was always über Christian and maybe slightly critical, but it was never loud and in public. Her parents are hard-core—her mom's wardrobe probably contains the entire Bible in printed quotes—but this all-Christian dialogue and showiness feels very "not Kelly." "This isn't really about Cecilia. But before we start," Kelly says, "we should probably pray."

"Most def," Dave says.

They bow their heads, so I follow. I think we're praying for our lunches, but we haven't ordered, and then Kelly prays for the server right as she's refilling waters at our table. I open my eyes to smile at her—*We're normal, I promise!*—and I see Dave squeezing Kelly's hand as he says, "Yes, Lord," and the small crack of Kelly's smile. I suddenly notice how much she uses the word *just*, over and over, as if it makes the prayer more sincere: "Father God, I just pray that you be present in this tough conversation, Father God, and I just know, Father God, you have just prompted our hearts, so please just tell her that it is out of concern and not criticism that we are just holding her accountable."

"Me?" I interject, but their heads stay bowed. I want to break the mood because Kelly and I often joke while we're praying. "Pssst!" I whisper. "Father God doesn't forget his name every other word." Instead of a giggle, I get silence, and that feels mean, so I say, "Father God, I'm sorry, I'm *just* confused, Father God, at *just* this new style of praying, Father God."

Kelly squints her eyes like she's trying to wring out more sincerity or maybe wring out my words from her brain. I stare wide-eyed at their bowed heads, wondering what I've done to require an intervention session. Dave blindly feels for her wrist and squeezes, like, *"You're doing great."* She nods once, fueled by it, and then continues as if I said nothing. "Father God, we just know that if you are disciplining, it is only because you are a loving father." I'm in trouble with God? "Just help us to hate the sin and love the sinner, and I just pray that you would release the claws of backsliding embedded in Lovette."

Whoa. I have claws in me?

"Oh," Kelly adds as an afterthought. "And please bless this meal, amen."

I look up. Still no food. Are we blessing the water? When the server tiptoes past, I flag her down and order a soup and sandwich, so this poor girl will at least get a tip.

Dave sneezes, and someone nearby says, "God bless you!"

"He does!" Dave responds. Oh boy. I offer a weak smile to the person, who looks at our table like, "Huh?"

Kelly sips her water, and I notice she has a ring on her wedding finger. They both do. "You get married and not tell me?" I joke, and Dave gives a one-syllable courtesy laugh, then sobers.

"These are purity rings," he states, as if I'm clueless. "We're reminding each other and anyone who watches—because everyone's watching, right? Right?—that we're married to God. It keeps Kelly and me treating each other like brother and sister in Christ."

"So you're siblings with feelings for each other?" I joke, but neither of them laugh. Kelly actually winces, her hair falling forward as she nods. Something is way different.

"Hey! Your strip of hair! It's not purple anymore!"

"Yeah, Dave and I talked it over and realized it might be distracting to the message of Christ."

What the heck? "Are non-Christians against purple?"

She glares at me like I should know better. "It might give the wrong impression, like I'm rebellious. I'm not. I don't want people thinking it's okay to defy Him or do your own thing and not care what God thinks."

"Kelly, that's crazy. You really think God cares about Kool-Aid hair?"

"Maybe not, but you shouldn't do things if it makes others stumble."

"I'm writing a song about it," Dave pops in. I turn to him, and for a second so many mean comments come to mind. Song titles about purple hair and the fiery purple judgment of God.

I swallow down the words and force myself to look back at Kelly, shutting him out. "Or your purple hair could tell people, 'See this? This is a reminder that God looks at the inside, not the outside. And, hey, this is me. I love purple, and I love the way it looks braided into this awesome blond hair God gave me because He's clever and creative.'"

Kelly warms at my compliment, but Dave says, "I dunno, bro."

Bro? I'm having none of this. "Look, if a person isn't going to accept Christ because of purple hair, there are bigger issues between him and God."

"Speaking of bigger issues . . ." Dave trails off.

Kelly gulps. My grilled cheese and tomato soup arrive.

"We're worried about you," Dave continues.

"What . . . about . . . me?"

He looks to Kelly, and suddenly she doesn't want to talk. With a nudge from Dave, she starts. "You signed a True Love Waits pledge."

I pause. "I did. Seventh-grade winter camp. February. So did you."

"Well, you've been dating Jake for three months now, and . . ."

"And?"

"A lot can happen in three months."

I ask her, "Haven't you guys been dating longer than us?"

Kelly's eyes dart to Dave before she says, "We were *courting*."

"*Were*?" I echo. I've asked Kelly how things are with Dave, and she always says, "Blessed." "Did you break up?"

Dave shakes his head. "We took a step back." I look at Kelly but she busies herself drawing squiggles in the condensation of her water glass. "We realized we needed to back up to stay on track with God. That's why we're just friends now."

"That sounds like a breakup."

Kelly sighs, like I'm changing the subject on purpose. "I'm just saddened that you signed a True Love Waits contract—"

"Pledge—" I correct.

"Same difference, and you're not even considering it."

"It says to wait to have sex. I haven't broken it."

They eye each other. Kelly speaks first. "I heard from Niles that Jake says he's not against sex outside of marriage."

I don't know what to say because Jake never answered about Hannah, which was an answer.

She leans down, her chin close to my soup. It steams in front of her eyes. She whispers, "He's not a virgin."

This part I know, and it makes me uncomfortable. But I won't tell them that. "So?"

"So he can't be your husband," Kelly says. "We talked about it in seventh grade." I'm mortified that we're about to rehash a seventh-grade conversation about boys in front of Dave. "You said you weren't going to date any guy, and then God was going to give you a boyfriend right after college, and that guy was going to be your future husband, and you would know because he wouldn't have dated anyone before you either. And then you would kiss for the first time at the altar when you got married."

I remember all of this, and she's right. I said every word of it. "For God's sake, Kelly, I was TWELVE!"

She gasps. "For *God's* sake?" she repeats.

"Sorry. Look, things change. My mind changes."

"I read the essay you wrote."

I close my eyes, trying to shut out the memory of those papers—the copies upon copies—plastered all over the school. Students laughing.

"Think of all the people who know now about where you stand on the issue."

"Not all of it was the truth," I say, thinking of the

humiliating stuff Cecilia added. "And I didn't *choose* to let them all know."

"Still. Maybe God let everyone know as a gift for you. Think of how bad you're going to ruin your witness."

"You guys, I haven't even kissed Jake."

Kelly coughs into her water as she's taking a sip. "What?"

"Really?" Dave says, incredulous, like I've told him that I have a pet platypus.

"Really." I take a huge bite of my grilled cheese, even though I've totally lost my appetite. I swam two miles, and my body needs it. I wash it down with a few spoonfuls of soup and then look at my wrist as if I own an invisible watch. "I gotta go." The chair clatters into the person's chair behind me as I get up, and I apologize. Kelly and Dave look at each other with "I told you so" eyes. I drop ten bucks on the table. "Please don't get change."

I walk out of the gate and slap my board onto the concrete, startling the leashed dog next to me. "Sorry, boy," I say and pat his soft Labrador head. He licks my palm, and I hear Kelly's faint, "Lovette, wait," but I'm off toward the pier without looking back.

When I roll up, I stop in front of the statue of Tim Kelly. I touch him—the bronze is warm across my palm—and it calms me. I look out at the waves. The Pacific Ocean here isn't aqua like postcards of tropical surf spots. It's dark gray-green usually, camouflaging seaweed and coffee-colored boardshorts, but it's home. I pull out my phone to text Jake: *Meet at H pier?*

He texts back a thumbs-up.

When I turn around, there he is, in the middle of the bike traffic and pedestrians and skateboards and dogs. Like in a movie, he's stock-still as everything around him crisscrosses in chaotic patterns. It makes him look taller, sturdier somehow. My smile's big and goofy, and I don't care if all the tourists in Hermosa see. I leave my skateboard and charge at him. He lifts me and spins me around, burying his face in my neck. Everything in me wants to kiss him and I wonder if he feels the same and I'm embarrassed, but there it is.

"How'd you find me?" I left Martha's in such a flurry that I never texted him where exactly to meet.

He holds his phone up. "FriendFinder app."

He laces my fingers with his and beams when he feels the fierce way I grip his hand. I've missed him this past week. This past hour. He looks at the ocean.

"It's too washed out today," I say.

"For surfing." He walks me back to my board and picks it up with his free hand. "Come on. I only have fifteen minutes on the meter."

He wiggles my phone out of my back pocket, and I jump, which makes him laugh. "Careful. Your phone's touching your butt. Better tell it to stop." He hands me my phone. "You've suddenly caught this one-day cold—maybe you should tell Billy's Buns you can't make it to work tonight."

Curiosity wins over my desire to be honest. "Okay. Where are we going?"

He grins. "Do you trust me?"

I text Kim. *Can't make it.*

Before I lie, she writes back: *Got you covered. Have fun*

Chapter Thirty-Five

"Are you taking me to the base?"

We've been on the 405 South for fifteen minutes now, drowning ourselves in Discover Weekly music on Spotify.

"To my home? To meet my dad? I'm not sadistic."

I turn up the heater. It's a cool day, and my sports bra is wet from either skateboarding or getting the third degree from Pope Kelly and Officer Dave. "I haven't met your family. I don't even know where you live in Manhattan."

He taps the steering wheel. "My aunt's home. She'll be awake when we get back if you want to meet her."

"I'd like that. A lot." I lean over and rest my head on his shoulder.

"Where'd you go this morning?"

I tell him about Alix, open-water swimming, and skating. I hesitate to bring up the rest, but I do. "I met Kelly and Dave for lunch."

"TFTI."

"I would've invited you! She actually made sure you *weren't* coming, so I thought it was going to be a girls' thing. Then I got there, and there was Dave. And it was pretty much an intervention to break us up."

"Huh," he says. He looks down at me leaning on his shoulder, and kisses the top of my head. "Looks like it worked."

I laugh. "I can't figure her out. Something's off."

"You're just noticing this?" he jokes.

"No. Like more than normal. I can't explain it. I know her. And . . ." I don't finish my thought because I'll sound mean.

"I'd say you could've texted me sooner and I would've rescued you, but you don't seem like a girl who needs rescuing."

"I will next year when you move away."

There. I said it. He looks at me, his eyes rich with concern. I bite my lip, and he sighs. "I hate it too. You have no idea." He rubs his forehead, uncreasing his wrinkles. "But I don't hate today." He smiles at me with resolve. "I'm not letting it ruin what we have right now."

I reach my right arm across his stomach, and it tightens at my touch. He presses his lips against the top of my head again. "Careful," he murmurs. "I've gotta get you there safely."

"Where?"

"You'll see. Your curfew's eleven, right?"

"It's a sliding scale since my brother's home. But yes."

"You might need to text for an extension."

He merges from the 405 to the 5 South, and after a while there are only freeway sounds and car music, vehicles blurring past on the north side. Tired from the long day, I'm starting to nod off when Jake says, "Boobs."

I open my eyes. "What?"

"We're passing the boobs."

He points at the San Onofre power towers, two massive

nuclear-reactor power-plant domes. I slap him playfully, but it's true. They do look like two huge, armored boobs pointing to the sky.

"Sorry, should I have said 'bosoms'? The nipples glow red at night." I slap him again, and he adds, "What? They guide me home. God speaks in different ways."

I laugh but say, "Do you believe that?"

"That God made bosoms? Yes. Some of them fantastic." He looks pointedly at me, and I blush.

"I mean the God part." My arm's draped across his stomach like a seat belt, and his body's warm. My head's on his shoulder, and it all makes me feel like I can be completely honest. "Not just that Jesus was a good teacher—most nonbelievers believe that. I know you come to youth group, but lots of kids go. Arnie comes every week and he's a total atheist, but he has the hots for Carrie."

"I get that."

"Hey! Be serious. Jesus means everything to me. And you mean, well, a lot. More than I ever expected a guy would. And I'm afraid that—"

I feel his chest inflate and his body tense. He lowers the volume of the music. "You think because I don't wear a 'Jesus Saves' T-shirt that I don't believe?"

"Hey! No, don't be like that." I straighten, turn my whole body to face him. "It's important to me because *you're* important to me. You seem kind of angry at Him sometimes. I honestly don't know what you think of Him. You could be an atheist for all I know."

"Eh, Carrie's not my type." It's a faint attempt at a joke,

but he still looks bothered. "Look, if you're asking, then yes, I believe in Jesus. I know what He did. I don't think—like nonbelievers—that He was just a nice teacher running around telling nice people to go be nicer." Even in the darkening twilight, I notice his knuckles whiten against the steering wheel. "I know He claimed to do some pretty serious stuff—like changing people's eternal destinies—and if that was all a lie, and He *knew* it, then He wouldn't be a nice teacher. He'd be the greatest dick in all of history."

I gasp inadvertently. "I've never heard someone refer to Jesus like that."

"Well, I don't believe that He was lying, so I'm not really calling Him that. Just saying. I get that we live in a fallen world." He waves a hand at the freeway outside our car windows. "I get that bad things happen and that God has to allow free will because the only value of love is in the choice. I get that." He's amped, and it's a side of him I don't normally see. Usually people would say this with joy, but he sounds mad. His eyes are fixed on the windshield in front of him. "I get that the only way to show us He loves us is by giving us the choice to love Him back. And sometimes we're the victim of someone else's choice. I don't blame God for any of that. I get my dad's best friend getting burned to death. Hate it, but I get it. My dad knew what he was getting into. War has consequences."

He pauses, and I swallow, but I knew what I was asking. What did I think I was gonna get from him, a simple "Jesus is awesome!" fist bump?

"What I *don't* get is that my real father died out there,

and God couldn't just let him be. No, He resurrected some other guy in my dad's skin—a head case and an alcoholic—and brought *that* guy back to me here in the States, and now I have to take care of him. With one grenade, God made me an orphan *and* a parent." He flicks on his right blinker with force and switches lanes. "Somewhere deep inside me, I know God's still good and I don't get the whole picture, and maybe that's the beauty of it. I know enough to believe He's real, and that this place isn't our final home. But I don't feel like lifting my arms up because God's good and gives me shelter, education, and lattes every morning. He doesn't need praise for that. And I'd rather spend my time praying for Him to protect future little six-year-olds riding their bikes near bombs, instead of asking Him to find me a parking spot or help me on a test. So you won't find me talking to Him about the little things. You're not gonna find me talking to Him about us."

"You consider *us* one of 'the little things'?"

He lets out a exasperated groan. "Are you even hearing me? Fine, let's talk about that, then. No, I don't care if we have sex."

"That's not what I'm—"

"That's exactly what you're asking. Do I love God enough to *wait*? There's other things that keep me up at night. Being closer to you doesn't." It should be a compliment, but his tone's frustrated and it makes me swallow. "Do I think God's *for* it outside of marriage? There's nothing in the Bible that says 'Go for it.'" He lowers his voice. "But I just don't care enough to run from it either. Not with you."

He said he believed in Jesus. But then he said he didn't get Jesus. He said he wouldn't have sex with me. But then he also said that he wouldn't care if we did. And as confusing as that should be, it somehow makes sense when I think of what he just said about his dad.

"Thank you," I say. "Sorry I made that about us. I can't imagine what it's like not to recognize your own dad. Really. I know it took a lot to share that." He doesn't respond—which I understand—so I turn to face the passenger window, lean my head against my headrest, and look out. I stay frozen that way, and he turns the volume up and drowns the tension with music. It's almost night, and it's a new moon so it's especially dark. I focus on the ocean to my right. I can just make out the crashing waves on the side of the highway. Something blue lights up but then dissipates. "What the—" I say.

Our car slows as we exit. I turn to him, expecting his face still to be tight, but he's watching me, his cheek dimpling as I gape.

"What was that?" I say.

"Red tide."

"But it's December," I argue.

"I know, right?"

I remember reading about this strange occurrence. It's some dinoflagellate that makes the ocean light up like a glow stick. When the waves crash, the microbes get agitated and give off a flash of blue light—some sort of chemical reaction inside cells.

He turns down a small road. "December's been warmer than usual, so the blooms multiplied, and then this storm pushed it all up and, voilà, red tide." He parks, unhooks his charger, and leans over me to hide his phone in the glove compartment. I feel his body heat, and I want to touch him, but I don't. The music stops playing and in the new silence, we can hear the muted surf through our closed windows.

"Are you okay?" I venture.

He puts a hand up to my cheek, then drops it and squeezes my hand instead. "Yeah, I mean . . . it's— There's a lot. I know the answers you want me to say, and I'm"—he looks out my window at the dark sky and then back at me—"I'm not you."

I nod. I keep thinking about what he shared about his dad. About us. About God. He clearly struggles with God, but that actually makes his faith *more* real. A sense of peace washes over me, soaks me until I'm drenched in it.

He hands me his sweatshirt from the back seat, then pecks me on the cheek and jumps out of the car. The smell of dead fish makes my eyes water.

I follow him down a dirt trail. I know we're near La Jolla Shores, but this little cove's tucked away from waves and people. It looks like a glassy lake. At the shoreline, small waves crash, creating an eerie neon-blue glow.

A guy at the shore waves at us, and he's standing next to one of the largest stand-up paddleboards I've ever seen. Jake introduces him as "Bill," and I shake his hand—a thirtysomething guy with a shaved head and a peeling nose. He hands the paddle to Jake and says, "An hour?"

Jake nods, and Bill walks away.

"How do you know him?" I say as we lift the board together with a grunt and set it in the shallow water.

"I don't." He responds to my quizzical look with, "What else am I gonna spend my hard-earned credit-union paycheck on?"

○))) ◗ ● ◖ ◖ ((○

Even if Jake falls off the face of the planet and I go on a thousand dates in the future, I don't know what could top this. I'm sitting with my legs crisscrossed on an SUP board the size of a table. It cuts through the night water like glass, and the fluorescent blue lights up the perimeter of the board. My back's touching Jake's legs. He stands directly behind me, a parted stance, and strokes the water with his paddle. Every time the paddle touches the water, an outline of bright blue ignites and melts away.

"It's like we're in a cartoon," I whisper. The blues are so bright, they look like they belong in an animated film. I could watch this all night: the gliding of the board lighting up the water. It's like our LED surfboards, except the opposite. Our boards were blue and the ocean was dark. This time, the board's dark, but the ocean around us lights up with its touch, the electric blue of the night sky in unicorn posters.

"Unreal, isn't it?" Jake whispers back. The board rocks from the rolling tide, but it's mostly calm. A line from a worship song comes into my head: *If the oceans sing Your praises, so will I.* I reach back and wrap my arms around his calves, leaning my head back on his legs.

"It's perfect."

He did this. He planned this. He spent his paycheck on

it. He made sure it happened on a new moon, because the luminescence would be the best if it contrasted the darkness instead of moonlight. We're far enough out that the cove and shore are shadowed outlines in the night. I dance my fingers against his calf. His leg tightens, but it's probably to balance.

He crouches, setting the paddle on the board, and then he sits down behind me and places a leg on either side of me. I can feel his chest against my back, and I press into him to feel more. He wraps his arm around me and pulls me in close, drinking in the scent of me with his nose against my neck. His lips press against my cheek, my neck, my ear, and I feel drunk from it. We float for minutes that I never want to end. We don't need to say anything. Words might ruin it, the bliss of feeling so close to a person that they feel like an extension of you.

He starts to kiss my neck again, small kisses, cautious, and I turn my head so that I'm facing more toward him than away. He pauses, rests his forehead on my temple, and then kisses my cheek. Once. Waits. My pulse quickens. I turn closer, and his lips brush the edge of my mouth.

I want it to be here. Not at an altar, or in a building. Not in front of hundreds of people, snapping photos and "aww"-ing at my stumbling first kiss. I want it to be surrounded by the ocean that makes me feel alive and so loved by my Creator, in the arms of the person who doesn't have it all figured out but admits it, who understands how it feels to be let down by your parents but still believes that good things can happen and that life's amazing and messed up and full of miracles. My thoughts are deep and swimmy from whatever Jake's making me feel. But I want to kiss him, right here, now, more than anything I've wanted in my life.

I lean back, turn my head more, our mouths a millimeter apart. His lips move away from mine and head back to my ear. "Stop moving, mannequin. You're making this difficult." He can sense what I'm leading him to do, and he backs away, crawls to his knees. I'm bruised by his rejection, and he must see my crestfallen face because he says, "I didn't bring you out here to take your first kiss away."

It takes a moment for his words to register. He's actually looking out for me, which makes me even more attracted to him. "What if I want to give it?"

He stands up. "No."

I turn around so I'm facing him, and then I stand up too. We balance precariously on the board. "Why not?" I try to step closer, but he holds the paddle across my stomach, his arms extended, forming a two-foot span between us.

"I want you to be sure of things," he says. "If you're doubting, or wondering—"

"I'm not." I pull the paddle down from my stomach and step closer. I close the gap between us. The paddle dangles in one of his hands, and I hope he doesn't drop it. I touch his chest with delicate fingers, and he stares at me. Controls his breathing. I trace my fingers down from his chest to his sides, and he brings his free hand around my waist and pulls me close. Our breath's hot and mixes together as we stand for several moments, our noses barely touching.

His eyes blink a question, and I know what he's thinking.

"I'm sure," I say.

A dimple creases one of his cheeks, then the other, and I know that he believes me.

I feel his lips barely touch mine, and I suck in my breath at their softness. My foot wobbles and I grasp for him, but the board's no longer under my feet, and I'm splashing into the nighttime water with an ungraceful plop, a ring of electric blue pooling around me in concentric circles and washing over my head as I go under.

Chapter Thirty-Six

"Give me your hand," he instructs. He's kneeling on the board; I'm neck-deep in the red-tide ocean. It's soupy and foamy, like grimy bathwater. I grab the far side of the board with one hand and let him pull me up by the other hand. We're both on the board, only he's dry. I'm a sopping mess in front of him, and the two of us look at each other, remembering what we were about to do, and burst out laughing.

"Oh my gosh," I say, wringing out my hair with my hands. "Is this stuff poisonous?"

"Nah," he says. "Well? It's not harmful like it is in Florida, but it's probably not amazing for you. We should get you to a shower."

"Awesome," I giggle. "I'm covered in algae."

"Algal blooms," he corrects and paddles us toward shore. "It's like flowers." I sit in a huddled ball as he stands over me. He leans down and sniffs my wet hair. "Is that roses I smell? Mmm . . ."

I laugh and swat at him. "Stop it." I know I smell like dead fish. It's bad.

We get to shore and heave the monstrous board onto the sand. Bill's nearby smoking a cigarette at his pickup and waves us over. He directs us to the nearest beach showers, about a block and a half away, and I'm shivering and goose bumped by the time we get there. "I'd offer you my sweatshirt, but . . ." Jake trails off, grinning at his sweatshirt that's clinging to me like a wet paper bag. I fake kick him, and he says, "Arms up." I shoot my arms up, and he peels me out of his sweatshirt. My T-shirt and sports bra are also drenched but not as heavy with cold seawater. He pushes on the shower, and the cool water feels warm against my chilled skin. I rub the ocean off me as best as I can, and he says, "I wonder if you're gonna sweat blue for a few days." I swat him and he swats back, and I catch him off guard and pull him under the shower. His hair gets wet, and he gasps from the shock. And then he doesn't care and wraps himself around me under the shower, and we're drenched and water's spraying everywhere and I'm warmer on the inside than if I were in a hot tub. We're holding our bodies close, our faces pressed against each other, our opposite cheeks kissing. I close my eyes and let the beach shower pour over me. I feel his head dip and his lips touch my shoulder. He waits, but I don't pull away. His lips move to my neck and then my cheek. He pauses, then traces them across my cheek toward my mouth. Our lips touch again, but I freeze. My eyes open. We're not in the ocean surrounded by God's beauty. This isn't a first-kiss moment. I'm wiping off algae and we're under a rusty outdoor shower and I'm shivering. The water automatically shuts off and he pulls away, muttering an apology.

But I grip his hand before he can move, hold him still, and reach behind me to push the shower back on. It pours over us, and he knows what I mean by turning it back on, knows it even before he sees the longing look in my eyes. He pulls me under the rusty showerhead, not holding back this time. His lips press into mine, four months of desire breaking through, and I reach for his chest. His T-shirt's wet underneath my hands, and I grab it in fistfuls. He reaches behind my neck, gripping my hair and holding on for dear life. Our mouths explore each other—our lips, our tongues, even our teeth— slowly, like we want to know every part and don't have to rush because we have forever now. The shower water pours over us like a waterfall, and it doesn't matter that I couldn't find this place on a map and there's salt in my eyes and sand between my toes. It feels like what I imagine Adam felt when he first laid eyes on Eve—how he broke into poetry.

We press the water back on many times, silently communicating that we don't want it to stop, and we don't. Minutes later, when we finally pull our lips away from each other, we stay there after the water shuts off, drenched and happy, embracing like we can't get close enough.

Jake breaks our hold first. It's like he wakes up two hours after his alarm. "Shit. Curfew."

"Right."

He wrings out his sweatshirt and then reaches for my hand. We walk together, the electric blue to our left, the highway above us on the hillside to our right. Our chins are tucked down, a little embarrassed by this new closeness. At least I am. Is he? What do you say after a first kiss? Talking about it would be weird, but talking about anything else would feel awkward and forced. As if he can sense my worry, he rubs the inside of my wrist with his thumb, and my heart calms again.

On the drive back, the heater's blasting, and he has to turn on the defroster because our wet clothes fog up the windows. Worry creases the edges of my tired brain, wondering what this kiss means for us, for God. I counter it by reaching for his phone and making him a Spotify playlist of my favorite worship songs. My eyes start to blur, so I lean my head on his shoulder and doze off. Some time later, he nudges me when we drive by the power plant.

"See?"

He points. Just the tips of the "boobs" blink red.

"Can't believe you woke me up for that." My words are slurred with sleep, but he knows I'm smiling.

"Yes you can."

I burrow back into his shoulder, and he turns just enough to kiss the top of my head. I must fall back asleep immediately because when I open my eyes a moment later, we are parked in front of my house and the car smells of strong black coffee. He must've stopped to grab one rather than make me stay awake to keep him up.

"We're here," he whispers.

Disappointment creases my eyes. "But your aunt. I was supposed to meet her."

He taps the car's clock on the dash. "Your dad's a military guy, and it's after twenty-three hundred. So." He opens his car door and walks around to open mine. "Next time."

I love that there's a next time. And infinite times after that.

We've reached my front door, and we stand under the porch light.

"What?" I ask. "Do I have seaweed on my face?" I wipe my cheek and check my nose with the back of my hand.

"You okay?" He clears his throat. "You know."

Oh. With the kissing. The only thing I'm afraid of is that he'll think because I'm okay with this one thing, I'm okay with all the things.

I lick my lips. "I'm not like that, you know."

"Like what?"

"Like, now that we've done this, we'll do other stuff. In fact, I think this was a one-off."

He cocks his head to the side, and my palms sweat even though I'm cold.

"Like, I'm okay that we did it," I ramble, "and I don't think God's against it, at least I can't find it anywhere in the Bible. But." I pull my shirt away from my stomach. It's still damp, chilled from the night air. "It doesn't mean I'm going to do it all the time now. Or even one more time."

"A one-off," he repeats.

I nod. "Our relationship's more than that. And I just don't want it to be defined by just physical stuff. It's just"—Oh no, I'm sounding like Kelly praying with all the *justs*—"I don't know, I still want to be an example, and . . ." I stop my sentence there. I don't know why.

"So you're like a kissing one-night stand."

I laugh. "That makes me sound like a player."

He holds out a hand to high-five me. "Well good night then."

I push his hand away, pull him close and hug him. "Don't you dare." He wraps his arms around me and we nuzzle.

"I got it," he murmurs into my neck and ear. "One and done. Harsh. But worth it."

I kiss him on the cheek. "Thank you." I start to pull away but he has a hand around the back of my neck, and he holds me still, quiet, against him. Desire's making me dizzy. I pull away and he lets me, but then I tug at the belt loops of his wet jeans and look up through my eyelashes.

"So," he starts and puts his hands on my waist. "Since this is a one-night stand—a *kissing* one-night stand," he clarifies, "then the night's not over for fifty-two more minutes."

He pulls me in, and I let him, our lips finding each other like they were meant to connect from the beginning of time. *Last kiss*, I promise Jesus. *After tonight, I'm done.*

Chapter Thirty-Seven

It's been four days since I swore off another kiss. I've only seen Jake once, so it's been pretty easy. Plus, his aunt was there. I finally saw his apartment, and it's small but cozy. Lots of gray carpets and pastel drapes. His aunt was sweet, her hair in a tight bun even when she wasn't on a flight, and she offered me water with lemon. His bedroom was like his coffee—plain. Sheets, two blankets, nothing on the walls, and a couple of books on one of his nightstands. He had to head back to the base that day, so we exchanged Christmas presents in front of his aunt. Pastor Brett dared the youth group to accept the five-dollars challenge—buying presents for our friends that were *thoughtful* rather than over-the-top, in light of the Christmas season and God looking at the heart rather than the outside fluff. Jake bought me a snow globe. It says HAWAIIAN ISLANDS across the bottom and instead of snow, it has sand. Inside the globe, there's a tiki pole flanked by two palm trees. The pole has five wooden signs with arrows pointing different directions: Waikiki, North Shore, Lahaina, Hanalei, and Kona. I grin. "It's like a Hawaiian GPS. I'll bring it if we ever take a trip there." I bought a pack of blue neon glow sticks—the color of our LED surfboards and the La

Jolla red-tide waters—and I made him a sign with seashells and the glow sticks that reads THIS WAY HOME. It's funny to me that we both got each other things that talked about direction. Mine was super cheesy, but he loved it. I could tell by the extra-long embrace down at his car before he headed back to Pendleton. He whispered, "You're my GPS." I turned to him to ask what he meant, but he turned me away and pecked my cheek. "One-off," he joked. Then he drove away.

It's now Christmas Eve, I'm getting ready for midnight Mass (I go every year with Lydia; it's tradition), and I'm in the bathroom I share with Matt. I run out of toothpaste, so I open his toiletries travel bag, looking for some, and I see four condom packages. Matt's in college. He'll be twenty-one on March 1. But still, it takes a second to process. Matt's *really doing that*? I thought maybe he was doing more stuff than me, but that's like *the most* stuff.

I don't know why, but I take one of the condoms out and look at it, reading the fine print. I figure he won't notice, so I open it and feel the texture between my fingers. It's slimy and kind of gives me the willies. I stretch it, and it snaps out of one hand, slingshotting to the other. Then I start unrolling it up my arm. I don't know what possesses me—it's not like I want to use it or anything—I think I'm mesmerized.

Just then, Matt walks through the doorway, and there I am, my tube of mascara open on the sink and my hand high in the air, gloved with his condom. We look at each other in the mirror. He probably would've laughed if he didn't suddenly remember how mad he's been at me. "What are you doing with that?" he growls, motioning at my condom arm.

"What are *you* doing with it?"

"You really want me to answer that?"

"No. Ew! Don't be gross!" I peel it off and throw it in the sink, then stomp out, embarrassed.

"It's not a party balloon," he shouts after me as I race down the hall. "Leave my stuff alone!" Then he adds, "Dad! Lovette's stealing my condoms!"

I careen back to the bathroom. "Shut up!" He laughs low and mean. I whisper, "Don't you have another country to go to?"

My words seem to punch him in the face. He tips back on his heels. "No. Haven't you figured that out by now, genius? I'm honest with our parents."

My heart sinks. "They said no?"

"Not exactly. I saved up. I had the money. Told them I wouldn't ask for a penny. I thought it would make them see how thoughtful I was. Instead, I was told that if I chose to spend my hard-earned money on studying abroad, Mom and Dad would choose *not* to spend their hard-earned money on tuition next year."

"No."

"I called their bluff and told them I'd take out loans. 'Oh,' Dad added. 'And you'll break Mom's heart.' How dare I put myself at such a health risk when they've been through so much already." He crumples the condom foil wrapper and throws it at the trash can. It misses. "You know how her headaches escalate when she gets upset."

"That's not fair."

"No shit, Sherlock." He hisses his words. "But your

comment at Thanksgiving got them asking questions about my plans. So I was honest, because *I* actually care about their feelings."

It's a low blow, and I know he's talking about my surfing. He's not outing me, but he hates me for it. I don't know which is worse.

Christmas is subdued. We're playing the part of the happy family that we usually are. The breakfast smells great, presents are under the tree, we all thank one another for our gifts as we unwrap them, but our smiles are strained, our conversations those of understudies to the usual actors on stage. Recited lines. Mom rubs her temples a lot, so we make an extra effort to pretend to be relaxed, stretching out on the couch, not looking at our phones. I'm relieved when a couple of Matt's friends show up to watch football. I retreat to my room and flop onto my bed. "Happy birthday, Jesus," I say. I pull out my Bible and read His birth story in the Gospel of Luke, lose myself in giddy angels and awestruck shepherds. Everyone who hears about the Savior's birth is "amazed" and probably talks about it like it's the latest TMZ story. But Mary "treasures up" all the things and ponders them in her heart. What does "treasures up" mean, anyway? Is it a good thing? I wonder what she thought about. I wonder if she was quiet about it because the angels told her that her son would someday die for the sins of the world, take the place of her and everyone else. I wonder how she felt knowing that God's wrath would be poured out on that child in her arms. That's a lot to think about for someone my age, and she was probably younger. Probably fourteen or fifteen. My eyes travel to the snow globe on my nightstand, and I lift it in my hands and shake it. Sand rains down on the palm trees, the signs with all their different pointing fingers. I hear and feel Jake's whisper against my ear, *"You're my GPS."* I suddenly feel selfish that I'm almost seventeen, and all I'm thinking about is when I can kiss Jake next. I push it out of my mind. Maybe God told Mary it would all be roses.

I last six days and four hours before I become a kissing bandit. I'm in love with kissing. Anytime I get a solo moment with Jake, I find his lips with mine. When he picks me up in his car. When he drops me off at night. When we both get bathroom passes at school and intercept each other in the math wing. When we walk through the Manhattan Beach alleys between the million-dollar houses stacked together garage to garage. Everywhere. It's fun and new and does something to the inside of me that I never want to end.

I try it everywhere. In the water, on dry land. Surfing, night swimming. Kissing in the water is salty but more serious. We can tread water, one hand on both of our boards and the other on each other, gripping the sides of our neoprene suits. Kissing while balancing on our skateboards is tricky, but I've perfected the "lean and peck" without smacking my nose against his cheekbone.

How's it already January? I think falling for someone is a time warp where you want every moment to last for eternity but instead it keeps jumping forward and you ask, *Where did the last hour go? Or the last day? Week? Month?*

I'm not planning on marrying Jake tomorrow, but sometimes I imagine myself after college marrying a twenty-six-year-old version of him, and that makes me feel okay about kissing him. I realize the slippery slope I can go down when it comes to that—how I could say that about sex, too—except I'm pretty sure the Bible's clear on that matter.

My brother is still in town. I wish he would go back already, but school doesn't start for him until mid-January. One-and-a-half more weeks to endure the looks and silence. We all tiptoe around our house, eggshells and tripwires everywhere.

I hate every moment because my brother's right. He did the right thing by telling our parents, regardless of how it turned out. And so should I. I feel it grate at my soul every time Mom closes herself in her room early for the night. My brother faced that head-on, and I'm terrified of it. Afraid of making Mom get stress headaches. Afraid of Dad's military rigidity. I'm letting fear guide me instead of God. I think back to the verse in the prayer room in church: "And we know that all things work together for good to those who love God. Romans 8:28." Do I believe that? What if God does allow my parents to cut me off from surfing? Do I love God enough to let him work that to my good somehow?

I should tell my parents I want to compete in the All Wave Junior Open. I should tell them how badly I want to surf again without feeling guilty and criminal. But I don't. Because the truth is, I love it too much to let it go. I'm willing to disobey God for the ocean.

At youth group tonight, Kelly's sick and Jake can't make it for some reason, so I'm in the front row all by myself, which makes me feel like Brett's talking directly to me during his sermon. He holds his open Bible with one hand. His other hand is in his pocket, casual, as if he's telling us about the weather. "Not many people from the Bible had hundred dollar bills falling from the sky just because they obeyed God. God wasn't poppin' bottles and makin' it rain whenever they did what he asked." A few of us chuckle at Brett's lame slang, others shift in their chairs. "Remember Joseph? Joseph did the right thing, and look what happened to him! His boss's wife was like, 'Hey, Joey-joe, you're a hottie with a body, get in my bed and let's do a little somethin'-somethin',' and he was like, '*Heck no!*' But the boss's wife didn't get that *no* meant no, and when she grabbed Joseph, he wriggled out of his jacket and headed for the nearest fire exit, but meanwhile she screamed. When her attendants came running, she said that the owner of the jacket attacked her in bed and tried to make babies. And did God clear Joseph's name? Nope. Joseph went to jail for twenty years!"

I already know where this sermon's going: trusting in God when things don't make sense. Obeying him regardless of outcome. AKA telling my parents and surrendering my board.

I zone out and imagine Joseph in jail. Twenty years is a long time. It's three years longer than I've been alive. I wonder if every year Joseph thought, "This *is the year that God's gonna get me out."* I wonder if he stopped thinking that after a while. Did he ever have a wave-crashing thought that maybe God had forgotten?

I know this story. Sometime in that twenty years, the pharaoh's cupbearer and baker were arrested and put into jail with Joseph. They both had dreams, and God told Joseph what the dreams meant. Joseph must've thought, *Finally!* I mean, if God started speaking to *me* like that, wouldn't I think He was up to something? Surely He'd get me out of jail. So Joseph told the cupbearer, "Hey, when you get out of here, tell the pharaoh about the cool dream thing I did." When the cupbearer was released like Joseph predicted, I bet Joseph thought, *"Any day now. Any day . . ."* But the cupbearer forgot to say anything! In the Bible, we fast forward through all that. But sometimes I wonder what Joseph thought about during the 365 days a year for twenty years. I get out my phone and do a quick calculation. Did he wonder on just one of those 7,300 days if God was still in control?

I get it, I tell God during closing prayer. *But not yet. I'll tell them after the competition. Maybe if I have an award to show them, they can see that I'm good at this, that I'm not going to get injured the way my brother did, that they can rest easy knowing that I'll be going to championships, not hospitals.*

When I get home, I change into my pajamas and crawl into bed, but first I wrap a piece of surf wax in cellophane and hide it under my pillow. I shake the snow globe and set it on my Bible, watching the sand float and flutter in chaos before it settles and clears.

Chapter Thirty-Eight

"You know what today is?"

Jake has stumped me. January 16 isn't our anniversary. It isn't anyone's birthday. I look at all the eyes directed at me around the table. Our lunch crew is at Two Guns Espresso in Manhattan Beach, a locals' hangout, and the only coffee shop in the South Bay that boasts its lack of Internet. Their hope is that people come here to talk, connect, not disengage. Aside from the few two-person tables bumper-boating the line of people that goes out the door, there's an extra room, narrow but wide enough to house one long rectangular table, where we sit with our lattes, schoolbooks, and about eight other patrons. No one minds. It's bright and comfy, and there's no stranger danger in Manhattan Beach, not with so many Uggs and yoga pants.

We were meeting here after school. I wasn't told why, and now it looks like everyone expects me to know. January 16? I hope I'm not forgetting something important. Lydia pulls out a pink cardboard box and opens it. Inside are six Beckers cookies in the shape of surfboards.

"Hmm," I say, sliding my backpack off. Jake's usual black coffee steams in the cold afternoon, already half empty.

They've been here a while. They all drove, but I skateboarded. Wanted an extra workout. He hands me my favorite, a milkadamia, which is a latte with macadamia-nut milk. I sip the delicious foam. "Is it that holiday where we eat lots of Beckers cookies and binge Netflix or watch *North Shore* on repeat?"

"Netflix and chill?" Niles says. "That should be a national holiday."

"If that's today, we're for sure honoring it," Kaj says, putting his arm around Lydia.

Kelly rolls her eyes.

"I swear, your mind's so comfortable in the gutter," Lydia says but then kisses him. "And who says you're getting Netflix and chill today?"

"It's one month till you compete," Kelly interrupts. "The surf competition."

"Even Kelly remembers," Jake says.

Lydia beams at me. "We all remembered. It's your debut! Your chance to bury Cecilia's boyfriend in the wake of your turns."

Trevor Walker. I think about what he said on the water. I've often wondered if I should tell Cecilia what I heard. *How would you handle that one, Jesus?* Back when I wore the WWJD bracelet in seventh grade, it was all about smiling at strangers and offering doughnuts to the homeless. That's what Jesus would do. I never imagined I'd be asking God what my responsibility was in telling my enemy that her boyfriend cheats on her.

"We should get some practice runs in," Jake says.

Lydia claps. "Yes! We could bring posters and rate you perfect tens!"

Kaj laughs. "I don't think that's how it's scored, baby."

"A perfect score would be a twenty," I explain. "Never happens, especially if you're up early. A judge won't throw a ten in the first heat." I recall my early competitions and watching my brother in his. There were three judges and a fourth as a "spotter."

"How much time do they give you?" Niles asks.

"Fifteen minutes, if I remember."

Jake nods. "It'll seem shorter when you're out there."

"So you pop up as much as you can against the others in your heat—say there's four of you—and the judges give you scores for each wave you ride." I take a drink, nibble on the edge of my cookie. "Each judge takes their top two scores for each surfer and, based on that, ranks how you placed in your heat: one, two, three, or four. Then those rankings are added to the other judges' rankings for you, and the lowest-numbered surfer or sometimes the lowest two numbers move on to the semis or finals."

Lydia eats her cookie, shakes her head. "Sounds like my way of scoring's much easier."

Kaj kisses the top of her head. "You're pretty."

She slaps his shoulder. "Don't you dare."

"What? What'd I say?"

She's all levels of irritated by his condescending remark. She stands. "Excuse me." She throws her backpack over her shoulder, grabs her half cookie, and whips her hair behind her, marching off without a backward glance.

"So Netflix and chill later?" he calls after her.

She responds with a middle finger above the back of her head.

Niles howls with laughter, and Kaj turns back to his iced latte as if she blew him a kiss goodbye.

"We can Netflix and chill later," I say, gently kicking Jake under the table, and he chokes on his coffee. He wipes the dribble off of his chin.

Kelly's eyes bug out like a cartoon, and Niles and Kaj cackle. Avoiding eye contact with me, she exits through the doors to the parking lot, maybe to find Lydia.

I look at Niles, Kaj, and Jake across from me, all grinning.

"Oh my gosh. So Netflix and chill means . . ."

"Sex," all three say in unison.

I slap my hand to my forehead, feeling like a moron for not putting it together. I should've known that. I mean, it's not like I haven't heard it. But in junior high, it was code for kissing. When did everyone get the memo that the definition changed? "How was I supposed to know . . ." My cheeks are beet red, I can tell by the heat in them, but when I look up and see the boys giggling, I can't help but laugh with them.

○))) ● (((○

The girls come back in, and Kelly still won't look at me. I'll have to explain later. Right now, everyone else is asking me about whether I'm nervous and what tricks I'm going to do, and I'm answering but also remembering Kaj's comment about honoring Netflix-and-Chill Day. Lydia telling Kaj his mind was in the gutter but also not denying anything.

When we finally leave, before I ride to my work shift, I text Lydia.

Hey

Whats up

I pause, stare at my screen. *So*

Yes?

Do you Netflix and chill for real?

Lol

She didn't write "no." She wrote "Lol." My head's dizzy. I knew they made out. But I guess I figured if they'd had sex, Lydia would've told me. I mean, I told her when Jake and I kissed. That night I sent her a text and she sent an emoji of hands clapping and wrote back, "It's about time." It makes me sad that maybe she didn't tell me about the sex because she knows what I believe about it. How many of my friends are going through changes and not telling me? Are they assuming I'll judge them for it? I mean, why else would she keep it from me? And is everyone having sex?

I text her: *But you're Catholic*

And?

I don't know what to say to that. I just assumed she wouldn't ever. I see Lydia's text bubbles. She's typing a lot.

Sometimes things aren't as big of a deal as you make them. You'll see soon enough ;)

Whoa! Soon enough? I text in all caps: *WHEN I'M MARRIED!*

She writes back: *Lol. Ok*

Why does everyone seem to think it's not a big deal? Well,

everyone except Kelly, who thinks I'm the worst of all sinners for dating a non-virgin.

Jake slept with Hannah. My brother's sleeping with his girlfriend. Lydia's sleeping with Kaj. Am I just some old-fashioned backward-thinking girl who's been drinking the Kool-Aid? I've known I was extreme by not kissing before marriage, but I didn't think I was the only one waiting for sex.

I think of the purity contract I signed in seventh grade. It made sense then. I remember when Tim Rainsforth accidentally touched my breast in ninth grade at the lock-in. Even then, I knew it wasn't something anyone my age should be doing. When did everyone decide it was okay to do all the things?

I need to clear my head. I slap my skateboard down to the ground, sling my backpack on, and head to Manhattan Beach Boulevard. I ride down the hill, fishtail skidding to brake, weaving in and out of the winter tourists. At the pier, I kick off my shoes and walk toward the water. The sand is cool, but the sun warms my neck. I stop at the edge of the dry sand, where the tide ends and the dark, wet sand begins. I set my board on my backpack to keep the sand off, and I lie down, close my eyes on the far too cheerful sun, and let it soak into me.

For the past five years, my answers have been found in Bible verses. But the questions were easier. Pastor Brett gave me my first Bible verse to memorize after I had told him I believed in Jesus. It was a Sunday morning a few months after Hume Lake, and he walked me out to the parking lot after service. I had so many doubts—I mean, who doesn't at eleven?—but he assured me God had accepted me. "But what if He changes His mind?" I asked Brett.

"He doesn't. 'I the Lord do not change.'"

"But what if I don't do enough good for Him?"

He laughed. "You can't. We don't do things in order to be loved by Him. We do them *because* we're loved by Him."

"But what if I do bad stuff in the future?"

"You will," he said.

"But what if He stops loving me?"

He squinted up at the glaring sun above us, the same sun I feel warming me right now as I lie on the beach. "Imagine the sun as God's love for you. You can hold an umbrella up to it and block out the sun, right?"

I nodded.

"So, technically, you can stop receiving it. But He never stops shining it. You gotta decide what your posture's gonna be toward Him. That will decide what your life's gonna look like."

He handed me a Bible verse and told me to memorize it and say it to myself whenever I started to doubt: "For it is by grace you have been saved, through faith—and this is not from yourselves, it is the gift of God—not by works, so that no one can boast. Ephesians 2:8–9."

That's when I started memorizing every verse I could. "How can a young person stay on the path of purity? By living according to your word. Psalm 119:9." Purity meant staying close to God. It was so simple. It worked.

I never could've imagined what I'd be wondering about on January 16, almost five years later. How purity started meaning other things. How questions got broader. More layered. *This was so much easier when it was just me and You,* I tell God. *Back when all I had to do was understand that You died for me, that I couldn't make it up to You, and how You didn't want me to. How You just wanted me to choose You. But choosing You was so easy back then. There wasn't all this other stuff.*

Wait. I think back to Pastor Brett when I wondered if God would change His feelings for me, and he quoted scripture: "I the Lord do not change." I sit up, resolved. I need to figure this out. If the Bible always held my answers, then maybe it still does. I need to look. The ocean splashes my toes, and they curl back on instinct. The tide's shifting, coming higher, inch by inch, unnoticeable, but soon I'll be soaked. I stand up and lift my things just in time. A wave pushes the water to my ankles, not as cold as the first time it splashed me. I insert my AirPods and lose myself in worship songs, walking north toward my work.

Your promise still stands.

Great is Your faithfulness, faithfulness.

I'm still in Your hands.

This is my confidence, You've never failed me yet.

It fills me like the first breath of air after being tumbled and held under by a wave. I walk along the shore all the way to Thirty-sixth, where I have to head up two streets to my work. The water's so comfortable as it splashes against my calves, and it calls me to leave my backpack and skateboard and dive all the way under. Just a quick dip, harmless. But I don't think Billy's Buns would appreciate a drenched employee dripping seawater onto their ciabatta loaves. I've got a job, I sigh, remembering, and I trudge away from the beckoning water and make my way to the world of hairnets and salami slices.

Chapter Thirty-Nine

Jake uses the thumb of his opposite hand to wipe the salt water off the face of his watch as a rolling wave raises and then dips his board. "Eight more minutes."

"Got it. You said 'nine more minutes' a minute ago."

We're between sets, so I tip off my board and go under, letting my hair slick back mermaid style.

When I climb back onto my board and paddle closer to him, I continue what I've been telling him since we entered the water. How I've been looking up every verse God has to say about sex outside of marriage.

"So it's pretty clear when it says, 'Avoid sexual immorality.' But I was like, *What is that*, ya know?" I sit up on my board, twirl my legs in the water, turning my surfboard back and forth. "Like why doesn't it just say, 'Don't have sex if you're not married?' Why's it all fuzzy about details? So I looked up the Greek, and it's this word *porneia*."

Jake arches an eyebrow at me. "Is that where the word *porn* comes from?"

"I don't know! I did *not* Google 'porn' to see what would come up. But, anyway, it's a whole bunch of things, including even"—I lower my voice—"bestiality."

"Great." He looks like he's lost his appetite.

"But in that pile is sex outside of marriage. It's one of the things. So God's definitely like, 'Hey, don't do this.'"

"I didn't know you ever doubted that."

"I just wanted to know *for sure*."

"I'd like to know that you're *sure* about competing."

"Of course I am!"

"Well, you just missed a great set because you were reciting your research paper."

"It's not a research paper. And I didn't want that wave."

"You know who *did* want that wave? The winner of your heat, that's who."

I splash him, but he seems nervous. He glances at me and then back at the horizon. I lie back down on my board, paddle so close to him our boards almost touch. "Gosh, it's like *you're* the one competing in two weeks." I lean on my elbow facing him. "Why didn't you, by the way? Sign up? You afraid of beating me, Hawaii boy?"

He gives a half laugh. "Nah. I just knew this was your thing. That you needed it."

I reach out and touch him with my toe. "I did. Thank you." And then I add, "There's one more competition in May. Sign up for that one with me?"

He looks at me, his eyes pained for a moment. "Maybe."

"What's wrong?"

But he answers, "Wave." I turn, and a perfect one's forming. I aim my board at the shore and go, then see in my periphery that Jake's racing me for it. I grin, seawater shooting into my mouth as I stroke my arms harder.

"Come on, mannequin!" he shouts. "Don't be such a statue. Move!"

We both pop up at the same time, and I smile at him over my shoulder. I'm in front, blocking out any move he can do. He rides slowly, I can tell, so he doesn't collide with me, and I gloat by making extra rail to rails, tic-tacking down the line like I'm on a skateboard. I wiggle my butt at him. The wave is kind to me as I make a bottom turn and shoot back up its face. At the top, just to rub it in with a finale, I arch my back, stick my belly to the sky, and throw my head back, trying for a soul arch. Of course that's silly to do on a shortboard, and I lose my balance and back flop into the water.

When I emerge, he's clapping, his applause sarcastic and slow.

"Why, thank you," I say, getting back on my board and meeting him to paddle back out.

"Congratulations. You just got eliminated."

"Sore loser."

"Who was closest to the peak?"

He obviously was closest to the breaking part of the wave, which meant he had the right of way.

"You, but I thought you were only fighting me for the wave so you'd light a fire under my butt."

"We're simulating competition. You just got penalized for interference, and they just dropped your best wave."

"Then I guess I'll have to have more than one."

"And don't do a soul arch. It's hardly worth any points. And you'll never pull it off on a shortboard. Not with these waves and the way they drop out."

"Aye, aye, captain."

He shakes his head and looks out at a distant sailboat. It's sweet how nervous he is for me. I decide to hold off on any more Bible verses until the fifteen minutes is over.

Another set comes in during the last minute, and I ride it clean and neat, one bottom turn, and then end with a simple tailslide. Decent. Comfortable. Not fireworks, but safe.

○)) ⟩ ⟩ ● ⟨ ⟨ ⟨ ⟨ ○

Back on the shore, lying side by side on our towels, I continue talking to him. "But all the other stuff I read in the Bible—about avoiding sex unless they were married—it was weird for them too. It wasn't like it was because they were all uptight back then. Guys could sleep with whoever, seriously, married girls, single girls, prostitutes—sorry, sex workers—and then Jesus comes along and he's like, nope. Not okay."

"Shame." My mouth falls open. "I'm kidding!" He pulls me close and reaches around the base of my neck. "Have I tried to have sex with you?"

"No."

He kisses my cheek. "Then why all the defense?"

"Because it doesn't start that way! It's not like you throw off your clothes one day and say, 'Hey, baby, let's do it.'"

His eyes widen, a mix of amusement and incredulity. "Is that what I'm gonna say?"

"No! I'm just giving an example. Be serious."

"I can't. Not with all the 'Hey, baby.'" He pulls me on top of him. "Hey, baby, let's touch lips."

I crane my neck away from him. "You're impossible."

"With God, all things are possible." He grins, knowing he took that verse way out of context. But I feel his muscles through our layers, and I wrap my arms around him and kiss him deeply. We lose ourselves, and the chill in the air becomes less as our body heat warms the thin layer of seawater trapped in our suits.

Lately at the beach, we've been kissing lying down on our towels, and it's my new favorite thing. We're in our wetsuits, so it's not like anything bad can happen. We lie side by side, or I lie on top of him, and when he lies on me, he's careful not to crush me. It's usually only from the waist up, but there's something different about our bodies connecting and not just our mouths. It's an intense feeling of closeness, like the best hug I've ever received. I told that to Jake the first time we lie-down kissed, asked him if he felt the same thing, and he smiled and kissed my forehead. "Something like that," he laughed. "Guys are wired a little differently. Sorry, *designed*." When I asked him what he meant, he shook his head.

"So, Six-Sport Saturday," he says, peeling himself away from me.

"What about it?"

I can't believe our annual lock-in is this weekend. It feels like just yesterday they were announcing the six-sport theme at youth group. We start at 6:00 a.m., drive to Mt. High eighty miles away, and snowboard for three hours. Then we drive back down the mountain and meet at the beach for lunch. The whole afternoon from 2:00 p.m. to 6:00 p.m., we compete in four other sports, each lasting an hour: surfing, volleyball, cornhole, and Ultimate Frisbee. We play Ultimate with a glow-in-the-dark Frisbee since it'll be pretty dark by then.

When we get back to church, we eat dinner and then play our final sport: capture the flag. I think the leaders hope we'll be so tired afterward that we'll all pass out in our sleeping bags as they play some John Hughes movie that they'll claim is the *best movie ever!* At 6:00 a.m., before heading home, we'll stuff our faces with too many doughnuts and hold an award ceremony to receive our official Six-Sport Saturday certificates, bragging rights to our non-California friends that we surfed and snowboarded in the same day.

"You know."

"You mean because it falls on Valentine's Day?"

Pastor Brett says it's perfect so that we celebrate the love we have for our friends and not just the romantic love we have for one other person. I'm excited I get to celebrate both.

"No, the whole surfing part—" Jake starts.

"Oh, that. Don't worry. I know, I know." There'll be too many eyes watching, too many people whose parents know my parents, who could run into them at Trader Joe's and say things like, *"Wow, your daughter's quite the surfer."* And then Dad would have a coronary and there'd be no surf competition, not with the funerals and all. His funeral first, then mine when Mom murders me afterward.

He brushes my cheek with the back of his pinkie. "It's too risky."

I nod, the pit in my stomach gnawing at me. I used to think it was my own guilt, but now I'm thinking it's the Holy Spirit bugging me to tell the truth. I know it's not coming from me because I feel fine about keeping it secret. What my parents don't know won't hurt them.

"Too bad it's not Five-Sport Friday, right?" I say, and he leans in and thanks me with a kiss. I lose myself for the next hour, lying next to him, on him, and under him, kissing until my face is raw and red and a single star appears in the twilight.

Chapter Forty

We arrive early at church on Saturday to make sure we get the good fifteen-passenger van and not the one that smells like chicken nuggets and spoiled milk. We all know which van's used for the elementary day-camp Youth Adventures, and whenever Pastor Brett takes two vans anywhere, it's the one time high-schoolers arrive early. A line forms outside the good van by 5:20 a.m. After we fill up, the overflow crowd groans and makes the funeral march to the Youth Adventures van. Many of us have our own boards and skis, so one of the leaders stashes our equipment in his pickup. A couple of students luck out and ride with leaders who are holding backpacks and beach supplies for later today.

The van's quiet the entire way, most of us sleeping with our foreheads against the row of seats in front of us. There's only one carsick incident, which of course happens in the chicken-nugget van.

At the mountain, Brett prays with us as a group, gives us check-in times, and then sets us free. It's only 7:30 a.m., and we're not meeting back at the vans until 11:00 a.m. We all disperse, grabbing our equipment, getting in line for passes, or heading to rentals.

"Hey, Kells," I say, as we buy our tickets. "You wanna board with us?"

She looks surprised. "Huh? Okay. I may slow you down."

"I'm not racing."

Dave looks at her, and there's this eye conversation that goes on. Then she says, "Nah, you'll probably be too fast for me, even on a slow day. Why don't you guys go have fun?"

"Come on, Dave," Jake says. "You afraid to be outboarded by a girl?"

"Me? Nah, nah."

"Okay, then, let's go!"

Dave hesitates and then lifts his snowboard. Kelly hoists her skis over her shoulder, and we trudge up the icy slush to the chairlift.

For the brief few hours that we glide on waves of white groomed powder, Kelly forgets she's "concerned" about my relationship with Jake, and Dave forgets he's supposed to remind her of that. And they both forget that they're supposed to be shunning him. He high-fives them and leads them through fun tree sections. Kelly smacks me playfully with her ski pole, and when she stops to adjust her glove, I carve hard and spray her with snow. When we finally take a break for hot chocolate and french fries, our faces are flushed from the icy wind, and Kelly's holding my hand and twisting my hair into ringlets. Carrie and Jessica join us, and we watch out the window and score people's wipeouts.

We're back to the vans and on the road by 11:36 a.m., record timing for thirty-five teenagers. Everyone passes out again but gets a second wind the moment we arrive in Manhattan Beach. Lunch is set up, and we scarf down sandwiches from Billy's Buns. Once the blue bags of Doritos are gone, we're fortified for our next sport.

For growing up near the ocean, we should be pros at beach volleyball, but you wouldn't know it. We punch the ball back and forth and hope it lands on the other side. Carrie's our ringer, spiking it like she's president of the AVP, but the rest of us fall over it mostly, rolling in the sand and laughing.

Meanwhile, the truck arrives with the rented foam surfboards, and the leaders disappear to bring them over. Kelly eyes me. "Don't worry," I say to her. "I'm not surfing today." She sighs with relief and then looks at Dave, like *See?*

I wonder if Kelly's told him I'm not allowed to surf. I wonder if he was planning on telling my parents if he caught me today. Or worse, I wonder if he was going to have Kelly do it. I shake that out of my head. I'm making up thoughts, judging people before they've even done anything wrong. I mumble an apology to God and jog into the water.

Dave yells, "I thought you weren't allowed to swim." I look at Kelly, who looks away. So she did talk.

"I'm peeing," I yell back. "Wanna come in? It's warm over by me."

"Ha. Ha," he says and splashes in, temporarily giving up his crusade. Jake and Kelly join me, and the four of us body surf and have the best time. The surfboards are brought in to the white water, and I watch as everyone gets tumbled.

Boards slingshot in every direction. I can't take it.

"Come on," I say to Jake. "We can at least help them."

We stay in waist-high white water and steady their boards, point the noses toward the shore, and help them wiggle onto their stomachs. We shove the boards to make sure they have enough momentum for the wave to take hold. Many of our friends crawl to their knees, or lose their balance and flop to the sides, but once in a while, someone will stand with shaky legs and airplane arms and everyone will cheer and applaud.

An hour later, cornhole's much more laid-back, with everyone tossing beanbags and just hoping they plop through the hole in the board. Dennis, who was sliding on his backside anytime we saw him on the mountain, and who couldn't even get on the surfboard without falling back in the water sputtering, is now shouting, "Who's your momma?" and landing every beanbag on the surface or in the hole. Jake and I lose in the semis to him and Tricia, and I run over to get a drink from the water fountain, hearing him yell, "Boom!" behind me.

Around the corner of the public bathroom, I notice Dave and Kelly talking heatedly about something. I'm too far away to hear, but she's waving her arms, and he keeps trying to calm her.

"Hey!" I hear Jake's voice and turn from them. He's by the outdoor showers. He places his palm on the shower knob and pushes with a jolt of his shoulder. Water shoots down from the spout. He wiggles his eyebrows. "I seem to remember this triggering something."

I grin and walk over to him. "You know we can't kiss here.

Not in front of our whole youth group. Can you imagine?"

"Yes. I like to imagine it very much."

I splash him with the water. The shower does its automatic shut-off thing. "Nope."

"Wait. Where are you going?" he asks, as I head toward the beach crew. "This is the part where you turn it back on. With your palm. And the eye thing. And then the kiss thing. And the water falling on us . . ."

When my eyes scan the public bathrooms again, Dave and Kelly are gone.

○))) ● (((○

During the first ten minutes of Ultimate, Abe Montez gets an elbow to the nose and a glow-in-the-dark Frisbee to the eye, so while the boys are "tending to him," but really just going in for a closer look at the blood, I find Kelly. "Hey, you okay?"

She scrunches her nose and eyes. "Of course. I wasn't even near Abe or the Frisbee."

"No, ya goof. I mean with Dave."

She hesitates. "Why?"

"I dunno, I saw you over by the bathrooms. You seemed— well, you *both* seemed bothered."

"Oh." She rolls her neck around. Digs a foot in the sand. "I mean." She clears her throat. Gosh, she's bad about hiding things. "Maybe it looked that way. But you know." She licks her lips. "Are you sure it was us? It's dark. Look what just happened to Abe."

"No, it was earlier. What's going on, Kells?"

Her eyes glisten. She opens her mouth, but then Dave comes lords-a-leapin' across the sand. "Duuuude. That was rough. Gonna leave a mark for sure. He got an *A*-kicking. But he'll have one *H* of a story."

When I look again at Kelly, the tears aren't there.

"Are you both okay?"

He looks at me and then Kelly. She shakes her head once.

Dave frowns. "Not sure what you mean."

I explain what I saw by the bathrooms. Kelly's flailing hands. Dave's soothing touches.

"Right. Right." He nods like it's all coming back. "We're wrestling through some things right now."

"Things? Are you back together?"

"No!" he answers so quickly, Kelly flinches. "Kelly's like a sister in Christ. I love her like a *sister*." I look at Kelly but she's looking at her hands, kneading them as if they lack circulation. "We courted for two months," he continues, "but then we prayed and we didn't feel prompted, so we're trying to be intentional. You know, I'm trying to guard her heart. Be a brother." This doesn't answer why they were arguing, but I let it go.

On the way back to the vans, I reach for Kelly's hand like old times, and she takes it gratefully, squeezing it as if to acknowledge that I'm not crazy. Something was going on.

At the church, after the pizza boxes are empty, we pick teams and turn off the lights for a capture the flag across the inside and outside of the church property. Students scurry in every direction, disappearing into the night. Jake's by my side, and as we creep along an outdoor walkway, I couldn't care less about the game. His arm's around my waist, and I keep feeling his finger trace my side, up and down, up and down.

A back door's open to the sanctuary, so we let ourselves in, hunters on the prowl. It's a good shortcut to the other side if you can make it through without getting caught, but we hear squeals and gasps in distant rows on the other side. It's going to be a hairy exit if we go that way. My hand moves along the back wall and I feel the door to the prayer room. I open it and pull Jake inside just as I hear footsteps padding down the carpeted hallway. The person passes, we wait a minute, and then I tug Jake's hand to go back out. He leans close, touches my neck with his lips. "Happy Valentine's Day," he murmurs, and I melt. He pulls away, but I pull him back, and then we are kissing, *really kissing*, and I whisper, "You okay not winning capture the flag?"

Still kissing me, he holds up his hands and whispers, "I surrender." We hear lots of muffled running outside the door, so I pull him down under the table, the same one I hid beneath in ninth grade with Tim Rainsforth.

I crawl on top of Jake, the two of us still kissing so silently—ninja-like—and the thought makes me grin.

"What?" He can feel my smile through the kiss.

I shake my head, pull away for a moment to put a finger to his lips—*shh*—and then my lips travel back to his.

There's this teeny voice, like a one-inch-high person shouting from the bottom of a well, reminding me that there's a verse on the wall, that this is where people come before God with their worries and heartache, but my head's swimmy and I'm exhausted from the day and nothing feels better than lying on top of Jake and kissing until the sun comes up. Which I would gladly do, if pot patrol wasn't going to take roll at midnight.

His fingers trace my sides again, but this time go higher, and I suck in my breath.

I think back to when a guy last touched my bra— ironically, in this same room. I remember feeling nothing. This time, I definitely feel something. Electricity shoots from my fingertips to my toes.

"Sorry," he whispers. He moves his hand away.

"Don't be," I whisper, and I move it back. He pauses, unsure, and then he becomes totally sure, and his hand moves freely.

I lose myself in the moment, the line between right and wrong growing hazier by the second, and then I'm jolted awake by a startling awareness. I roll off of him and sit straight up.

"What is it?" He crawls out from underneath the table. "What's wrong?"

The reality of what I've just done hits me. What I've done *in the prayer room.* "You don't have, like, a Bible with you? Like in your pocket."

I'm speaking in code, hoping he gets it without me having to explain. It takes him a minute, he looks down at his jeans, and then he chuckles.

"How can you laugh about that?" I hiss.

"Well, I'm kind of used to it. You see, there's this natural reaction—"

"Can't you control it?"

"Uhh . . . I don't really know how to answer that."

"That can't happen. That's, like, bad. That's like *bad* bad."

"It happens every time we make out, Lovette."

"Then how come I never noticed?"

"Because it's trapped in a wetsuit! And between your wetsuit and mine, it's like inches of padding."

"Millimeters," I correct.

"How many times do I shift off of you or move to the side? Come on, you seriously didn't know?"

I look up and see the cross, next to it the verse on the wall: *"And we know that all things work together for good to those who love God. Romans 8:28."*

"We shouldn't have done this." I stand up and walk out of the prayer room. No sooner than I get out, Carrie tags me. "Yes!" she squeals. "You're on my team now!" She pulls me by the arm, half running to the nearest exit. I look behind me. Jake has exited the prayer room too, but he doesn't follow. He watches me go, his shadow getting darker as we travel down the hallway.

Chapter Forty-One

After midnight, we're into the second '80s movie, something about a tomboy drummer girl who discovers she's got the hots for her best friend when he starts dating this popular girl. We're all in our sleeping bags, girls on one side of the youth room and guys on the other. A large glow-in-the-dark strip of tape runs down the middle of the linoleum carpet and the leaders park their pillows there, in case anyone thinks of "accidentally rolling" in their sleep. I can't get what happened in the prayer room out of my head, so I'm searching through my Bible with my phone flashlight.

"Sorry, Lovette, it's lights-out."

Candy appears in my face like a pop-up card. It's like she has sin sniffers.

"Sorry." I close my Bible.

She sees my phone flashlight against the pages of scripture, and her face drops. "Were you having your quiet time? Well geez, Louise, Holy Spirit breeze, I can't believe that I just told you to stop reading His word."

"No, it's fine. I was looking up some passages. It can wait."

"Like H-E-double hockey sticks it can." She leans in close. "Okay, top secret, just for you. Head to the women's restroom.

The one with the three stalls, not the single. That's my patrol area."

I don't want to get out of my warm sleeping bag, but Candy's breaking rules for Jesus, so I feel a responsibility to her faith to go study scriptures in a cold bathroom. I shimmy out of my sleeping bag, and she stops me.

"I heard you're dating Jake."

I gulp. Nod once.

She smiles wide, her teeth bright in the moonlight, which reminds me that we're gonna have a full moon in two days.

"That's so wonderful! No one can even tell. You're an example to our youth group on how to act in a relationship."

I see a flash of me and Jake making out in the prayer room, mauling each other like we were wild animals on National Geographic. "Thanks."

"I'm talking to the youth group in two weeks on purity. Why don't you share? Just like five minutes or so."

My palms are sweating and clammy. I need air. "Uh, I'll pray about it."

"Great!" As I crouch-walk toward the doors, she motions at me to hide my Bible under my shirt.

After a quick check under the bathroom stalls to make sure no one's there, I sit, legs crossed, on the bathroom tile. *Purity?* What a joke. I look up one of the verses I studied last week: "You are not your own; you were bought at a price." That's a rough one. I definitely didn't remember *that* in the prayer room. God exchanged my ugliness for His beauty. But it was done on the cross, not through some happy hand-holding kumbaya campfire. It came at a price. And if I felt the weight of that, I'd probably listen more to the conclusion: "Therefore honor God with your bodies."

I skip back to the top of the paragraph: "Flee from sexual immorality." *Flee.* So funny how everything's about fighting the good fight, standing firm in our love for God, being proud and not ashamed of the gospel, but this verse says to *run.* Get outta Dodge. In terms of fight or flight, it says *flight.* Not *fight.* I think to the prayer room when I lost myself in the moment, and I get it. I think God gets it. We can't fight. I look up at the fluorescent lights in the ceiling. *But why would You make our passions so strong if You only wanted us to resist?* It doesn't add up.

Kelly pushes the door open and startles when she sees me on the floor. "Hey. How's the weather down there?" Her voice sounds different, slurred. She stumbles into one of the stalls. Over the sound of her peeing, I hear her curse.

"Kell?"

"What do *you* want?" she snaps.

The toilet flushes, and I stand when she emerges. Before I can say anything, she throws her arms around me. She smells like the patrons at the Venue after two hours in front of a bartender. "Kelly, are you drunk?"

"Phhhhsssh." Then she laughs. "That's the sound of a fish with no eye. Phhhhhsssh."

Oh boy. "Does this have to do with Dave?"

She throws her head back. "Dayyyyve! My bro." She says

"bro" like it's two syllables, *bah-roh*. "I'm his sis. 'Hey, sis.' 'What up, sis?'"

She leans against the wall and slides to the floor.

"These tiles are cold." She slaps the wall, but she's done talking about tiles. "You know we didn't even kiss when we dated?" I squat down beside her so we're eye level again. "Then he broke up with me, and I was crying and he felt bad, so he kissed me to make me feel better. And then he was like, 'Babe, we can't do that, nah, nah,' so then we didn't talk. But then he'd say he missed me and then, then we'd just do more"—she motions with her hand in a circle to demonstrate *more*—"and then he'd cry after because he felt guilty." She grabs my head and presses her forehead against mine. "Don't tell him I said he cried." Then she pulls away, and I'm grateful because the fumes of whatever she drank are pouring out of her mouth like dragon fire. "And then we'd pray and we'd both cry. But later, we'd just do more again."

She starts to cry. I'm missing some of this booze-muddled story. Gosh, I wonder how much she drank. She sniffles, whips up her head.

"So he's like, 'She's my sis.' 'Hey, everyone, this is my sis.' 'Sister from another mister.' 'Meet my favorite sis.'"

I sigh. "Yeah, it's funny he calls you that. After you dated."

"Funny. You know what's funny?" She opens her purse and pulls out a tampon. "*This* is funny." She holds the tampon like a cigar between her fingers. "I needed this, like, six days ago. But magic trick. I *still* don't need it!"

Oh. *Ohhhh.*

That's what she meant by "more." Geez, that's quite a few

steps past kissing. All this time these past few months after they ended things, when she was pulling me aside—her Jake misgivings, the disapproving looks, the intervention at Martha's—all that time she and Dave were having sex.

Oh man.

She puts her head on her knees and begins sobbing, big, heaving sobs. I try to shush her quiet. The last thing I need is Candy coming into the bathroom and smelling the liquor. She wouldn't be offering any "Be blessed!" exclamations. There's so much wrong with this scene, not the least of all that Kelly's drunk while possibly pregnant.

"What am I gonna tell my parents?" she says, hiccuping.

"Slow down."

"And God must *hate* me."

Whoa. Now that's something I never thought I'd hear from Kelly. "What? Kelly, you're letting the alcohol talk." I reach for her hand, but she recoils.

"No! He does. He's getting back at me. For this. For Dave. For you."

"For me?"

"Duh, Lovette, how do you think Cecilia knew what you wrote on your essay?" she snaps. I see a stream of spittle spray from her mouth like aerosol perfume. "Who do you think stole it and helped her make copies?"

I'm stunned. Mouth slightly parted, eyes unblinking, body stiff with disbelief. Jake would be proud of my mannequin skills. Betrayal courses through me, a cold, mean animal that leaves my heart limp, my spirit deflated. *Not my best friend. Please not my best friend.* I think back to my tears, the rotten emptiness in the pit of my stomach, the shame that the school saw me as a laughingstock.

"You," I can barely whisper. "But why would—"

"Because I was mad! Because I don't know! Because why do we do *anything*?"

Wait, now she's getting philosophical? Anger builds, a slow roiling boil. "That doesn't even make sense—"

"Of course it doesn't!" she growls. "All you see is your perfect life. I kept trying to warn you about Jake, and you were like whatever, whatever, and I wanted him to stop messing with you because I knew he was gonna break your heart."

I sigh. This is about Dave.

"So I thought if I made you not so perfect, he'd be embarrassed by you, or not want to be seen with you or something because I figured that was the way he was."

Because that's the way Dave *was.* She pulls on her hair and shakes her head.

"But then the joke went further than I expected and I felt so bad and I wanted it to stop and I told Cecilia don't write those things, but she already made copies and said she'd snitch on me if I didn't help her." Her eyes plead with mine for mercy. "But I helped afterward. Remember?"

I do. She was with my friends, helping clean up the mess. Turns out she made the mess too.

I want to scream at her. I open my mouth to tell her how she's controlling and horrible and spiteful and worthless and cruel.

But I look at her, this broken shell, face puffy, confused,

afraid, completely alone. Something triggers in me, and I see that's how I probably look to God most days. Still, so much in me wants to lay into Kelly right now. My brother would call it "ripping her a new one." I'm forming words, but they're mean. Mean like Cecilia's tongue. And that's when I hear God ask me, *Are you any different?*

People talk about standing up for Jesus. Is this one of those moments? Not standing on a street corner with a Bible and a microphone. Maybe it's all about standing in the face of betrayal on the cold bathroom floor and choosing forgiveness when you have every right to choose wrath.

It's not about me. Isn't that what He's always trying to teach me? *You are not your own. You were bought at a price.* I have this single moment to be what He would be to me. What He has been to me. What He is now.

My love for her is bigger than my anger. Not by much, but one of them's got to win out if this friendship is worth saving. I take the deepest breath of my life, deeper than when I've been tumbled by back-to-back waves and finally came up for air, the kind of breath that reaches beyond my lungs and into my soul. My arms stretch up toward Him and then out to wrap around her, drawing her whole crumpled body into my embrace. She hides herself in me like a burrowing bunny, hiding in the folds of my compassion, and says *sorry* over and over.

"It's gonna be okay," I whisper. "No matter what."

"You promise? I've messed up so bad."

"Welcome to the club. He knows. He knew before the cross."

She exhales like I just poured bathwater with lavender over her. I don't know if He's going to erase the aftermath, like the stuff that might already be set in motion. But she'll be okay. She's loved by Him.

○)))) ● ● (((○

When she calms down, she falls asleep on my shoulder and doesn't stir for thirty minutes. When my arm's asleep, I nudge her awake, make her stand, and lead her back to the youth room. I tuck her in her sleeping bag next to mine.

I think she's out, but then she says, "How do you do that?" Someone nearby shushes her. The movie's almost over.

"What?" I whisper.

"That's why people like you. You put them first. It's never about you."

I think of making out in the prayer room. Swimming at night. Surfing with Jake. Keeping it all from my parents. *Never about me?*

"Hardly."

"Hmmph." She reaches out her hand, light as a pixie, and rests it on my cheek. It's sweet at first, like being touched by a fairy, until she falls asleep and her hand becomes dead weight across my face. She may think it was my words that did the trick, but I think we're both a little different after tonight.

Chapter Forty-Two

Sunday morning, Jake leaves before I wake up, so I don't get a chance to say goodbye, which would've been nice, considering how we left things last night. Everyone's waking up. The volume in the youth room has gone from silent to roar in less than five minutes. Kelly opens her eyes and touches her head gingerly. I hand her a water bottle as feet zigzag between our sleeping bags. The smell of doughnuts wafts through the room, and Kelly turns pale.

"You okay?"

She shakes her head, peers up at me with sleepy eyes. "You mad?"

She's talking about Cecilia, not the drinking. "Yeah. A little."

She tucks her chin down. I should hug her, but I hug my knees instead. It still stings. Sober Kelly hurt me.

"The All Wave Open is tomorrow. Presidents' Day."

"Yeah." I roll up my sleeping bag. She fidgets with the zipper on her purse.

Most kids are staying for big church, but I need to skip service today and take care of some things before I lose my nerve. I grab my belongings, but she keeps her head down.

Guilt stabs me as I reach the double doors. Above the exit it says, WELCOME TO YOUR MISSION FIELD.

"Hey," I say, and she looks up. "You'll text me if you"—I motion to a certain item in her purse—"find out anything?"

She swallows and nods. I jog back and kiss her on the top of the head, then race out, praying it's a false alarm. Oh, Kelly.

Once outside, I'm awake and aware that it's the day before competition. My nerves are one of Dave's guitar strings ready to snap with the first strum. Jake texts: *Hey can we talk?*

I call him. He picks up without a hello.

"Hey, you," I say.

He doesn't respond.

"Jake?"

"Hey, Lovey." His voice is sandpaper. "What's up?"

"I dunno. You just texted if we could talk."

"Right," he says. "I meant in person."

"Oh. You okay?"

"It's my mom."

My shoulders tense against my neck. "Oh my gosh, what happened? Is she okay?"

"Yeah."

My whole body exhales, not just my lungs. "I'll stop by," I offer.

"I'm down at the base."

"Already?"

"Uh-huh." He probably had to take care of some things before the competition tomorrow. "I'll be up by you later today."

"Yeah, of course. I'm gonna go for a run anyway. My

stomach's having major butterflies."

"I'll bet. You're gonna do great."

"Yeah, well, I've got a great coach."

Again, silence.

"Jake?"

"I love you."

My brain halts. I think my blood stops flowing. My heart's the only thing working, pounding like a steel drum. So loud in my ears. So fast.

"You can't say that over the phone," I whisper. "Not the first time you say it."

"I had to. I wanted you to know. I didn't want to wait two hours."

"Okay, well, wait. I'll be there."

"Hey, Lovey?"

"Mmm?"

"I'm sorry."

I smile. "It's no big deal. I mean, as long as you say it again in two hours."

"No, I mean . . ."

"What?"

"Nothing. I'll see you in two. Text me when you're back at home."

He hangs up. My body feels like Jell-O. I thought he was calling to tell me he was feeling conflicted about the prayer room, and I was ready to tell him that it was as much my fault as his. "It's okay. So we messed up," I planned to say. "We don't have to repeat it." But instead he floors me with . . .

I sit down on the curb to catch my breath.

I think I love him too.

When I regain the strength in my legs, I walk back to my house and into the usual Sunday morning scene. Dad and Mom sipping coffee at the kitchen table—Dad with his newspaper keeping the printing presses in business, and Mom on her iPad looking at Pinterest for home-design ideas.

"Hey, honey," Mom says, "you're home early. How was the church slumber party?"

"I think you should let Matt go." I say it before my knees give out and I take it all back. "To study. I think you should let Matt go to the study-abroad program."

Mom's finger lifts from scrolling. Dad peers up at me from the business section. I crack my knuckles.

"He did the right thing by telling you. He's not *just* over eighteen. He'll be twenty-one in two weeks. You don't have to sign any papers anymore—he could've just gone and called you when he got there. But he didn't. Not because he was scared but because he loves you. Isn't that worth considering? He didn't *have* to. But he chose to do the right thing." It takes me a second to force the next two words out. "Unlike me."

Dad folds his newspaper in half. Mom turns her iPad facedown.

"I was told I couldn't surf again. That I wasn't allowed to go in the water even."

"We made those rules so that—"

"I've been swimming in the ocean four to five times a week for four years now." I say it in one breath, and they look confused, like they're hearing a foreign language. "And surfing for the past five months."

"No." Mom's shaking her head, disagreeing with the truth.

"And there's a surf competition tomorrow. I signed up. I'd love to have you come watch." I look from one to the other. They're mute. "Look, I didn't choose the right thing. I get it. But Matt did. Don't make him regret it. Let him go. That's his dream. Surfing's mine, and I've made my dream happen without you. So don't make him suffer for including you in his decision."

"Enough," Mom says and stands. She presses her temples and closes her eyes tight.

"You're grounded." Dad finally speaks.

"I'm sorry?"

"Your phone." He holds out a hand. I reach in my back pocket, and I feel it vibrate. A text comes through from Jake.

Home in 30

"Can I answer this?"

"Your phone!" he bellows, and I hand it over like it's on fire.

He squeezes my cell, a grenade with the pin removed. "Passcode?"

"One four five three," I answer. He checks it in front of me to make sure I'm not lying.

With a low voice, he says, "You will not leave this house today. For the next month, I will drive and pick you up from school. You will put in your two weeks' notice for your job. And you will not compete in any surf competition tomorrow or any other day. Do I make myself clear?"

My voice feels strained, like I'm suddenly a falsetto. "Yes," I squeak.

My body tenses, and my nostrils flare. I did the right

thing. I was honest. So what just happened? Everything I've worked for this whole year. If I'm a no-show, Cecilia will think she's won. Trevor Walker will gloat that I couldn't show my face. But it's more than that. It's all the hours of training. The hours running and skating, working out on the sand. The paddling, the hundreds of waves, the constant refining, the techniques, tricks, style. The talks with my friends about strategy. Was it all for nothing?

My father's deadly calm. "Your mother and I need to talk. Go to your room."

For the first time, I look my father in the eye and say the word that sums up all of my emotion.

"No."

And I run out the front door.

Chapter Forty-Three

I show up at Jake's aunt's apartment and slap an open hand a couple of times against his door. Though my lungs burn from running the four miles from my house to the apartment, all the months of training in the sand have paid off. As soon as I hear the bolt unlock, I push hard against the door, and he stumbles back a step as I enter the living room. I fall onto his couch and drop my head into my crossed arms, curling my body down against my knees, and cry like a levee has broken. My shoulders shake, my face is drenched. I don't look up as I feel Jake sink into the couch next to me. Without a word, he rubs my back as I cry.

"So Niles talked to you?"

I peer up at him. "About?"

His face is blank. "Nothing. What's wrong?"

"My parents."

"They found out about surfing," he guesses.

"I told them."

His hand stops on my back mid-rub. "Really."

"Really." I clear my throat of tears and snot. I'm a gross mess, and I lift up the bottom front of my shirt, already drenched with my sweat, and blow my nose in it. "I did it for my brother. I used to think it would be great to be him, the center of attention, but he's almost twenty-one and still on a leash." I reach for my shirt again to wipe my face, but he stops me. Hands me a Kleenex. "Thanks." I blow my nose, and some of it drips onto my hands. I don't even care. "I didn't think they'd be so extreme. I mean, I knew they hated it, but what's done is done. I've trained for this every day for months. My *gosh*, the waves are one- to two-foot breakers! My dad went all military and took away EVERYTHING."

"They called."

"How did they—"

"From your phone. Looking for you."

"What did you say?"

"I told them I'd call if you came. I thought you left because you were upset at what you heard. But you haven't talked to Niles?"

"What? Niles?"

"I was on the phone with him when I got it. That's the only reason he knows." He gets up, retreats to his room. I follow, my curiosity and worry piqued. When he sees me in the doorway, he sits on the edge of his bed, holds out a fat envelope to me. I see the University of Hawaii seal on the back.

His voice is flat. "I got in."

I think I'm going to be sick. No, no, no. I take the envelope, pull the letter out. *Congratulations, we are pleased to offer you enrollment for Fall '20 at the—*

I drop the letter. It's real. "So what does this mean?"

"It means my mom is doing everything she can to get me in-state tuition."

"Okay." I try to process that Jake's leaving in five months. Five months is still five months. I look down and see the corner of a suitcase. A full suitcase.

He looks at the suitcase and then at me. His eyes are glassy.

"When?" My question is quiet. Lifeless.

"If I finish out the school year there, it'll be half the year." He speaks slowly, each word causing him pain. "If I do more than a semester out here, it gets dicey. Their new semester starts Tuesday."

That's two days from now. "But—"

"Don't worry, I told her no, that my girlfriend had a surf competition." He rubs his eye sockets with the heels of his hands. "She bought me a plane ticket for tomorrow morning at six fifteen. Before she talked to me. I told her I was going to push it back, pay the difference myself. But—"

"But now I'm not competing." I sit down on the bed next to him.

"It's a lot of money. Pushing it back one day." He kisses my shoulder, then rests his chin on it, caresses my arm with his hand. "If I were spending it just with you, I'd sacrifice all my paychecks. But somehow I don't think your dad's gonna let me see you tomorrow. Not after you went AWOL."

I close my eyes. Let myself feel his breath on my neck, his chin with its stubble on my shoulder. "Then I won't go back."

He lifts his head, eyes me warily.

"I won't. I'll stay here. He'll never know. We'll surf tomorrow—the heck with the contest—we'll make our own with the LED boards and light up the ocean in the day."

He smiles, but only one side of his mouth lifts. "I had to

return the boards," he says. "They weren't mine. Just on loan." Our matching blue boards are gone? It's as if a piece of us, part of the fabric that built us into what we are, just ripped. My throat tightens. "Fine. We'll tour the South Bay tomorrow, have the date of our lives, eat every cookie at Beckers, taste every flavor ice cream at the Creamery. Have milkadamias at Two Guns until we're flying from the caffeine, and stay up all night in each other's arms."

I'm crying again; my heart hurts, physically aches like I miss him already, even though he's right here. I wrap my arms around him and kiss him while I cry, and our tears exchange cheeks and drip down our chins. My shirt's cold against me. With one tug, I pull it off. I'm in my sports bra, but I feel closer to him this way, his hands on my bare skin. I tug at his shirt and he reaches over his back and pulls it over his head. He lowers me onto the bed, and we are lying where he dreams every night, kissing and holding each other's bodies for dear life. I'm afraid the second I let go, he'll already be on a plane.

Before this school year, I couldn't have imagined walking through high school with a boyfriend. It seemed wrong. Five months later, I can't fathom what a day will be like without his fingers linking with mine through the school hallways. Maybe Lydia's right. Maybe I'm making a bigger deal of things than I need to. As we kiss, I feel the same reaction from him that he had in the prayer room, and he moves off me. "Sorry," he says.

"I'm okay with it." He checks to see if I mean it, looks into my eyes. I roll on top of him to prove it. His breathing's getting throatier, and I'm not sure when it started, but there's a slow rhythm to how our bodies are moving against each other. It's like what I see of couples on the dance floor of the Venue sometimes, only our version is horizontal. It feels incredibly good. I want more. I move my lips to his ear. "Be with me tonight," I say, and a sound comes from him, like a growl.

"Are you sure?" he says.

"I think so," I whisper. I reach for his jeans' button. But he stops me. I try again, but he grips my wrist. "What?"

He moves me off of him and rolls to the side of the bed. He sits up. His back muscles are flexed, and I can see his elevated breathing, his rib cage expanding, his chest filling and releasing. He rakes a hand through his hair. He mumbles, "I can't believe I actually stopped."

I wrap an arm around him from behind. "Then come back."

He removes my arm and looks at me. "There's nothing more that I want to do. Please know that."

The words feel like rejection is coming.

"Hold on," he says. "I need a minute." He gets up and disappears into the kitchen, leaving me alone on the bed. What did I do wrong? He returns with two bottles of water, hands me one, and takes a long drink of the other. He sits back down on the edge of the bed. "I remembered you from when I was younger—how fearless you were—that's what first drew me to you when I moved back. You helped me forget how crappy things were." He sips his water, puts the cap back on. "I'd been through it, my dad and all. But when you told me about your brother—I was like, hold up. You—you'd been through it too. Only I saw how much you believed God, not just believed *in* Him. And I dunno, I was like, that's what strong is. And it made me think maybe I could, too. Maybe I didn't have to be so pissed at Him for everything." He takes my hand in his. "Whenever you talk about God, what you love is who He is. When you talk about Him, it's like He's real, not just something you do on Sundays. He's not just a bunch of don'ts. Kelly's about the don'ts. You're about the dos. God's not a drag to you. He's exciting. The ocean's exciting. Doing new things is exciting. But it's because you include Him in everything. You like working *with* God, like He's your teammate. But this"—he motions behind us at the bed—"if you're not sure He's *with* you on this one—and believe me, thanks to Bible One-Oh-One that you recited to me while we surfed—I don't think He is. So maybe He has something else in mind."

I turn my water bottle end over end. "Like what?"

"I dunno! I wish I had the answers. I just know that I don't know."

I look down at my sports bra. I feel naked right now, even though I've spent hours around Jake in a bikini. I take a pillow and hug it to cover me. He tugs on it affectionately, but I don't let go. "Two years ago," he continues, "I didn't know anything but Hannah. A year ago, I didn't know that I'd move to California. Five months ago, I didn't know that I'd move back." He hands me one of his hoodies to put on, and I push my arms and head through it. It's the smallest one he has, but it hangs on me like curtains. When I pull the hood off my head, he cups my face with his hands, kisses me gently. "All I can see right now is you. You make me make sense." His eyes glisten again. "But I'm leaving tomorrow. And I don't know. I don't know what God's gonna do five years from now, a month from now, tomorrow. I don't want to assume I've got Him figured out." He holds me tighter. Won't let me look away as he says, "Because one day, if I'm not the man standing beside you at that altar, I want to be able to shake his hand and look him in the eye and not feel like I stole anything from him."

"*Stole?*"

I pull his hands away from my face, and he lets them drop, but he interrupts my anger with, "Stop. You *know* me. I'm not talking about your virginity or your purity, like it's a game, or some other bullshit. I'm talking about an amazing *moment* which was maybe"—he closes his eyes and breathes deeply through his nose—"maybe meant for you to share with *him* rather than me. You know how hard that is to admit? That forever might be some other guy? That whatever guy you pick is gonna be so damn incredible that you'll want to have every memory with him?" He licks his lips, and his eyebrows crease, like he's already jealous of this imaginary husband. "We're not there yet. We just have right now." He finally looks at me, gently reaching his hands around my waist, so I lift my puffy eyes to meet his. "So I want you to be able to look back on *this* moment, and be thankful that we made the right decision. Because if I *were* that man, and I want to be—God, I want to be—then I'd want every single boyfriend of yours leading up to our day to be able to shake my hand and say the same. And it's you, dammit, who's made me realize that."

It's probably the greatest thing a guy has said or will ever say to me. I want to hold it close, tuck it in my pocket where I can always feel it against my hip every second of the day.

I want to post it on a billboard, write it in a song, shout it through the barrel of every wave. But another very different thought creeps up and finds a way to my lips. "So Hannah gets something from you that I won't?"

This time, it's Jake who pulls away. "That's not fair."

He's right, it was a crummy thing to say. But I'm angry with my parents and lost that he's leaving and embarrassed that he rejected me and so in love with him in this moment, and everything all together makes my head a jumbled mess. I hear my next words like they're coming from another person. "So how do I know you won't be weaker in the future with some other girl?"

"I might," he answers truthfully. "I can't make any promises. Only one tonight."

"Right. Okay, well, thank you." I don't mean to sound stiff, but my words are cardboard.

He tilts his head, unsure of my response. His phone buzzes. The caller ID says: Mannequin. My lip quivers.

"My parents," I say. "I should go."

"Can I give you a ride?"

"No. I have time. I'll walk. Figure I'll be locked in once I get there. It's almost a full moon. Might stay out until then."

"Two moons," he says and reaches for me. I let my arms hang. I don't hug him back. He kisses me, and I refuse it, press my lips together hard, new tears starting. I blink them away.

"You sure you don't want a ride? It's five hours till sunset."

"Text them I'm on my way. I'll be there in five hours."

Chapter Forty-Four

Even though we broke up, I should be happy. He did the right thing. Isn't that what matters? The Christian phrase keeps looping through my mind: "Guard your heart." *"Rejoice!"* Kelly would say. *"He guarded your heart."* I offered Jake the chance to be closer to me than anyone, and he refused. He denied me so that he could make sure God protected me. Now that I'm alone away from the moment, I'm embarrassed by it all. I was willing to deny God for it, but Jake wouldn't let me, and now everything feels like a loss. Jake's gone. Surfing's gone.

I walk to the Redondo Pier, but I no longer see the kiosks along the boardwalk or even the restaurant above the ocean, Old Tony's. I see all the spots we rode our skateboards, the rails and curbs he made me try to jump. *"How's it feel?"* I hear him ask me the first time we rode.

"Exceptionally amazing."

"Exceptionally?" I can still hear him laughing. *"Who says that?"*

I remember how I shoved him playfully. *"Lots of people."*

I head north toward Hermosa and, on the way, stop at a familiar house. The brick on one wall, the navy-blue wood and framed white windows. *"This one,"* I hear him say, and I see him pointing at it. *"Your house-lottery game. I'd pick this one."*

"If you saw inside, you may not want it for your lottery house."

"What if it was the worst inside, and I didn't care?"

I walk on to the Hermosa pier, stop at the statue of Tim Kelly. Died in a car crash. How many people die untimely deaths? Yet he's the only one with a statue. Something about him was far greater than surfing, and that gives me a little solace. *What did you stand for, Tim? Was it worth it?* I pat him on the shoulder and trudge on.

I leave the beach and walk up to Hermosa Avenue, walk along the street with all its cute storefronts, but I hear the music playing in Jake's car the first time we drove together, passing the bookstore Pages, the Creamery with its line out the door.

I head back down to the Manhattan Beach Pier and travel north, my eyes fixed on the ocean, on the hundreds of waves we rode together. I hear him clapping, whooping, slapping the water in excitement. I remember him talking about how I headed up the wave with speed but wasn't extending enough at the top.

"You're on your haunches like a bunny rabbit."

I can hear my laugh, the way it echoed in the windless night as I splashed him.

At Twenty-sixth, I make my way up to Old Man Mike's, and my heart sinks when I don't see the LED boards, even though I know Jake said they'd be gone. But Mike's boards are gone, too, and so's my wetsuit. I go through the gate and knock on the sliding glass door. Mike slides it open. "Hey, kid," he says. He looks sad.

"Oh, no, you get robbed?"

His eyes open wider than their usual half lids. "No. No."

"Where are your boards?"

His face drips with apology before he speaks. "Your father—"

"My dad was here?"

"He was looking for you. He's really worried."

I cross my arms. "I'm sure. Like he kept a close eye on me that year after Matt's accident."

"That's a lot for a parent to know what to do with."

"I can't believe you're defending him."

He raises his hands in surrender.

"Where's my wetsuit?"

"He, uh, had me put the boards away. He has your wetsuit."

"I bought that with my own money!"

He holds his hands higher like I'm aiming a gun at him.

"Sorry." I slump into a lawn chair. "My boyfriend's moving away tomorrow, and we just left on a really bad note."

"What about?"

I laugh, embarrassed. "Sex, actually."

"Huh. That's a doozy."

"We didn't," I say. "Have sex."

"Good on ya." He nods like I've shared a similar view on politics. Then he adds, "I waited."

I turn in the lawn chair. "Really?"

He laughs, and it's guttural and ends with a hack. "Yes, ma'am. That was a thing back then. Waiting." He nods at the sun, disappearing with its last thin line of orange on the horizon. "Seems like a foreign concept nowadays. Best choice

I ever made. Only memory I had was with her." He searches the horizon like she's out there somewhere. "When you love someone that much, you don't want other memories creepin' in. Least not me, I don't."

He taps the back of the lawn chair. "I'm gonna tell your parents you're safe, if that's okay."

"Please don't. They'll come pick me up. I'm going home, I swear. Just want to stay to see the moonlight. It's almost full tonight."

"That it is. How 'bout I tell 'em you stopped by on your way home. Just so they stop worrying."

It's a compromise. "Yeah, okay."

He heads inside and tosses a beach towel out of the glass door, then slides it shut. I wrap myself in it like a taco blanket and turn the chair to face the rising tide. Thirty minutes later, the moon shines on the water, creating a pathway straight to me, shimmering the way it always does, the way it did before I met Jake.

"Two moons," I murmur to God. I set down my towel and head home.

○))) ◗ ● ◖ (((○

When I finally step onto my driveway, I look up and know I'm royally busted. My house is lit up like a Christmas tree, every window a beacon to guide me home. If my parents owned flares, they might've set them off by now. I know they must be worried, but they have to know I'm okay. I'm sure they've talked to Jake and Mike by now.

I don't have any strength left to stress out about this, so I push through my front door to face the music. Mom's sitting at the dining table and she springs up, toast out of a toaster, and Dad rushes in from the bedroom.

"Oh thank God," Mom breathes.

Dad slows to a halt. Says nothing.

I decide to save them the speeches. "I was irresponsible, thoughtless, and selfish. If you want to ground me forever, that's fine. I don't have anywhere to go, anyway."

"Where were you?" Dad's voice isn't the threatening calm from before. It's quieter, a scared child.

"First Jake's. And yes, I know I'm grounded, so you can doubly restrict me from seeing him in the future, because he's moving back to Hawaii. Tomorrow."

"Tomorrow?" Mom repeats. "Your boyfriend?"

"Yes." For the first time in front of my mom, he is actually my boyfriend when she says that. Well, was.

"Tomorrow? Monday?"

Today's still Sunday, so I'm not sure what other day of the week tomorrow would be, but I politely nod.

"Oh." Her shoulders sag, and her eyes look like they understand what I'm going through. Her face makes me teary, so I look away and kick at the wood floors.

"Don't scuff," my father says.

I stop.

He looks like he hasn't slept for two days. "Jake called us hours ago, saying you'd left."

"Then I walked."

"Where?" Mom asks.

"Nowhere, really." *Just the places that remind me of Jake.* "Everywhere."

"Oh?"

I can't explain. Maybe another night. "Then I went to Old Man Mike's. Sorry for pulling him into this. He didn't know, by the way. About the you-can't-go-into-the-ocean rule. Or that I wasn't allowed to surf."

Dad says, "We figured."

"Anyway, I'm sorry. I'm not sorry for going, but I'm sorry you got worried. You haven't been worried about me in five years, so—"

Mom gets huffy. "Lovette, that's not—"

I hold a hand up, and Mom stops. "No, it's true," I say. "But it's okay." And I actually mean it. "God used it for His good." I know my parents have no clue what that means, and I'm not sure I do. But it makes sense right now.

I take my shoes off by stepping on the backs of them with the toes of the other. "Can I go to bed? I haven't exactly had a good day."

"Me neither," Dad quips.

I don't know why today was any different—why it would worry them—but they look like real parents. The kind that get concerned, who age ten years when their kid disappears.

"Okay, well." I start to walk away.

"Don't leave angry," Dad says, and it's an order.

"I'm not."

"I mean earlier. You gotta leave, then you leave. But not." His words choke on each other. "*That* way. Not when you're mad." He's speaking through gritted teeth, and he's holding back something I've never seen from him. Tears. "If something would've happened . . . and that's the last . . ." He turns away and clears his throat. He turns back and his voice is steady again, the military man I know. "You're free to go."

"Sorry you had a bad day," I mumble. I walk toward my bedroom but then turn. They're still standing at the table, heads down, limp wilted leaves. "Dad?"

He looks at me.

"Remember when I won the Under-Tens Surf Rider Days?"

Dad nods. "You were eight."

"That was a good day."

I make my way to my room and shut my door for the night.

I lie in bed hugging myself in Jake's hoodie, staring out the window at the glowing moon. For at least fifteen minutes, I shake Jake's snow globe and watch the sand settle, then repeat and watch it again. My Bible lies open on my bed, unread. A soft knock raps on my door. Not waiting for an invitation, Mom enters on tiptoe. I shake the snow globe one more time.

"Hey."

"Hey."

She walks over to the chair by my window and sits.

"Can I ask you something?"

I look at her, and she takes it as a yes.

"Why this contest? Why the ocean? I mean, most kids lie about drugs, you know?"

I sit up in my bed, pull my knees up. There's no fight left in me. My words come out tired, unfiltered. "When Matt was in his accident, I thought it was my fault."

Mom looks shocked.

"He and I had argued that day. I thought maybe he was still mad and that's why he fell. And when you both ignored me and stayed at the hospital, I figured you found out somehow about our fight, and that I deserved it."

"Oh, honey—"

I lift my palm up. She quiets.

"I thought if I was good enough and did everything right, you'd come home and Matt would be okay. But it didn't happen. At least not right away. Then one day, I got in the ocean—trying to let a wave hurt me—thinking if I suffered, then maybe Matt would get better in exchange. But the waves were soft."

This is a lot for Mom to process, I can tell by the crinkle between her eyebrows, the disbelief in her concerned eyes.

"I left my hair wet, hoping you'd notice and get mad—something. Only you guys never came home that night. That's when I realized it didn't matter—whether I did good or bad—your focus was Matt. And that's fine—it needed to be—only I was twelve and didn't get it then."

I close my Bible and set it on my nightstand, rub the cover and smile ruefully. "Luckily, I was going to church with Kelly, and God pointed out my twisted thinking. He didn't work that way. Doing good to cancel out the bad, or vice versa. I started hanging out at Bruce's Beach when you weren't around, which was always. Old Man Mike gave me a wetsuit. And once I got back in the water for real—like not just to punish myself—I felt like it was keeping me alive. God rescued me, and the ocean that you told me to stay away from ended up being where I connected with Him. I can't explain it, other than my life came into focus."

I scooch under my covers, lying down, but I turn my head on my pillow so I can face her. "First it was just the water. Where I felt God most. But when I started surfing again, I felt I could do more than I'd thought possible. Like I'd been created for a purpose. And not just surfing. Bigger than that. This competition represented that, you know? The start of something big."

Mom looks at me for a long moment. For someone who usually has something to say, her words are missing. She stands and leans over me, kisses my cheek tenderly. "You want me to leave the light on?"

"No, that's okay. Moon's bright tonight."

She looks out at it, then scans my four walls, her gaze drifting from the Hume Lake Christian Camp photo to the postcards of the waves to the poster of Kelly Slater. She picks up my snow globe, scrutinizes the tiki pole inside with its signs for Waikiki, North Shore, Lahaina, Hanalei, and Kona. A look of recognition flickers, connecting it to the boyfriend who's moving back there. She frowns, shakes it, and sets it back on my nightstand.

I hear her pause at the door after she turns off my light, but I keep my back to her, my eyes fixed on the sand in the snow globe swirling and swirling and then settling to the ground.

Chapter Forty-Five

I'm dreaming that I'm in a pinball machine. I realize why when I wake up to a hand shaking my shoulder.

"Lovette." No, still dreaming. It's Matt's voice, and Matt's away at college.

I swat at the hand and grunt.

"Lovette, wake up. I'm Kelly Slater."

This wakes me up, but only to annoy me, because it's most definitely *not* Kelly Slater. "Very funny." I rub my eyes and turn to him. It looks like Matt. This is confusing.

"Get up, butthead."

It *is* Matt.

I drag myself up to a sitting position. "What are you doing here?" I whisper. I look outside. It's still dark, but the moon's no longer in my window. I reach for my phone on my nightstand, and then remember why my phone isn't there. Jake. The surfing contest.

"Had the day off. Thought I'd make sure the dust had settled. You almost caused World War Three here yesterday."

"Yeah, I feel pretty beat up," I mumble.

"Not you. Them. Mom and Dad went at each other. Brought me into the whole thing."

"Sorry."

"I heard what you said about me. Well, the gist of it." He grabs me by the back of the neck, shakes a little. "Thanks."

It feels good, even at zero o'clock in the morning, to know your older brother thought you did a pretty cool thing by standing up for him. Still—"You couldn't wait for the sun to come up to tell me this?"

"Wow, how about, *'Hey, Matt, thanks for driving seven hours to wake up Mom and Dad and convince them to let me compete.'*"

"WHAT."

"Shh! God, they finally went to bed two hours ago. Get up."

I shake my head. "I don't have a board."

"No, but you have friends." He tosses me my cell phone. "By the way, that's on loan for the day. Dad wants it back at fifteen hundred."

I'm confused. Matt groans. "Couldn't find Old Man Mike's cell. I got ahold of Lydia and asked about borrowing boards, but she told me about Jake moving away, sorry, that sucks, and said to call Kelly, and Kelly didn't have a board—how's it that none of your friends surf, it's like they live in Kansas—but then Kelly said you talked about some surfer named Alix with an *I.* Her number was in your phone, so I called—middle of the night and she actually answered—and I explained and asked her if I could pay her to rent her board. She said she has a few and you could use one of hers, but she couldn't fit the extra in her car. So Lydia and her boyfriend, Guy?"

"Kaj," I correct.

"Lydia and Kaj picked it up twenty minutes ago. They're meeting you at the check-in booth in"—he looks at his phone—"T-minus thirty." He walks out of the room, walks back in with my wetsuit and throws it. It slaps my face and lands on my lap in the bed. "Dad says that's yours." He walks out of the room.

I'm stunned. He pops his head back in. "Party bus is leaving in five. Let's move."

I look at my phone: 5:43 a.m. There are texts from Lydia, Niles, Kaj, and Kelly that show up at the top of my text stream. They've all been read by my parents. There's one generic text written back to them all: *This is Lovette's father. Lovette will not have her phone for a month. Thank you.*

There are no texts from Jake. He knows my dad has my phone, so why would he text? Still, my heart hurts at seeing nothing.

I text him frantically.

Competing. Mom and Dad said ok. You still here?

I wait. My text doesn't register as delivered. That means he's boarded the plane and turned off his phone. *Please, Jesus, tell him to turn it back on.* His flight isn't until 6:15 a.m. That means he has time to get off the plane. He can still make it. But would he? I think of the way I left him last night, and regret weighs my eyelids shut.

He's not coming.

With slow movements, I change into my bikini and put the wetsuit halfway on, just the legs, letting the top half hang at my waist. I throw on Jake's hoodie over my bikini top, and find my ball of wax, still wrapped in cellophane, under my pillow. I slip my flip-flops on and jog out to the car.

"Are they coming?" I ask Matt as we click our seat belts on.

I motion with my chin toward the house.

"They're letting you compete, but only because I'm taking you. Watching you might be a little much for them right now." He puts the car in drive. "One heart attack at a time."

○)) 🌒 🌑 🌑 (((○

The sky's a molten white when we step out onto the sand, the marine layer creating the gray emptiness of February skies. It makes the water look colder somehow, and I walk numbly to the judging tents. There are at least thirty people here, parents and teens, holding surfboards in one hand and coffees in the other. The competitors all with wetsuits half on, sweats and beanies in every direction.

I sign in, and they tell me I'm in the first heat in the prelims. They hand me a blue bib, and I choke back a sob. Blue.

The color of our LED boards.

I'm a mix of emotions this morning. This is it. It's what I've been wanting. But my head aches from all the tears of yesterday, my sinuses a clogged mess. I can still feel my swollen, puffy eyelids every time they blink. My heart feels hollowed out. It's real. He's gone. Jake's really gone.

"Lovette!" I hear a chorus of screams cutting through the quiet crashing of waves. My brother and I turn to see Niles, Kelly, Lydia, and Kaj all waving madly from a couple of lawn chairs and canopy over by the lifeguard tower. When I see the joy on their faces and think back to the lengths they went to make this happen, my emptiness evaporates like the marine layer at noon. I give my cheeks a quick slap, and Matt and I walk over.

Kaj holds up Alix's shortboard when I approach. "Your chariot awaits."

I take the board and give him a hug. They all surround me in a hug huddle, which is never our MO, but they know how eroded I feel after yesterday. Lydia takes a poster off the sand and holds it up. In fat Sharpie, she's written *9.9*.

I giggle.

"I woulda given you a ten, but I don't want to raise any suspicions that I'm biased."

"Looks fair to me."

Kelly tosses me her purse. "Look."

I look inside. "It's empty."

No keys. No wallet, phone, tampon.

No tampon.

I look up at her, a question, and she nods. She needed the tampon. She tackles me—her normal, affectionate, huggy self—but when I let go, she holds on.

"Clean sets today," Matt says, watching me check out the water over her shoulder.

A pod of dolphins dodges through the surf, and my friends open their mouths in awe. I tap Kelly to peel herself off of me so she can see.

Niles asks, "Does that happen all the time?"

I think of that one morning surfing with Jake when a bottlenose shot through the wave next to my board. "No, but when it does, it's magical."

The air horn sounds, indicating ten minutes until the

first heat, so I blow them all a kiss and take off on a short jog to warm up.

I slow when I see Trevor and Cecilia under a red canopy. Trevor catches my eye and smirks. "Looks like I'm not in your heat."

"Good thing," I say, "you might distract me."

He recognizes my dripping sarcasm, but he's usually the one dishing it. Before he can offer a retort, I spot Alix and jog over to her. Immediately, she hugs me like we're old friends.

"Thank you so much."

"Me?" She throws a hand across the air, shooing off the compliment. "Did you see what your brother and your friends did? Who are you, like the second coming of Tim Kelly?"

My breath catches. There's no way she knew all the times I thought about Tim Kelly, stopped at his statue, talked to God about him. It feels like God just hugged me too.

"Well, there's no way any of this could've happened if you didn't loan me your board."

Again with the hand shooing. "Bum deal about your boyfriend. Your brother filled me in."

I don't know what to say except, "I better finish warming up," and she shoos me off again with the one hand.

Back at our canopy, I remove Jake's hoodie and shrug on the rest of my wetsuit, zip up, and attach the Velcro leash to my ankle. Kelly puts the blue bib over my head, and Lydia hands me her latte to sip, simultaneously, like they're my pit crew. Niles pats me on the back, and Kaj holds his phone up to my face, blaring an Eminem song.

"Seriously?" I say.

"Just getting you pumped."

Matt stands away from my friends, arms folded, checking out the surf, checking out me. I see his stance. Stiff and unmoving.

"I'll be fine," I say to him.

"Course you will," he says. He looks back out at the mighty waters, and his jaw tightens. He's facing the ocean that took him out of life and rearranged his future. It's different for him.

I walk over to him, set my board down at my feet, and put my arms around him. "Thank you."

He pats me twice on the back, and then the air horn sounds again. I pick up the board and sprint out toward his nemesis, my peace.

○))) ● ● ● ● ● ○

The biting cold of the February water seeps into the crevices of my wetsuit neck, and instantly I'm wide awake. The rumbling surf growls at me, and I attack with windmill strokes against the current. The tide pushes back, but I'm stronger and I cut through the first set of white-water roughness and head to the outer break. I see the three other competitors in their individual red, yellow, and white bibs: all guys. I'm not used to Alix's board—it's narrower and feels a little wobbly until I get my sea legs and discover how it moves with my weight. The tip of her board spears the crest of a wave, and it splashes in my face. The salt burns my eyes and nostrils, and I spit and dig past it.

I made it.

I prop myself up and look out at the endless expanse of water, the wild undulating beast that God quiets with a word. *I'm not taking your waves, Jesus, just borrowing them. It's all yours, and I'm grateful to have it as my playground this morning.*

Jake's right. Fifteen minutes feels a lot shorter when you're out here. Moments tick by, and there's a lull in the surf. I see a swell forming way back. I've gotta take it. But no. Everyone's probably desperate too. Sure enough, all three start to paddle. Red looks over at me and slows, but he's almost caught it. I don't know why he stopped. Yellow and White make it, catch the wave, but Yellow pulls out because he's in White's way. It goes soft on White, dies out, but he scores for the stand and the riding it out.

Behind that wave, another one's looming, and none of the guys are in position. Red looks like he's paddling more toward me than the wave, but he can't make it to either in time. It's forceful; I catch it and ride left, doing a quick bottom turn but then going back up, staying high for a longer ride. It's clean, only two small tricks, but the bottom turn and the length of the ride will get me a good score.

The next set comes, and I pop up, but Red sees me and paddles for it too. I'm closest to the peak, so I don't know why he even goes for it, and I shout for him to pull out, but he stands anyway, blocking any possible ride that I could have. He'll be called on interference for sure, but I was set up perfectly. I could've had a solid point total.

I get three more rides in, but I have to pull out of two because of Red. He's obviously new to contests and doesn't understand the interference rules. Still, it's frustrating.

The air horn sounds. The heat is over, and I know before I look at the tabulations that Yellow has outscored me. Only the top score moves to the finals. The deep pang of disappointment makes my strokes toward shore feel heavier. All I've worked for this year. Every 6:00 a.m. workout. Every wind sprint. The drills I repeated, the hours I invested. The shivering I fought through when my wetsuit was done but I still wasn't, swallowing sea water through chattering teeth but always going back for one more wave.

It's yet another loss to add to the past day and a half, but when I take a breath and look up at the sky, I'm reminded of how lucky I am that I got to be out here at all today. "Thank you," I whisper. My friends cheer for me when I approach our canopy, and it fills all the crevices in my heart that my disappointment created. I shrug my shoulders like, *"Oh well."*

"You got robbed," Niles shouts.

Lydia puts her hands on her hips. "Why'd Red keep cutting you off? Pendejo."

"Who *was* that idiot?" says Kaj.

"Relax," I say. "Some newbie."

"Tough break, Lovette," Trevor calls out, snickering as he walks by. His canopy's on the other side of the judges' tent, so he's only over here to gloat at my defeat. "Shoulda known not to compete with the boys."

"Who's that ass-wipe?" my brother says, but Trevor's out of earshot.

"Nobody of consequence," I say. "Let it go. Not even worth your time."

Alix isn't up until the third heat, so I carry her board over to where she's stretching on her towel.

"How'd it go?"

"It went," I say, kneeling as I set her board down.

She scrunches her nose. "Sorry."

As I stand, I notice Cecilia behind her canopy talking with some guy. "Hey," I say to Alix. "That's the guy who cut me off every wave. The red-bib guy." Alix and I watch as Cecilia hands him money, more than a few bills.

"What's she doing?"

"I think she's paying him for making sure I didn't move on."

"Are you gonna say something?"

The injustice rises in me, wants to scream *unfair!*

"Who'd believe me?" I say. "There's no proof." And I don't feel like fighting. I'm so over it. "Listen, get ready for your heat. Good luck, okay?"

I walk away, then take one last look at Cecilia, so tickled with herself as she and the red-bib guy laugh, and I say out loud to God, "She's *your* battle. I hope you win her over."

I got to surf today. God made the impossible possible. That's *my* victory.

○)))) ● ((((○

Back at our canopy, we watch the rest of the heats. The second heat consists of three girls and a guy, and the guy cleanly wins. In the third heat, we cheer for Alix and she comes close, but she's eked out by a few points. Trevor wins his heat by a landslide. Kaj and Niles ask if I want to stay for the finals. I'm about to say no when I see Old Man Mike emerging from the judges' tent and making a beeline for me.

"Mike!" I shout.

He pats me on the shoulder. "Hey, kid." He shakes Matt's hand. "Long time no see." He smiles at my friends and then focuses back on me. "Good news. You're in the finals."

"Wait, what? I got eliminated."

"Rules state that if no girls win the heats, then the top four guys move on PLUS the highest-scoring girl."

"But Alix—"

"Below you by half a point."

Everyone's quiet for a moment, then they erupt in cheers.

"Hurry up, come grab your bib. Finals are in two."

I follow him at a brisk walk back to the judges' tent. They hand me a black bib, and I barely have time to run back and get the board from Alix again. I start to explain but she does the mosquito-shooing hand again.

"I heard. Go! And do me a favor." She motions toward Trevor's canopy, where he's busy putting on a white bib. "Kick his ass."

○)) ❭ ❭ ● ❰ ❰ ❰ (○

I jump back into the water, and the five of us paddle out. We're strong paddlers, strong wave riders, strategic in our positioning along the line. The sets are consistent, giving us plenty of waves to choose from, and we're all getting our share of style points.

When Trevor's paddling back out after one of his rides, he gives me a combination of a bunch of different angry faces, trying to set me off. He looks ridiculous. I feel the corners of my mouth lifting, so I turn my cheek away from him. Did Jesus turn the other cheek because he was afraid he'd smile and make everyone angrier?

A wave comes and rescues me, but Trevor goes for it, too. I crane my neck to see how fast it's coming, and we both stand. It turns out to be an A-frame wave, breaking both directions, so we split the peak and ride down opposite lines. The wave's holding a nice face, so I hit the lip, turning my surfboard toward the lip as it falls. It smashes my surfboard down, but I maintain control and ride it down the face into an extended bottom turn.

When I paddle back out, I see that Trevor's starting his return, which means he had a long ride as well. When I sit up on my board, I turn it toward the shoreline. My friends cheer with wild arms, and I wave back. Lydia shakes her *9.9* sign high above her head. Next to them, my brother watches me, tall and proud. Mike's there, too. But back away from all the crowds, from the clumps of competitors and friends, Dad stands, arms crossed, a lone soldier in a desert of sand. My heart skips ten thousand beats. *He came.*

I wave, and he salutes back.

Tears join the salt on my face, and I gear up for one more ride.

I'm ready to take the next set to a new level. I remember Jake's coaching, everything he taught razor sharp in my brain, as loud as if he were next to me reciting every word from September to February all over again. My body knows the perfect ride, breathes it, can execute it.

The sun shoots through the gray, three fingers of light reaching down to the water. It reminds me of Pastor Brett talking about God's love. *"Imagine the sun as God's love for you. You can hold an umbrella up to it and block out the sun, right? So, technically, you can stop receiving it. But He never stops shining it."*

I let the sun hit my face. I bask in its warmth, soak up what was there all morning, hidden behind the clouds. *"You gotta decide what your posture's gonna be toward Him. That will decide what your life's gonna look like."*

Posture's everything. It's everything on a surfboard. It's everything in my relationship with God.

I see the approaching set. The other four aren't positioned for the first wave. Besides, it looks small. They don't want it. But I know it's coming for me, just for me, a hill of sea forming in height and growing in speed. I drop to my belly on the fiberglass and soar forward. My arms reach deep into the water and pull until my neck feels the strain. In my periphery, I can sense the disappointment of the guys who wished they had trusted their gut that this nothing would become something, that this rolling water would become a mighty wall of ocean crashing and daring the bravest.

I'm breathless at the top, looking down at the sheer cliff, but I see my line and I take it, standing and tipping over the crest, weightless for a moment. Just enough to know that this wave's mine to either take on or be devoured by.

I think of all the tricks, how I could own this wave, destroy my competition, leave them in my wake.

I could win.

I could win.

And it's enough to know. Because Brett's voice whispers in the waves again, *"You gotta decide what your posture's gonna be toward Him. That will decide what your life's gonna look like."*

I take off fast and ride the wave high, like it could lift me to heaven if I stayed high enough. I purposely miss everything except for a floater, and then I counterbalance and extend. I throw my head back, arms out, palms up, arching my soul up toward my Maker.

This is my posture toward You, I tell Him. *This.*

I'm so extended that I have to land the floater hard, slapping my board against the bottom of the wave with such force that my knees ring from the shock. The soul arch is brief, not technical, and not worth many points according to Jake. But before today, I'd never succeeded at it on a shortboard.

I start to paddle back out, but the air horn sounds. End of finals. I exit the water and walk straight to Dad.

"You came."

He clears his throat. "Studying abroad. Matt. We're gonna try again next year. Provided we get the okay from the doctor. Matt's invited us to help him move into his new apartment. We're doing a family vacation. I guess you could come. Kidding. You're coming."

I smile. "Dad—"

"Eh. Get back to your friends."

"Thanks. For coming."

"Nice move with the arch. Fancy."

"Not a lot of points. I won't win."

"There's one more of these, right?

I pause. "In May. The final of seven."

"Put on by Spyder."

"How did you—"

"Your surfing coach told me. We've signed you up."

I throw my arms around him. "Thanks for talking to Mike."

He awkwardly pats my back, still rusty in the hugging-his-daughter department. "No. Your other surfing coach."

I blink. The air's gone from my lungs.

He grins at my gaping mouth, throws a thumb over his shoulder. "He said he'd meet you over by the showers." I look behind Dad at the restroom. Jake stands, his back foot resting against the wall behind him. I leave my surfboard. I can't run through the sand fast enough.

When I get there, I'm breathless, but not from running.

"How long have you been here?" I gasp.

"Long enough to see you tank. A soul arch? Really?"

I smile, relief coursing through me. I can't believe he's standing here. "Yes. Really. But how did—"

"Kelly called me in the middle of the night last night. Then Niles. Then Kaj. Then Lydia. I didn't want to make you nervous, so I stayed out of sight. They knew I was here."

I turn and look back to our canopy. Dad's there too, now, and everyone's watching. They all knew!

"Unbelievable."

"No. What is unbelievable is this shower. You push it and crazy things happen."

I laugh. "Oh really."

He pulls a hand around my waist, and I reach up around

his neck. He's warm and inviting, like a gulp of water after being parched for days. He leans in. "My flight still leaves tonight." My stomach sinks, but I know. I mean I knew if he postponed his flight, it was postponed, not canceled. "But I couldn't *not* be here for this."

I lean into him. "I'm in love with that."

"I'm in love with you."

He says it with such confidence, I can't say anything in response. My body becomes rubber. I can't speak. I can't form words. So instead, with a shaky hand, I reach up behind him and press the shower button. Water pours out like a hose on full blast. He steps backward into it, and water gushes over him, drenches his hair, his clothes. I step forward, and the water cascades over me too, the spray making it hard to keep my eyes open. But I do just long enough to find his lips with mine, losing myself in his kiss, his embrace, this moment.

"Breast to breast!" I hear my friends shouting from under the canopy.

We laugh through our kiss, and he pulls me behind the bathroom wall where we can share a moment alone. We look at each other for a really long time, our gaze unblinking, searing and powerful and speaking so loudly of a love that words would minimize.

"I don't want to leave," he finally says, wiping the beads of water from his face.

"I don't want you to go." We grip each other tightly, and he presses his lips to my forehead. I feel a tear drop from his chin to my cheek. "This year has been"—he stops to clear his throat—"more than I expected."

"*Exceptionally* more?"

He laughs, and it gets garbled in the back of his throat. It's him who's crying for once, not me. I take his hands, link my fingers firmly with his.

"Hey," I start, "I'm not ready to do 'us' apart. I don't know what that looks like."

He looks away.

"But," I add, comforting him with a slight squeeze of my hands, "I wasn't ready to do 'us' *together*, and we figured that out, right?" He nods and looks back into my eyes. I notice his nose is running, but he doesn't care, and he's not letting go of my hands. "I don't know what God has for us. But right now is good—really good—so let's ride that wave, okay?"

He smiles through shiny eyes and manages, "Okay." One more tear escapes from him before he kisses me again, and I hold on to the kiss for a precious moment. I think back to the competition today, how hard I fought, and how full I felt, even though I didn't think Jake was there. Then I release him, a strange strength not entirely my own filling me, and I lead him back out from behind the bathroom wall, back toward our friends—our tribe—the family who's had our backs from day one. Sure enough, they cheer in the distance when we emerge. Tonight's another story, a chapter that will begin without him. And I'm worried and terrified and sad and all the things. But I also know my posture when the sun's shining, so I know ultimately I'll be okay, with or without Jake. God's brought me this far, and He hasn't failed me yet.

I'm still here.

Acknowledgments

Michael Bourret, you are a man of character, wisdom, professionalism, and kindness. You're a brilliant agent, and anyone in YA will attest to that. I can no longer joke with you about how you can sell everyone's book but mine! Lol. I wish I had enough words to encompass my gratitude for your faith in me.

Francesco Sedita, I love that you reached out to my agent with a simple, "So I have this idea . . ." Thank you for being bold in your creativity and vision. Nathaniel Tabachnik, thanks for the coffee meetings when I flew to New York for the day just to ask you all the rookie questions. As editors, you both have been so supportive and insightful through this journey.

Sometimes I've read books and wondered how errors still made it in. Now I know. Caroline Press wasn't their copyeditor! Sara LaFleur and Vivian Kirklin, if proofreading interiors doesn't work out, you really should become crime scene investigators. Rebecca Behrens, do they give prizes for copyediting? You'd podium for sure. I thought my manuscript had zero errors. So many times I would say to Nathaniel on the phone, "How did they find that?"

Lynn Portnoff, I've no clue how you climbed into my head and designed a cover that was better than I imagined, but I'm grateful for your magical powers.

Lesley Downie and Scott Sussman, you were my filters, soundboards, thesauruses, and way better wordsmiths than I could ever hope to be. There aren't enough margaritas to repay you, even if we were college students on spring break in Cabo with an open bar. Seriously. You made this book happen.

Phil Blyth, thank you. For constantly asking me for another chapter. For telling me, "You've got this," when I clearly felt like I didn't. For taking notes as I read aloud so you could point out the good stuff. For trying your darndest to stay up with me as I finished the last page at dawn. You almost made it. Haha. You were this book's momentum.

Lori Polydoros, thanks for the Long Beach writing dates! Mark Cole, thanks for explaining all the scoring rules for surfing. Kayla, Cora, Josie, Melody, Shannon, and Anna, thanks for being stoked at the first chapter. Mom and Dad, my constant cheerleaders, set your pom-poms down for a sec and pick up a brandy. I did it!

Vanessa Hernandez, you win for the best pep talks ever: "This isn't a Pulitzer, so get over your writer's block already." Ha! Twenty years ago, you told me to write a YA novel. I'm tardy, but I listened.

Jesus, I've written so many books and offered them to the world, but this one you offered to me. Humbled that you'd entrust me to give everyone a glimpse of what I see when I see you. You are complicated, but I'm not going anywhere.

And last, but far from least, Dawn Brooke Owens, you left me an index card that reads, "Please don't ever stop writing. My world needs you to be an author."

I didn't stop, B-town. :) See you on the flip side.